DROWN
HER
SORROWS

ALSO BY MELINDA LEIGH

BREE TAGGERT NOVELS

Cross Her Heart

See Her Die

MORGAN DANE NOVELS

Say You're Sorry

Her Last Goodbye

Bones Don't Lie

What I've Done

Secrets Never Die

Save Your Breath

SCARLET FALLS NOVELS

Hour of Need

Minutes to Kill

Seconds to Live

SHE CAN SERIES

She Can Run

She Can Tell

She Can Scream

She Can Hide

"He Can Fall" (A Short Story)

She Can Kill

DROWN HER SORROWS

MELINDA LEIGH

Published by Montlake, Seattle

www.apub.com

Amazon, the Amazon logo, and Montlake are trademarks of Amazon.com, Inc., or its affiliates.

ISBN-13: 9781542007009 (paperback)
ISBN-10: 1542007003 (paperback)

ISBN-13: 9781542007023 (hardcover)
ISBN-10: 154200702X (hardcover)

Cover design by Shasti O'Leary Soudant

Printed in the United States of America

First edition

To Ladybug,
for "helping" me with everything

CHAPTER ONE

Behind the wheel of her official SUV, Sheriff Bree Taggert stared at the screen of her ringing cell phone with regret. At six thirty in the evening, she was almost home, but her deputies didn't call her cell unless it was important. She answered, "Sheriff Taggert."

"I'm sorry to disturb you, ma'am, but I have a situation." Deputy Laurie Collins's voice echoed through the Bluetooth speaker. "Approximately thirty minutes ago, I responded to a report of an abandoned car at the bridge on Dead Horse Road." The deputy paused. "The car is not disabled in any way. There's no sign of the driver, but her purse and cell phone are in the vehicle. I'm concerned the driver might have wandered away from the vehicle and gotten lost. Or worse."

The hairs on the back of Bree's neck quivered. She lifted her foot from the gas pedal, and her SUV slowed. Collins was a new hire, but she was hardly a rookie. She came with six years of patrol experience. She had good instincts, and Bree felt lucky to have hired her. If Collins was concerned, there was likely a reason.

Bree pulled over to the shoulder of the road. "That is strange. Are you still on scene?"

"Yes, ma'am."

"On my way. ETA five minutes." Bree ended the call.

She squinted through the windshield. She could see her sister's farmhouse—now Bree's home. A ball of emotion welled up in her throat. Four months after her sister had been murdered, grief still flared at random moments. Bree had taken charge of her sister's two kids along with the farm. The kids sometimes needed more guidance than Bree felt capable of providing. She did her best, but in the real world, an "effort" grade was bullshit. Experience told her she'd be tied up with this call for the rest of the evening. She'd miss dinner with the kids and reading bedtime stories with Kayla.

But response time could be critical if the driver of the car was injured or lost. Early May in upstate New York meant thirty-degree temperature swings. The days were warming, but the nights still hovered near the freezing mark. Hypothermia was a real risk. The area around the bridge on Dead Horse Road was densely wooded. Bree didn't really have a choice. She had to go.

When she'd been a homicide detective with the Philadelphia PD, Bree had used cases to blot out personal issues. Avoidance had always been her preferred coping mechanism. If compartmentalizing were an Olympic event, Bree would be the gold medalist. She was almost grateful that the sheriff's department she'd been appointed to run three months ago was a total disaster. Between work and raising her niece and nephew, Bree had little time to dwell on her own loss.

Now, her priorities had changed. Her job was important, but there were days—like this one—when she resented its intrusion into family time. On the bright side, she had live-in childcare. So, that was one less worry.

She turned her vehicle around and punched the gas pedal, and her SUV raced down the road. She called the house to let her family know she'd be late, then turned her attention to the job. The back road and its namesake bridge were only a couple of miles away.

A few minutes later, Bree slowed down and turned onto a narrow county lane. Dead Horse Road had earned its name. Cutting through a thick section of old forest, it wound around massive trees and boulders. Bree crested a hill, eased down the steep decline, and navigated two final dogleg turns before the bridge appeared. She flipped down her visor to cut the direct glare of the sinking sun. At the base of the bridge, a small wooden cross decorated with a dead wreath marked the location of a vehicular accident fatality.

A Toyota Camry sat on the shoulder of the road. Deputy Collins had parked her patrol car behind the Toyota. Bree slowed her vehicle and pulled over. She climbed out of her SUV. Collins wasn't in sight.

"Sheriff!"

Bree spun.

Fifty feet away, Deputy Collins emerged from the trees and scrambled up the embankment. Her face was flushed with exertion, and a few blonde hairs had escaped her neat bun.

Bree waited for the deputy to hurry closer.

Collins took two deep breaths. "A passing motorist called in the abandoned vehicle. He claimed he saw the car Friday evening on his commute home from work and again today on his way into work this morning. When it was still here tonight, he reported it."

"Did he say what time he saw the car on Friday?" Bree asked.

Collins pulled a small notepad from her pocket and flipped it open. "Around seven o'clock."

Today was Monday.

"So, the car has been here for at least three days," Bree said.

Collins frowned at the Toyota. "The doors are unlocked. The key is inside. The tires are sound, the vehicle has plenty of gas, and the engine starts with no problem."

"What do you know about the driver?"

"I ran the plates. The vehicle belongs to Holly Thorpe. She lives in Grey's Hollow. Her registration is valid, and she has no outstanding tickets. Her driver's license is in the purse."

"Have you called her residence?"

"There's no landline." Collins pointed down the embankment. "I searched the downhill slope in case she stepped out of her car for some reason and fell. The rain was heavy Friday night. The ground would have been slippery. I didn't see any sign of her."

Bree's gaze tracked to the car, then the bridge. "As a rule, a woman doesn't leave her purse and cell phone behind."

"No. Her phone is passcode protected, but I could see that the battery still has a little power. It also has decent cell reception." Collins was methodically covering the bases.

Bree scanned the area. On one side of the road, thick woods covered an upward slope. On the other, a steep wooded embankment sloped down to the river. Just ahead, the bridge arched over the Scarlet River. Bree's instincts waved a red flag. Barring a breakdown or flat tire, there was no reason for a car to be parked here. No hiking trails. No park. The bridge was narrow, with no overlook. This was a back road used mostly by locals.

She walked to the car and peered in the driver's window. A purse sat on the passenger seat, the top unzipped. A cell phone rested on the console. A wallet poked out from the top of the purse.

"I opened her wallet to look at her ID," Collins said.

Bree donned gloves and opened the vehicle door. Leaning in, she tapped the cell phone's screen. The Face ID lock screen appeared. A few seconds later, it shifted to request a passcode. Bree touched the "Emergency" button on the bottom of the screen. "Owen Thorpe is her emergency contact."

"Yes, ma'am. I'm assuming he's the husband. According to his motor vehicle records, he's the same age as Holly, and he lives at the same address. He didn't answer his phone. I left a message asking him to return my call."

Bree chewed on the information while her gut churned. There was a remote possibility Holly had become ill and called for a ride. Perhaps she was so sick, she forgot her purse and cell.

For three days?

Seemed like a stretch. Bree surveyed the rest of the vehicle's interior, then ducked out. The temperature was dropping with the sun. If Holly had wandered away—or had been taken—from her vehicle on Friday, she'd already been gone for three nights. There was no time to waste.

"I'll send a deputy to her residence," Bree said. "If she's not there and her husband doesn't have information, we'll call for a search party and put out a BOLO." Bree accessed Holly's social media accounts and clicked on "About" in one of her profiles. "She lists Beckett Construction as her employer. I know it's late, but call the company and ask if they've seen Holly."

"Yes, ma'am." Collins returned to her patrol car.

Bree went back to her vehicle and called dispatch to request a welfare check at Holly's address. "Have the responding deputy call me on his cell phone instead of using the radio. I don't want the situation made public just yet."

Reporters monitored police radio chatter via scanners. In the event the worst had happened, Bree didn't want Holly's next of kin learning of her status via the news.

While she waited, Bree accessed Holly's motor vehicle records and reviewed her driver's license information. Holly Thorpe was thirty-four years old and five two. In her driver's license photo, her shoulder-length hair was straight and blonde.

In a few minutes, Bree's phone buzzed. She answered the call. "Sheriff Taggert."

"Deputy Oscar here. I just spoke with Owen Thorpe. He hasn't seen his wife since Friday evening. They had a fight, and she walked out on him. He says he's been drunk since, and he looks pretty rough. Seems I woke him up."

"Ask him if you can walk through the house to verify his wife is not there," Bree said.

"Yes, ma'am," Oscar responded.

5

Over the connection, she heard the deputy asking and a man's response of "Sure. Whatever."

"It's a two-bedroom town house," Oscar said to Bree. "This won't take long."

"I'll wait." Bree listened to Deputy Oscar open and close doors for a few minutes.

Then he said, "She's not here."

"Does the husband remember what she was wearing when she left?" Bree asked.

She heard Oscar repeat the question for Owen Thorpe.

Oscar said, "A blue blouse and jeans. Her raincoat is red. He doesn't remember which shoes she was wearing."

"OK. Stay with the husband for now. Keep him away from the news. Just tell him we're looking for his wife." Bree's mind was spinning when Deputy Collins rapped on the driver's-side window.

Bree stepped out of her vehicle.

Collins shook her head. "The construction company's office is closed."

Bree lifted her phone. "I'll call the chief deputy." She made the call to Chief Deputy Todd Harvey, who was on the local search-and-rescue team. After speaking with Todd, Bree turned back to Collins. "His ETA is twenty minutes. Use your cell to request additional units. We need to do an immediate foot search of this area. I'm going to scout around."

While her deputy used her cell phone to contact dispatch, Bree stood on the road in front of Holly's car and turned in a circle. Trees and rocks made up most of the landscape. *Why did Holly stop here?* The rush of water over rocks caught Bree's attention. Her gaze shifted to the bridge. Holly had fought with her husband. Their argument had been serious enough for her to walk out on him. She must have been upset, possibly despondent.

Shit.

Bree strode toward the bridge. An old iron structure, the bridge was less than a hundred and fifty feet long and probably should have been replaced years ago. But rural county budgets didn't prioritize little-used bridges until they collapsed in a storm. When Bree reached the middle, she looked over the railing. Thirty feet below, water rushed under the bridge.

Was the drop high enough to be fatal? Bree eyed the water churning below. Recent heavy rains had flooded the river beyond its usual depth. She didn't know if a jumper would die on impact, but they wouldn't swim away without injury. The current was swift. Downstream, boulders dotted the white water. It was unlikely many people would be able to make it to shore.

Bree followed the current. After passing under the bridge, the waterway turned to the east. A small offshoot curved to the west, continued to bend, and disappeared behind the trees. She would have to send deputies downriver along both banks.

She glanced at her watch. It was seven o'clock. The sun would set around eight. They had precious little daylight left. She strode back to where Deputy Collins stood next to her cruiser.

"Three units responded," Collins said.

Bree inclined her head toward the river. "Did you walk all the way to the riverbank?"

Collins shook her head. "No, I just checked the bottom of this embankment in case she fell."

Bree started down the slope. "Stay here and wait for backup. Tell Todd I'm walking down to the river."

"Yes, ma'am." Collins cast a glance over her shoulder at the bridge. "Do you think she jumped?"

"I don't know." Bree didn't like to make assumptions. Preconceived theories interfered with a good investigation. But why else would Holly have parked *here*?

Bree scrambled down the rocky embankment and picked up a game trail. She trod carefully. Long evening shadows obscured the footing. After about fifty yards, the ground sheared off, the trees growing at acute angles straight up. The path doubled backward for twenty feet, then turned around. It must zigzag down the steeper terrain. Bree navigated the first leg. Ahead, the skinny trail forked. One branch turned toward the river below. The other offshoot headed up the slope in the opposite direction. At the turn, she heard something large rustling in the underbrush ahead. She stopped and pulled out her weapon.

Her senses tingled, as if there was a predator nearby.

Holly Thorpe's killer?

Or Bree's imagination?

Relax. It's probably a deer.

This *was* a game trail.

Holly Thorpe's car had been there for three days. If foul play had been involved in her disappearance, then the perpetrator would be long gone. But Bree's instincts wouldn't shut up.

Ahead, a twig snapped. Sweat broke out between her shoulder blades. Something was around the next bend. She squinted into the shadows down the trail, regripped her Glock, and aimed it toward the sound.

She backed up a step, easing one athletic shoe onto the trail, wary of making any noise. Glancing to her left, she saw a fat tree trunk. Decent cover if necessary.

More rustling headed up the trail—right for Bree.

She held her breath as a dark shape rounded the bend and stepped into a ray of sunlight.

A black bear.

Bree froze. The bear stopped. It was probably on the way to the river too, and she'd surprised it.

Trying to be quiet had been the absolute worst thing she could have done. Black bears were shy. They didn't like people. If she'd made plenty of noise coming down the trail, the bear would have likely gone in the opposite direction.

This animal was lean, thin, possibly only a month out of hibernation. It would be hungry, but black bears were rarely aggressive unless they felt threatened. Or they had cubs.

It'll be fine.

Two small black shapes moved at the bear's feet. Bree spared them a quick glance.

Cubs.

This was a mama bear, and Bree was only twenty-five feet away from her babies.

Mama bear rose onto her back legs. Her nose lifted as she tested the air. The big head turned, and the animal sniffed in the direction of the river. She'd caught the scent of a competing odor.

The area might be trying to become a suburb, but right in front of Bree was a sign that much of it was still untamed. This was not the first bear she'd seen. Until her parents had died when Bree was eight, she'd run half-wild in the woods of Grey's Hollow. She knew enough not to run now. Fleeing would engage the animal's prey instinct.

People who ran from bears got caught.

But as much as her brain knew what she needed to do, her body was primed for a fight-or-flight response. Unfortunately, both of those options sucked.

Bree raised her hands and spread out her arms, trying to appear larger. She took a slow, easy step backward, and said in a loud, mostly calm voice, "Easy, there. I won't hurt you or your babies."

Bree's Glock felt like a peashooter, but it was all she had. Her can of bear spray was sitting uselessly in the back of her vehicle. A black bear could charge at thirty miles per hour. Her chances of stopping the bear with well-placed, meaningful shots during that panicked nanosecond weren't good. And she did not want to shoot this animal. Bree's heart sprinted in her chest, but she forced her feet to move like molasses. She could hear little but the desperate pounding of her own pulse in her ears.

The bear dropped to all fours, slapping the ground as her front paws landed. Huffing, the animal took two quick steps forward, then retreated.

Bree slid one foot backward, then the other. The bear swung her head in a low arc. Bree took another step back, putting one more precious foot of space between her and the animal.

Above, she heard a siren approach. The bear heard it too and pivoted in the opposite direction. She retreated at a run, with her cubs at her heels.

The breath left Bree's lungs in one hard *whoosh*, making her light-headed.

She'd been lucky. So lucky.

On shaky legs, she turned to walk up the trail to the road. She'd wait for backup—and bear spray—before searching the riverbank. Rocks shifted under her feet. The ground gave way, and Bree plunged down the slope. Struggling to keep her feet aimed downhill, she smacked into a sapling and slid between the trunks of two larger trees. She landed in a heap at the bottom of the slope. Loose dirt and small rocks settled around her.

The rocky riverbank was just ahead. Bree got to her feet and brushed some dirt from her pants.

An odor drifted toward her on the breeze, unsettling her stomach, and she knew what had attracted the bear.

She walked onto the rocks that lined the waterway. She had a clear view of the entire bank all the way to the bridge high above. Ahead, something red peeked out from behind a boulder on the shoreline, then retreated.

Her stomach knotted.

She quickened her steps. Rounding the big rock, she stared down. Knowing what she was going to find didn't make the discovery easier.

In the rocks and mud at the river's edge was the body of a woman wearing a red rain jacket and jeans. The bear had picked up the scent. Black bears will eat anything from bugs to grass to berries—to bodies.

She reached for her phone and called Deputy Collins. "I found her."

Bree approached the body. The victim lay on her side, wet hair swirling in the water around her face, the body limply shifting position as the current lapped around it. Bree reached into her pocket and pulled out a pen. She used it to lift the hair off the victim's face. She was small, blonde, and definitely dead.

CHAPTER TWO

Matt Flynn sat in the passenger seat of his sister's minivan. An abandoned industrial park stretched out on one side of the street. Small, run-down houses lined the other.

"Thanks for coming with me," his sister, Cady, said from the driver's seat.

"I'm glad you called me. I wouldn't want you in this neighborhood alone." For many reasons. A former sheriff's deputy, Matt had been to the area before. He'd busted a meth lab on the next block. But he also knew this was the neighborhood where Cady's ex-husband's family lived.

In the back seat, Brody barked once and pressed his nose to the window. The German shepherd had been Matt's K-9 partner before a shooting had ended both of their careers. Matt had taken a settlement from the county, with the stipulation that his dog retired with him. Brody was his partner. Matt had refused to leave him behind to be used by the careless and corrupt former sheriff. Matt wondered if Brody recognized the blocks as they cruised by.

"I didn't want to wait until tomorrow," Cady said. "The caller said the dog was in bad shape, and it'll be dark in an hour." Cady ran a dog rescue. She often received anonymous calls about neglected or abused animals. "Usually, I just get one of the girls to go with me, but I thought you might be a better option tonight."

"I'm happy to help, even though you're no damsel in distress." Matt said a silent thanks that his sister had plenty of street smarts and common sense. Not that she wasn't capable. A former collegiate rower, Cady now taught kickboxing and self-defense. Nearly six feet tall, she wore faded jeans and a hoodie emblazoned with the logo for their older brother's MMA gym. She didn't exactly look fragile.

"I'd rather not get into distress at all, if I can help it." Cady pointed to an overgrown lot. "This is it."

A small house sat in the middle of a suburban jungle. Weeds and foliage grew over the front porch. Mold covered the peeling white siding.

She pulled over, adjusted her long, strawberry blonde ponytail, and reached for the door handle.

"Hold on." Matt scanned the street. "Do you know who owns the house?"

"Yes." Cady gave him a name he didn't recognize. "I already spoke to him and got permission to remove the dog from his property. The house is supposed to be knocked down next month. Whoever is living here is squatting."

Matt hoped that was all they were doing. If he and Cady ran into drug dealers, they could be shot on sight and their bodies dumped in the river.

He turned to the dog in the back seat. "Stay." He didn't want Brody stepping on a crack pipe, needle, or broken glass. The dog was strictly backup.

Brody wouldn't like it, but he'd obey. Matt lowered the window to give Brody fresh air—and so the dog could get out of the vehicle if necessary. Then he opened his own door and stepped into the street. The hairs on the back of his neck shot to attention.

Someone was watching.

In this neighborhood, someone would always be watching. Criminals kept a close eye on their surroundings. Residents who weren't criminals would be equally as worried about strangers.

The sun was dropping low, casting long shadows. Matt followed Cady to the broken sidewalk. A rusty chain-link fence encircled the property. Unlatched, the gate hung on its hinges. It squeaked as Cady opened it. They went through the opening, the foliage closing in on them and obstructing their view. A prickly shrub snatched at the legs of Matt's jeans.

"Did the caller say where the dog was being kept?" He stepped in front of his sister in case any surprises waited for them.

"The back porch."

Matt's pulse thudded as they walked along the side of the house. He listened hard, but all he heard was the spring breeze in the trees and the distant rumble of a freight train. He held an evergreen branch aside for his sister, and they emerged into the rear yard. Broken bottles, cigarette butts, and fast-food wrappers littered the weedy ground. Glass shards crunched under Matt's boots, and he was glad he'd left Brody in the van.

A low whine sounded from behind a thick juniper bush at the corner of the building. Matt and Cady stepped around it to view the back of the house. A porch spanned the rear of the building. Half of the railing spindles were broken, and the wooden steps were rotted.

Cady pointed. "There."

A young white-and-brown pit bull mix stood near the sagging back door. He was tied to a post by a thick, dirty rope. Piles of dog feces surrounded him. The smell was overwhelming, and there wasn't a clean spot big enough for him to lie down. His ribs protruded, and his coat was matted and filthy.

"Poor baby," Cady crooned in a high-pitched voice. "You're so thin."

Matt approached the bottom of the steps slowly, looking for signs of aggression. The dog whined softly again. Matt pulled a piece of chicken from his pocket and extended it toward the dog. Its posture softened as it sniffed Matt's fingers and carefully took the food. No snapping but also no hesitation or distrust. *Amazing.*

Matt scanned the thin body. "Young male. Forty pounds. At least ten pounds underweight. Infested with fleas."

"There's no food. Do you see water?" Cady stepped around Matt to get a better look. She'd have none of his overprotecting. He should have known better.

"There's an empty bowl." Matt snapped pictures. Documenting cases was an old habit from his days as a sheriff's investigator.

"I've seen enough," Cady said, her voice final. "Let's get him out of here."

Matt leaned forward and untied the rope on the dog's collar. "Are you going to be a good boy?" he asked in a high-pitched tone. The dog responded with a wag.

"Watch your face, Matt."

The dog seemed friendly, but most dogs didn't bite out of aggression. It was usually a reaction to fear or pain.

Not wanting to risk falling through the rotted steps, Matt leaned forward and scooped an arm around the dog's middle. "Don't bite me, OK?"

The dog didn't struggle at all as Matt lifted him off the porch. Instead he licked Matt's face.

"OK. There's a good boy." Matt set him on the ground and gave his square head a rub.

Crouching to the dog's level, Cady opened the loop on her lead and slipped it over his head. "You're such a pretty boy." She gave him a treat from her pocket.

Unbelievably, the thin tail whipped back and forth, and his skinny body wriggled with joy.

"How can these neglected dogs still love people after what's been done to them?" Matt scanned the rest of the dog for injuries, but he seemed sound.

"Humans don't deserve dogs," Cady agreed.

Matt patted the dog's side. "Let's get him out of here."

"You are going to feel so much better very soon." Cady stood. The dog seemed happy to fall into step beside her, as if he knew he was being rescued.

She led him alongside the house back toward the front yard. Matt brought up the rear. They emerged onto the sidewalk. The setting sun blinded Matt, and he held up a hand to block it.

"Hey! You can't just take that dog!" a tall bald man yelled from across the street. He pulled his head out from under the hood of a battered F-150 and stepped around a toolbox on the ground.

Matt reached for Cady's arm, pulling her behind him. The dog pressed his body against her calf.

"We have permission from the owner of the house," Matt said.

"Well, that dog belongs to my friend. It ain't yours." The man was in his fifties, in saggy jeans and a T-shirt stained with what looked like motor oil. Despite being older and lean, he had a wiry and wary look that put Matt on alert. The man walked a few steps closer, clearly not afraid. He held a wrench in one hand and slapped it into his opposite palm.

Matt wished he still wore a badge and gun. "Where's your friend?"

In the background, Matt saw Brody's dark form leap silently from the open van window onto the sidewalk.

"He went to visit somebody," the man said. "He'll be back in a day or two."

"He isn't supposed to be living here." Matt kept his voice even. "You know he doesn't own this place."

"People do what they gotta do." The man shrugged. His tone dropped lower, more threatening. "You still can't just take a dude's dog."

Cady slipped out from behind Matt. "Hi, I'm Cady. What's your name?"

"Cady," Matt warned under his breath.

She ignored him.

"I'm Dean." The man's posture softened as she smiled at him.

Cady's face went serious. She gave the dog a worried look. "The dog is in pretty bad shape."

Dean frowned. "He looks OK to me."

Brody padded down the walk until he stood about fifteen feet behind the man. Matt gave him the hand signal to *stay*. He obeyed, but his focus was 100 percent on Dean. If Dean acted aggressively, Brody would take him down.

"He's underweight. He's covered in so many fleas he's lost some of his fur." Cady pointed to a bald patch on the dog's hindquarters. "Your friend left him without any food or water. When did he leave?"

"Yesterday." Dean's gaze swept over the dog, as if reassessing him. "No food or water, huh?"

"No." Cady reached into her pocket for a business card. "I run a dog rescue. You can give my card to your friend when he gets back, and he can contact me about the dog. We're going to take him to a vet for treatment."

Dean waved off her offer of a card. "Nah. I ain't never really looked good at the dog, but I can see you're right. He's way too skinny." He stepped back, his voice full of respect. "You go on your way. I'll go back to minding my own business."

"Thanks." Cady led the dog toward the van.

Dean gave her a quick head bow, then turned back to his truck repair. He hesitated as he caught sight of Brody on the sidewalk. With his ears pricked forward and intelligent eyes riveted on Dean, the dog was intimidating.

"Brody, *fuss*," Matt called.

Brody jogged past Dean and fell into a heel position at Matt's side. Shaking his head, Dean leaned under the raised hood of the pickup.

Matt opened the cargo door and picked up the pittie. Cady opened the crate in the back, and Matt slid the dog inside and closed the door. The dog turned around once and curled up on an old towel.

Matt lifted Brody into the rear seat of the van. "You're not supposed to jump in and out of vehicles since you hurt your shoulder, but thanks for backing us up."

Brody wagged his tail.

Matt and Cady climbed into the vehicle. Cady opened a bottle of hand sanitizer. Matt held out a hand, and she squirted some into his palm. The pittie was covered in filth and fleas, and Matt was glad they'd brought Cady's vehicle.

"Good thing one of us has people skills. That was masterful de-escalation," Matt said as Cady pulled out onto the street. "You turned a potential confrontation into a positive encounter." He had been ready to go all brawn, no brain.

Cady laughed. "I've done this a few times."

"More than a few, I'm sure, and that worries me." Matt glanced at his sister. Her profile was misleading. Her freckles made her look younger than thirty-three. But she'd been rescuing dogs for six years, since her disaster of a marriage and subsequent nasty divorce. Just thinking of that time made Matt's hand curl into a fist as he remembered the satisfaction of plowing it into her ex's face. But he didn't bring it up. One, she didn't know about that. She thought her ex had decided to stop stalking and harassing her on his own. And two, except for never dating, she seemed to have gotten past that terrible time.

"You sound like Dad." Cady shook her head. "I can handle myself, and I try not to do stupid things."

"I know."

"I called you tonight, right?"

"You did," he acknowledged. "And for that, I'm grateful, but you're still my little sister."

Cady barked out a short laugh. "I'm hardly little, and I rarely run into problems. Most people don't like seeing a dog mistreated. I've encountered some pretty badass dudes who got weepy or angry over an abused dog."

"But there are plenty of assholes who don't give a damn, like the one who left him with no food or water." Matt glanced over the back seat at the crate containing the little pittie. Through the holes, he could see the dog was still curled up. He reached over the seat to give Brody a head scratch.

Cady didn't argue.

A short while later, she drove back to Matt's house. "So, can I keep him here until I can place him with a foster?"

Matt rolled his eyes. "Of course. There's an empty kennel. Why not fill it?"

After Matt had recovered from his shooting, he'd bought the house and acreage and built the kennel with the intention of training K-9s, but his sister had immediately filled it with rescues. More than three years later, she was still keeping it full.

"Thank you." She leaned over and kissed him on the cheek.

"I'll help you get him cleaned up." Matt let Brody out of the van while Cady helped the pittie out of the crate.

They walked toward the kennel. The door opened and a thin man stepped out. Matt had known Justin since childhood. Recently released from a drug rehab facility, his friend looked rough. But then, he'd weathered a car accident, a subsequent opioid addiction, and the murder of his estranged wife, during which he'd been shot and kidnapped. Justin was still standing, but there wasn't much left of him. Emotionally, he was drained.

"Hey, Justin." Cady summed up the dog's condition.

Justin just nodded. He'd been unable to get a job since his release, so Matt had put him to work in the kennels. Dogs were the best therapy he could think of, and his friend needed to be occupied. Too much free time would not help him stay sober.

Justin kneeled on the concrete and held out a hand to the pittie. The dog walked closer. Justin stroked his head, and the dog leaned on him.

One wounded soul recognized another.

Matt's phone buzzed in his pocket. He pulled it out. *Bree.* His heart did a happy little skip. Their relationship was still new and shiny, and he hadn't adjusted to the effect just hearing her voice had on him. Did she want to see him tonight? "I need to take this call."

He stepped outside and answered the call. "Hi."

"Hi," she said.

He'd hoped her call was personal. They were past due for a date night. Her family and job kept her busy. But he knew instantly from the tone of her greeting that the call was official business. "What happened?"

"We found a body in the river near the bridge on Dead Horse Road."

"Are you still there?"

"Yes. It's a fresh case. I'm still waiting on the medical examiner."

"OK. I'm on my way." Matt ended the call. He ducked back into the kennel. "I have to go to work."

Cady frowned. "I'm not telling Mom. She's not happy that you're working for the sheriff's department again, since that's how you were shot."

"I know." But Matt had tried retirement. It hadn't suited him. He was only thirty-five. "But this is who I am." He called Brody.

"You can leave Brody with me. I'll put him inside before I go."
Cady gave him a quick hug. "I love you. Be careful."

"I will." Matt went into the house and changed into his civilian-consultant uniform: khaki-colored cargoes and a black sheriff's-logo polo shirt. Then he went out to his SUV and headed toward a dead body.

CHAPTER THREE

Bree climbed the slope back to the road. She swallowed a mouthful of evening spring air. Cold water had slowed—but not stopped—decomposition of the body. The smell, like meat just beginning to spoil, penetrated her nose and coated the back of her throat.

Collins was standing in the open door of her cruiser, talking on the radio. She spotted Bree, signed off, and jogged over.

"I called the medical examiner," Bree said, breathless. "And our criminal investigator, Matt Flynn."

Budget restrictions prohibited hiring a full-time investigator. Matt worked as a civilian consultant to the sheriff's department on an as-needed basis.

A sheriff's cruiser parked on the shoulder of the road. Chief Deputy Todd Harvey stepped out and walked on the gravel shoulder toward her. He adjusted his duty belt on his lean waist. At six feet tall, he had the long, easy stride of an outdoorsman. He stopped in front of her.

Bree summed up the situation in a few quick sentences. Then she opened the passenger door of her SUV and took out her camera. "We're losing daylight fast. You and Collins utilize additional deputies as they arrive to search the ground around the vehicle, between the vehicle and the bridge, and the bridge's surface. Bag anything you find as evidence. Photograph everything." Bree eyed the line of law enforcement vehicles. The press would be here shortly. "Set up a perimeter for media. Be careful. I saw a black bear and two cubs on the trail. I doubt they'll be back, but be mindful."

She closed the door, moved to the rear of the vehicle, and opened the cargo hatch. She retrieved her bear spray, just in case. "According to the initial caller, the car has been parked at the bridge since Friday. The heavy rain over the past weekend probably washed away any footprints." Bree doubted any evidence would have survived the storms, but they would go through the procedural motions anyway.

"Yes, ma'am," Todd said.

The wind kicked up across the river, and Bree could feel the chill in the air. The temperature was dropping with the sun. She put on her jacket and shoved gloves and evidence bags into the pockets. "Direct Matt and the ME to the body."

Todd and Deputy Collins turned back to their vehicles. Bree headed down the slope toward the body. She took pictures from multiple angles and distances. The corpse's left hand extended onto the rocks. The victim wore a silver wedding band with a brushed texture channel. Bree leaned closer and snapped a close-up. By the time she'd finished with her photos, the sun had dropped behind the trees. The medical examiner would also take photos of the body in situ, but Bree liked to have her own. Besides, the ME would be dependent on artificial light. Bree would take advantage of the remaining daylight. You couldn't have too many crime scene photos.

Footsteps caught her attention. Bree turned to see Matt and the medical examiner emerging from the woods. Broad-shouldered and six three, Matt was an impressive figure. He hefted two battery-powered floodlights on tripods. The portable lights were specifically designed for illuminating remote areas where setting up a generator wasn't practical.

Dr. Serena Jones was a tall African American woman with close-cropped hair. Her short, stocky male assistant half jogged to keep up with her. The ME and her assistant each carried a plastic kit.

"Sheriff." The ME stared at the body, assessing. "What do we know?"

"Her car has been parked at the base of the bridge since Friday night," Bree said.

Matt set down the lights. The sunset turned his short red-brown hair and tight beard the color of burnished copper. His gaze caught Bree's. Despite the gruesome situation, something inside Bree warmed as their eyes met for a few seconds. If they weren't—once again—standing over a dead body, he would have kissed her. But standing over a dead body seemed to be their norm, and Matt was aware of how she felt about PDA. She blinked away, afraid everyone else would see how much she liked him.

How did you greet the criminal investigator you were dating when no one else knew you were dating him?

"Matt." Bree cleared her throat. "Thanks for responding so quickly."

He nodded as he helped Dr. Jones set up the lights on the riverbank, flooding the body and area immediately around it with day-bright light. The ME's assistant moved in with his camera. When he'd finished, Dr. Jones crouched next to the body. Water sloshed around the ankles of her rubber boots. She reached one gloved hand toward the head, lifting the wet hair off the face as Bree had done. "The water temperature is probably somewhere in the fifties. So, the body isn't classically bloated, but she's starting to get soupy. She's been in the water at least a couple of days."

"Her husband says she left home Friday evening." Bree wondered if she would be able to verify the timeline given by Owen Thorpe.

Dr. Jones looked thoughtful. "I'll be able to give you a better answer after the autopsy. Let's turn her over."

Bree tugged on gloves and helped turn the body onto its back. A bloodless gash started on the forehead and extended into the victim's hair.

Dr. Jones pointed to abrasions on the victim's head and hands. "Most of these injuries look postmortem, possibly from hitting rocks and other debris in the river. Not sure about the head wound. I'll need X-rays and better light to assess it." She sat back on her heels. "There are too many variables for me to give you any more information now. I'll schedule the autopsy for tomorrow afternoon." The ME issued orders for her assistant to collect temperature readings and samples of the water and soil around the body. She drew a scalpel from her bag and opened the victim's jacket and blouse to make an incision in the abdomen. Body temperature was the most accurate when obtained via the liver.

To give them room to work, Bree and Matt moved away from the remains.

"What do you think?" Bree asked.

Matt shrugged. "I'm not going to think anything until the autopsy, but circumstances do suggest suicide is a possibility. She could have hit her head on a boulder in the water."

An hour later, the remains were transferred to a black body bag and secured to a gurney. Matt, Bree, the morgue assistant, and Deputy Collins carried the gurney up the slope to the ME van. Two news vans were parked down the road. Crews gathered on the other side of the sawhorses. Lights flashed as they photographed and videoed the gurney being loaded.

"Are you going to interview the husband tonight?" Dr. Jones asked Bree.

"I am," Bree said.

Standing next to the van, the ME exchanged her rubber boots for athletic shoes. "In case the victim doesn't have fingerprints on file somewhere, it would be helpful to collect her hairbrush or toothbrush from her home for a DNA comparison." Dr. Jones stashed her rubber boots in a plastic bin and closed the side door.

"I will." Bree nodded.

"Thank you." The ME climbed into the driver's seat and drove away.

Two additional deputies had arrived and assisted with the ground search. As Bree expected, they hadn't found much. She walked back to Holly's vehicle. Collins had the trunk open.

Bree joined her and stared down. The trunk contained a carry-on-size suitcase and an ice scraper. Bree took several photographs, then reached down and opened the suitcase with a gloved hand. A laptop computer sat on top of a pile of unfolded clothes. She snapped another picture.

"She didn't take the time to fold anything," Collins said. "She just shoved her stuff in and left."

Bree closed the suitcase and walked around the vehicle to open the passenger door. Crouching, she moved the wallet aside to get a better look inside the purse. The contents were typical: lipstick, hand sanitizer, nail file, mints. Bree spotted an envelope at the bottom and pulled it out. The flap was tucked in rather than sealed. She gently opened the flap and slid out a folded piece of paper. Scrawled on the paper were the words *I can't anymore. It's too hard.*

"A suicide note?" Collins asked.

"Maybe." About 30 percent of people who died by suicide left a note. Bree took a picture of the note, then returned it to the envelope. "Bag and tag it." Then she gave instructions for Holly Thorpe's car to be towed to the municipal impound facility, where it would be held as evidence until Bree released it. She turned to Matt. "I'm headed to see Owen Thorpe. Want to come?"

"I do," Matt said. "I can leave my truck at your place."

They dropped his Suburban in front of her farm. Bree cast a longing glance at the glow of lights in the kitchen windows.

Matt climbed into the passenger seat of her SUV. "You don't want to run in and say good night to the kids?"

Bree checked the time. After nine o'clock. "Kayla will be in bed. I don't want to wake her. She's finally back to sleeping through the night. I don't want to do anything to jeopardize her routine." Her eight-year-old niece had suffered terrible nightmares for the first few months after her mother's death.

Bree entered Holly Thorpe's address into her GPS. Then she pulled out of the driveway and onto the dark country road. She felt Matt's scrutiny on her profile in the dark.

"Is everything all right?" he asked.

"Yeah. Why do you ask?"

"You just seem . . . tense."

Bree tilted her head. "Just thinking about the case."

"You're not feeling any awkwardness working together now that we have a romantic relationship?"

Along with solving several cases together, she and Matt had been on a few dates over the past two months. "I don't feel awkward with you at all. In fact, I think we make a good investigative team. But with my deputies and Dr. Jones . . ." Bree searched for the words. "I feel like people suspect something and are watching us."

And judging her.

"Or you're just hyperaware of how our relationship will be perceived by others," Matt said.

"Or that." She laughed. "I've only been sheriff for a few months." Bree had been appointed to the empty position after she'd solved her own sister's murder.

"This is a small town. People are going to gossip."

"I don't like being the topic of their rumors." Bree halted at a stop sign, then made a left turn.

"First of all, I don't think anyone knows. This might just be in your head. Secondly, there isn't much you can do about it, except break it off with me. I really hope you don't want to do that."

She could feel his gaze on her profile, as if he was waiting for her reaction. She rubbed at a twinge in her chest. She didn't like the thought of not seeing him. He was the first man she'd ever felt a real connection with. On their last date, he'd taken her dancing, the old-fashioned kind. They'd been the only couple on the dance floor not in their seventies. "I'm not going to do that."

"I don't think keeping our relationship a secret is a good idea." He frowned. "It implies we're doing something wrong when we're not."

"It's not that I want us to have a secret relationship."

"Then why do we have to drive to the next county every time we go out?"

"I don't want people to stare at us. We're entitled to some privacy." Bree turned onto a tree-lined back road. She switched on her high beams to counter the utter darkness of the woods. "People already stare at me when I'm alone, like I'm some kind of novelty."

"I know you were born here, but you haven't lived in Grey's Hollow since you were a kid. So, you're a newcomer from the big city. You've made quite an impression on the town. People are curious."

Bree's takedown of her sister's murderer and her first case as sheriff had garnered her a rush of publicity. The local press had delved into her family history, and people were morbidly curious about her parents' murder-suicide. At age eight, Bree had hidden with her younger brother and sister under the back porch as it happened above them. As much as she personally hated the attention, she would have to run a campaign when her term ran out, and the good press she'd earned would help with her current budget negotiations.

"Look, my family has been under the local microscope for decades. I guard my privacy." Bree bit back a rush of bitterness. People wanted to know all the dirty details of her family's suffering. Didn't they realize the Taggerts were real people, who had suffered real loss? This wasn't a reality TV show.

"I understand why you guard your privacy." Matt inhaled and blew out a hard breath. "But I'd rather walk down Main Street holding hands and say the hell with anyone who doesn't like it."

They emerged from the woods. Bree turned onto a rural highway. As they approached the small town of Grey's Hollow, they passed a strip mall, the train station, and other signs of civilization.

"My office pays you," Bree said. "There are people who would call our relationship a conflict of interest and accuse me of funneling money to my boyfriend."

"In all fairness, you don't pay me enough to qualify as 'funneling' funds. I'm not doing this for the money." Matt had been shot in a questionable friendly-fire incident. He'd gotten a substantial settlement. He didn't need to work.

"I know." Suddenly too warm, Bree loosened the top button of her collar. The discussion with Matt was more stressful than finding a dead body. What did that say about her? She lowered her window an inch, letting a stream of cool fresh air into the vehicle. She wanted to be judged by her job performance, not her boyfriend. But Matt was right. They had every right to a relationship. She had a right to a private life, and hiding their involvement would only lead to problems. She was going to have to suck it up and deal with the intrusion into her personal life. "You're right. I'm sorry."

"You don't have to apologize to me. It's you I'm worried about. Nothing's going to happen to me. I don't need this part-time, poorly paying investigator's job. Wouldn't you rather the news about our relationship come from you, instead of someone else?"

"Yes." Bree loosened her too-tight grip on the steering wheel. "But I'm in the middle of trying to sweet-talk more money out of the county. Let me get through my budget negotiations with the board of commissioners, then I'll figure it out."

Matt reached across the console and took her hand in his big, warm one. "OK. But at that point, we'll figure it out together." He squeezed her hand, then released it.

A few minutes later, the GPS announced their destination was five hundred feet ahead. Bree turned into a small complex of town house–style condos. Yellow with white trim, the units were two stories each. Bree parked in front of the Thorpes' condo, next to Deputy Oscar's vehicle.

The relationship conversation with Matt had been out of her comfort zone, but it had taken her mind off the impending interview.

This was not an official death notification. The medical examiner had not formally identified the remains as Holly Thorpe. But her husband would know the truth, even if Bree had to couch the message with legalese. She shoved open her vehicle door. It was time to confirm a husband's worst fear: his wife was dead.

CHAPTER FOUR

Matt followed Bree into the condo. The place smelled like stale grease and whiskey.

Deputy Oscar had opened the front door. With a heft of his duty belt, he gestured down the hall. "He's in the kitchen. I've made coffee, but now he's just a more awake drunk."

A man sat at a small table, sobbing into his folded arms.

The second Bree and Matt entered the room, Mr. Thorpe jerked upright. He wore ripped jeans and an old university sweatshirt. Both were wrinkled and stained, as if they'd been slept in for days—maybe the entire weekend. His bloodshot eyes locked on Bree without blinking.

"Mr. Thorpe . . . ," she began.

"Call me Owen, please." He drew in a shaky breath. "Deputy Oscar said my wife jumped off the bridge, and you found her body in the river."

Bree stiffened. "We're not sure what happened." She tried for a measured tone, but her frustration was palpable. "The medical examiner hasn't issued a cause of death. All I can tell you is that your wife's car was parked near the bridge, and we found a body we believe to be Holly nearby in the river."

The glance she cast at her deputy was sharp enough to have sliced him in two. Oscar had clearly been in contact with deputies at the scene, and he'd relayed their assumptions to Owen. But assumptions were not facts. Death was hard enough on families without receiving conflicting information, and suicide was particularly difficult to accept.

Matt scrutinized Oscar. The deputy looked away, his mouth tight. He knew he'd fucked up.

"You can go back to your patrol duties now, Deputy Oscar." Bree's tone was dismissive, and the deputy slunk out of the kitchen.

"What do you mean 'believe to be Holly'?" Owen looked confused. He reached behind him for a framed snapshot. He held the picture in both hands and turned it toward them. "Is it her or not?"

In the snapshot, a close-up of Holly was framed by a brilliant blue sky. She was looking over her shoulder at the camera. One eyebrow arched, her expression flirty and mock-serious, as if she and the photographer were sharing a private, sexy joke. Matt guessed that Owen had taken the picture from the almost reverent way he held the frame.

Oh, no.

Either Owen didn't know his wife had been in the water for three days or he wasn't thinking about the effects—that submersion and the beginnings of decomposition had distorted his wife's face.

Holly didn't look like that anymore.

Bree was going to have to explain it to him. Her face went grimmer. "May we sit down?"

Owen nodded, fear clouding his eyes. Matt and Bree slid into chairs facing him.

Bree began, "Owen, the remains were found at the edge of the river. She had been in the water for several days. Submersion and time change the physical appearance—"

He groaned, interrupting Bree. Resting his elbows on the table, Owen dropped his head into his hands. If he was crying, it was silent. Maybe he'd reached the end of his ability to absorb the gruesome truth. The quiet ticked by, punctuated only by Owen's deep, quivering inhalations. Finally, he lifted his head and swallowed. "Does this mean there's a chance that Holly might still be alive?"

Pity shone in Bree's eyes. "That's *extremely* unlikely. I'm sorry. But in order to complete a death certificate, the medical examiner will need verification. Does your wife wear any jewelry?"

"Her wedding band." Owen coughed, then swallowed.

"Can you describe it?" Bree pulled out her phone.

"It's silver with a stripe." He lifted his hand and showed them his own. "It matches mine."

Bree opened her phone and showed it to him. "Is this it?"

He closed his eyes for a few seconds. Opening them, he nodded.

Matt glanced at the picture. The rings matched.

"Does your wife have a local dentist?" she asked.

"No," Owen answered. "She's terrified of them. She hasn't seen one since she was a kid."

Bree frowned. "Does she have a doctor?"

Owen gave her a name.

Bree made a note in her phone. "Either the medical examiner or I will keep you apprised on the official identification process. I'd like to take your wife's hairbrush and toothbrush with us."

He nodded, wiping his eyes on his sleeve. He gestured toward the nearby stairwell and choked out, "Sure. Her stuff is on the left side of the sink." His shoulders slumped, and his hands fell into his lap.

She took a small notepad and pen from her pocket. "When was the last time you saw or spoke to your wife?"

"Friday night around six or six thirty. I don't know the exact time." Owen's tone had gone flat. "We had an argument. She walked out."

"Did she say where she was going?" Bree asked.

Owen shook his head.

Bree took notes. "When did you expect her to return?"

His shoulders lifted and fell in a jerky motion. His gaze dropped to his hands, still in his lap. "She packed a bigger bag than usual."

One of Bree's eyebrows lifted. "This has happened before?"

Owen gave them a short nod. "It's no secret we fought. She'd left a couple of times before. She usually went to her sister's place for a few days. But she always came back after she'd cooled off."

"Did you call her over the weekend?" Bree asked.

Owen didn't respond right away. Nor did he lift his gaze to meet Bree's. Was he hiding something, or was he simply uncomfortable with the answer to her question—that he didn't try to locate or find his wife, and she killed herself?

"No," he finally said. "I was determined not to beg this time. I did all the apologizing. Never Holly." His jaw jutted forward, then he stared at the floor.

"What did you do after Holly left?" Matt prompted, hoping to jar Owen out of his own head.

"I walked down to the Grey Fox." He looked up. "That's a bar a few blocks from here."

Matt nodded. "How long did you stay there?"

Owen glanced away again. "I don't know. I woke up the next day on Billy's couch—he's the bartender. I don't even remember what time that was." His pale cheeks flushed. "I drank a lot of Jack Daniel's." He quieted, contemplative again.

Bree jumped back in. "What did you and Holly fight about?"

"The usual." His tone went bitter. "Money." A whole-body sigh heaved through him. "We're behind on the bills. Holly's mother is dying, and insurance covers a lot less than you'd think. We've been splitting the costs with Shannon—that's Holly's sister—but the bills are killing us."

"So, you don't want to pay for her mother's care?" Bree asked.

"Geez, no. That's not it. I don't want anything to do with those decisions. She's not *my* mom." Owen lifted his hands palms out, in a back-off gesture. "I can't even visit her. Her place smells like death. It makes me sick." His face creased in disgust. He gave his head a small shake, as if physically clearing it of the memories. "I keep telling Holly that her sister needs to pay the biggest portion of her mom's bills. We're using credit cards for groceries, and Holly's paying a thousand dollars a month for nursing services. We don't have that kind of disposable income. Our debt is climbing every month. I've already spoken with a lawyer about declaring bankruptcy. I don't see any way out from under our bills. On top of that, Holly isn't the best at keeping to our budget. She likes to shop." Anger colored his cheeks as he looked around his kitchen. "This place isn't much, but it's our home, and we're probably going to lose it."

"Did Holly understand your financial situation?" Matt asked.

"Yes. She's a bookkeeper. She understands money." He frowned, as if unsure. "She wasn't being rational. I know she's been depressed about her mom and shit, but it was like she couldn't reconcile what she knew to be true with what she wanted to be true. And Shannon just keeps pressuring us for more money." He covered his mouth with his fist. His shoulders shook as he fought back a sob.

As if by silent agreement, Matt and Bree gave Owen a minute to compose himself. Then Matt switched gears to a less sensitive topic. "What do you do for a living?"

"I'm the assistant branch manager of Randolph Savings and Loan," Owen said in a tired voice. "The branch on Plymouth Street."

Matt asked, "Did you go to work today?"

"No, I called in sick." He looked ashamed. "Before you ask, I don't make a habit of it."

"And where did Holly work?" Bree asked.

"She's a bookkeeper for Beckett Construction." Owen's eyes drooped. Grief was exhausting. Any adrenaline surge he'd experienced from the night's stress had clearly drained away.

Now that Owen had calmed, Matt circled back to the family drama. "Did you talk to Holly's sister over the weekend?"

"Shannon?" Owen's brows shot up.

"Yes," Matt said. "You said that's where your wife previously went when you'd had a fight."

"I wouldn't call Shannon unless you put a gun to my head, although I guess I'll have to now." Bitterness pursed Owen's lips. "She hates me."

Bree made a note. "Do you know why?"

"Probably because Holly has bad-mouthed me to her so many times in the past," Owen snapped.

"How many times has Holly left you?" Bree rested her folded arms on the table and leaned forward, intruding into Owen's physical space to apply additional pressure.

Owen pushed his chair a few inches back from the table, trying to recapture his personal boundary. He glanced away from both of them. "I don't know. I don't keep count."

But Bree didn't allow him to evade the question. "More than five times? More than ten?"

"More than five, fewer than ten." Anger lit Owen's eyes as he met Bree's gaze with an insolent glare.

Matt chimed in, forcing Owen to break off the staring contest. "Was your marriage always rocky?"

"No." Owen's voice softened, as if he was remembering the good times. "In the beginning, everything was great. We've been married five years, but the fighting only really started after her mom got sick."

"Had you talked about divorce?" Bree lifted her pen.

"No! Never." Owen shoved a hand through his hair. "We both knew the fights weren't really about us. This is just a temporary thing. Once her mom's situation passed, we'd be fine again." But his voice was weak, and he stared at his hands.

So, once Holly's mother died, everything would be rosy? They'd magically forget all the fights? Matt didn't think that was true. Based on the lack of confidence in his statement, neither did Owen.

Owen leaned back in his chair, his posture sagging and defeated. "I guess none of that matters now. Holly's gone. I can't believe it." He rubbed his eyes. "I shouldn't have yelled at her. I should have been more patient and understanding. But I can't go back now, can I?" He began to cry softly.

"Is there anyone we can call for you? A family member or friend?" Bree asked.

Owen wiped his eyes. "My brother is on his way. He'll be here soon."

"I'll also need the contact information for Holly's sister and employer," Bree said.

"Her sister's name is Shannon Phelps." Owen pulled out his phone and read off the numbers for Shannon and for Beckett Construction.

Bree wrote down the information, then closed her notepad. "We'll let you know when the medical examiner makes an official identification."

She slipped upstairs and returned with a round metal hairbrush and a pink toothbrush in evidence bags. She showed the bags to Owen. "Are these Holly's?"

Owen confirmed with a nod. Then they left him waiting for his brother, staring at the photograph of his wife and crying.

Outside, Bree paused on the sidewalk to scroll on her phone.

Matt glanced back at the house. "Seems cruel that he has to go through this again when Holly's ID is verified."

"It does," Bree agreed.

"What now?" Matt asked.

"I'm emailing Dr. Jones to let her know Owen identified his wife's wedding band. I'll give her the name of her family doctor as well." She tapped on the screen, then slid her phone into her pocket. "Next we drop the brushes off at the ME's office, go home, and get some sleep. No point in getting ahead of ourselves. We'll talk again after the ME issues a cause of death."

CHAPTER FIVE

Bree sprinted down the country road, her breath steaming in front of her face. The coming dawn streaked across the gray horizon in shades of yellow. On her right, early-morning fog hovered over a meadow. When the sun rose, the mist would burn off. Digging her feet into the pavement, she drove herself forward until her lungs screamed. A half mile from the house, she slowed to a walk, her lungs still burning. She unzipped her light jacket and let the damp air cool her.

Ahead, the farmhouse sat still and quiet. Light glowed in the kitchen windows. Bree's best friend and former partner, Dana Romano, was up, so there would be coffee. Dana had retired and moved to Grey's Hollow to help Bree raise her sixteen-year-old nephew and eight-year-old niece. Bree quickened her pace to a brisk walk. By the time she jogged up the back steps, her heart rate had returned to normal.

Inside, she toed off her running shoes and left them on the boot tray. Then she stripped off her jacket and hung it on a peg. She turned to face the glorious smell that promised caffeine.

"Morning." Dana stood at the counter, working the fancy coffee machine she'd brought with her from Philly. She was a morning person. At five thirty, she was fully dressed, her short gray-streaked blonde hair was stylishly tousled, and she was already wearing bright raspberry lipstick. "Did you have a good run?"

"Good but cold." Bree rubbed her hands together.

"In two more months, you'll be bitching about the heat." Dana dusted a large cappuccino with cocoa powder and handed it over. "It's a double."

Bree wrapped her cold fingers around the mug and sipped. Her body hummed in anticipation of the caffeine like one of Pavlov's dogs. "If I don't get my run in early, it doesn't happen. The day gets away from me before the sun comes up." Plus, Bree had needed to burn off her stress from the previous night's crime scene. She drank more cappuccino. "Thanks for this."

"You're welcome." Dana poured steamed milk into her own mug. "Wow. You're pale."

"Kayla was up last night." Thankfully, Bree had been able to get the little girl back to sleep in her own bed.

"Ugh. I thought she was over that stage," Dana said.

"They made Mother's Day cards at school yesterday." The crack in Bree's heart deepened.

"Shit. Poor kid."

"Yeah." Bree sighed. "A little warning from the school would have been nice. I could have prepared her."

Dana nodded. "She's still moving forward in general. There are bound to be small setbacks."

"I know, but each one breaks my heart. I should have stopped home at bedtime last night. The change in routine set her up for a restless night." Guilt poked Bree like a sharp stick. She was unprepared to be a parent. She felt like a pinch hitter who'd never played baseball. Even when she did her best to make the right decision, she sometimes failed miserably.

"You can't be with her 24/7," Dana said. "It's not possible for anyone to never be away from their kids."

"I know." But Bree didn't have to like it. She turned toward the doorway. "I'm going to shower."

"Put on some lipstick!" Dana called after her. "You look like a corpse."

Bree carried her cup with her upstairs and finished her cappuccino in the shower. After blasting her hair with the dryer for a few minutes, she dressed in dark-brown tactical cargoes and a uniform shirt. She removed her gun from the biometric safe in the nightstand and slid it into the holster on her hip. She secured her backup piece in an ankle holster.

She sat on the edge of the bed and put on her socks.

"Aunt Bree," a small voice said.

Bree looked up. Kayla stood in the doorway. The little girl was teary-eyed. A chubby white-and-black pointer mix stood at her side. The dog's worried eyes shifted back and forth from Bree to the child's face. Still in her pajamas, Kayla dragged her stuffed pig by one leg. A memory slammed into Bree's mind: her sister, Erin, age four, clutching her stuffed bunny as they listened to their parents fight. A short while later, their father had shot their mother, then turned the gun on himself while the children hid. Bree blinked away the image. She couldn't let the past drag her backward when she was needed in the present.

She focused on the little girl. "You're up early."

"I had another nightmare." Kayla rubbed an eye. "I dreamed you were gone."

"Oh, baby. Come here." Bree stood and padded across the room. She hugged the little girl close and patted Ladybug's head. Usually, the dog was attached to Bree, something Bree had almost gotten used to, but Ladybug always seemed to know when Kayla needed her more.

Kayla's body trembled for a few seconds, then she sighed and stilled. "I don't want to go to school."

Bree would get another chastising call from the vice principal. Kayla had missed more than three weeks of school over the winter. The little girl needed time to process her grief, but she was improving. It had been only four months since she'd suffered a tragedy that would have brought an adult to their knees, let alone a child.

The hell with the vice principal. Bree would deal with him. She would continue to make the best decisions for Kayla, not the school district.

"OK." Bree crossed the hall and knocked on Luke's door. "Time to get up."

He answered with a groan.

"Luke is grumpy in the morning." Kayla rubbed her eye again.

"So am I." Bree led her niece downstairs.

Dana looked up from her coffee mug and checked the time on the wall clock. "What's wrong?" she asked.

"I had a nightmare." Kayla's lip quivered.

"It's OK." Bree wrapped an arm around her shoulders and hugged her. "Let's get you some juice."

"Eggs, toast, bacon?" Dana believed food could solve most problems.

"Toast, please." Kayla's voice was sad as she slid into a chair at the kitchen table. She curled one arm around her pig and held it against her cheek.

Dana popped bread into the toaster and poured the beaten eggs into a pan.

Bree heard thumps on the floor overhead. A few minutes later, footsteps thundered on the stairs. Her nephew, Luke, hurried into the room dressed in jeans and a flannel shirt.

He poured himself a glass of milk. "Morning."

"Morning," Bree said.

Dana slid a plate in front of him, and he shoveled its contents into his mouth. He seemed to burn calories faster than he could consume them, and his milk habit had increased to three gallons a week. He'd grown two inches since January. At this rate, he'd need new jeans every three months.

"I'll be late tonight," he said between bites.

"Baseball practice?" Bree asked.

"Uh-huh." After pushing his empty plate away, Luke grabbed a jacket and headed for the door. "I'll feed the horses."

Luke was still sad, but he seemed to have adjusted to their new normal. For the past week, though, he'd been abnormally quiet. Bree stepped into her boots and followed him outside. She walked into the barn, where the smell of horses, grain, and hay greeted her. She paused to scratch Pumpkin's forehead. The Haflinger was pony size, though Kayla had informed Bree he was technically a horse. True to his breed, he was a willing, friendly, and sturdy animal.

Luke was not as talkative as Kayla. Rather than pry his feelings out of him, Bree found directness and honesty the best approach with the teenager.

"Kayla is having a tough time with Mother's Day coming up." She leaned on the stall door and waited.

Luke emerged from the feed room with three plastic containers. He went into each stall and dumped pellets. The barn filled with the sounds of horses nosing in their buckets and munching feed. Next he dumped and refilled water buckets. Bree gave each horse a few flakes of hay.

Luke stopped in the middle of the aisle. "I'm just trying to keep busy."

"It's OK to be sad, and it's OK not to be OK."

"I know." He sighed. "The thing is, I'm tired. I don't want to be sad anymore." His brows drew together into a low V. "But it feels like I'm being, I don't know . . ." He struggled for a word. "Disloyal."

"That's natural, but your mom would want you to be happy. You know that. She would want you to have a good life. Your happiness was her priority." Tears clogged Bree's throat. "We'll never forget her. She'll live in our hearts forever. But we also need to find a way to move forward."

"I don't know how to do that." Luke looked lost.

"Me either. Maybe we can figure it out together." Bree cleared her throat. "Maybe we should think about spreading your mom's ashes somewhere she loved."

The wooden chest full of Erin's ashes had been in a closet since her death in January. The kids hadn't been ready to make a decision then, but maybe it was time to lay her to rest. Maybe by doing so, Luke could put aside his guilt over moving forward.

Luke's eyes misted. "Yeah. It feels wrong that she's in a box. She wouldn't like that."

"Think about a place."

He wiped a sleeve across his face. "Mom would want to be outside."

"I agree." Bree pushed off the door. As she passed her nephew, she put a hand on his shoulder. "No pressure. There's no rush. Take your time. I'm always available to talk if you need it."

Luke nodded. Bree left the barn, giving him space. Unlike Kayla, the teen needed alone time to process his feelings. She went into the kitchen and left her barn boots by the door.

Kayla ate half her toast, then slipped out of her chair and carried her pig into the living room. Bree mentally tried to reshuffle her schedule, but she saw no outs. She dragged a hand through her hair, shoving still-damp strands behind her ear. She waited for Kayla to turn on the TV in the other room, then lowered her voice and summed up her conversation with Luke for Dana.

"This feels like a major move forward for him," Dana said. "But we should keep an eye on him for signs that he's not handling it well."

"I can't take off today. I have a meeting with a member of the county board of supervisors." Bree lowered her voice further. "And an autopsy."

"Ugh. Politicians." Dana clearly thought the meeting would be worse than attending the autopsy.

"Right?" Bree agreed. "But I have to play nice. This is about the budget, and I need money."

"Even worse." Dana waved a hand. "I'll hang with Kayla. No worries. All I had on my schedule was a spin class. I'll go for a run later. Kayla can ride her bike with me."

"Thank you. I'll try to come home on time." Bree had a whole new appreciation for working mothers. "Unless this new case turns out to be more than a suicide."

Dana said, "She needs to learn to adjust to you not being here occasionally. You're almost always here in the evenings."

"I know, but I don't have to like it." Bree went into the living room and crouched in front of Kayla, who was snuggling with her pig and Ladybug on the sofa. A cartoon played on the TV.

"I'm sorry, sweetie. I have to go to work." Bree kissed her head.

"Is it something bad?" Kayla's eyes went wide.

"No, of course not," Bree said quickly. "I have a very boring budget meeting today. But I'm the boss, and people need me to make decisions." She kissed her niece again. "I love you. I'll see you later."

Guilt tugged at her heart as she left the house and closed the door. She was halfway across the lawn when her cell phone vibrated. She glanced at the screen. Nick West, a local reporter. No doubt he was calling about the body.

Bree answered the call. "Hello, Nick. How can I help you?"

"I heard you pulled a body out of the river last night. I'm putting the story on our social media and online edition shortly. Is there anything you would like to say?"

"The sheriff's department is investigating the death." Bree climbed into her SUV.

"Can't you do better than that?" Nick sounded disappointed. "Can you confirm the victim's name is Holly Thorpe? Did she jump off the bridge?"

"Sorry, Nick. The truth is, we don't know yet. The medical examiner hasn't declared a cause of death." Bree cleared her throat. "Last night, the sheriff's department received a report of an abandoned vehicle near the bridge at Dead Horse Road. A search of the immediate area resulted in the discovery of the body of a woman in the river. The cause of death is unknown at this time. The sheriff's department is investigating. Is that better?"

"A little," Nick said without enthusiasm. "I assume the autopsy will be today. Can I call you later for more information?"

"You can call, but I can't guarantee what I'll be able to share." Bree started the engine.

"OK." Nick sighed and ended the call.

Bree drove to the sheriff's station on autopilot. Her administrative assistant, Marge, met her in her office with a huge cup of coffee. About sixty, Marge had been with the sheriff's department longer than anyone else. She knew everything about everyone.

"Thanks, Marge."

"You're welcome." Marge looked like everyone's grandma. But her soft exterior covered an iron will and a mind sharp enough to cut through bullshit like a hot scalpel through butter. "The county commissioners canceled your meeting."

Son of a . . .

"Did they give a reason?" Bree asked.

"No. They just asked to reschedule."

"Again."

"Yes, again," Marge agreed. "If they keep putting you off, they don't have to make a decision."

Frustrated, Bree turned to her computer to type up her reports from last night's call. On the bright side, now she had time to prepare for Holly Thorpe's autopsy.

CHAPTER SIX

Ten minutes before one o'clock, Matt parked in front of the medical examiner's building. In the next space, Bree was stepping out of her SUV. Despite the grim reason for today's meeting, he was still happy to see her.

He joined her on the sidewalk and stifled the urge to kiss her hello.

"Ready?" she asked.

"Yes," he lied. He would never get used to seeing a human being sliced open like a fish being cleaned. Oddly, looking at the body in the morgue was worse for Matt than viewing it at the crime scene. At the scene, there were often signs of passion, rage, or other motivations that had led to the person's death. The corpse was a person who'd had a life until something cut it short. With the violence of the crime on display, Matt would experience sadness, anger, or frustration. The morgue's cold sterility made the victim seem less than human.

He took one final breath of clean spring air as if he was stocking up and turned toward the building. He held open the door for Bree. As she passed in front of him, the corner of her mouth turned up, as it always did when he exhibited any of the old-fashioned gestures his mother had drilled into him since birth. The manners were ingrained and as automatic as breathing for him. Her expression was surprised but pleased, but maybe also surprised that she was pleased.

They signed in, made their way to the antechamber, and collected personal protective equipment. Matt drew on a blue gown over his clothes. When the bone saws came out, bodily fluids and fragments of flesh and bone could go flying.

He glanced through the small window that looked into the autopsy suite. Dr. Jones was bent over the stainless-steel table. On it, the naked body lay faceup.

"She got an early start," he said, reaching down to fix the elastic of a bootie.

"Shit." Bree pulled down her clear plastic face shield and rushed through the swinging door.

Matt followed, less upset about missing part of the autopsy. As always, the smells hit him like a blow, immediately turning his stomach. He took two shallow breaths before sucking it up and moving into position next to Bree. His breath fogged the face shield, making him oddly claustrophobic.

The body was scraped and banged up. The bridge was more than thirty feet above the river. At that height, the fall was survivable and the water deep enough that the jumper wouldn't bottom out. But a hundred feet downstream, there were boulders and other debris the body could have struck while being tumbled in the current.

The Y-incision flayed the chest like a wide-mouth duffel bag. The chest plate had been removed, and the internal cavity gaped empty. The organs had been removed, weighed, examined, and samples taken. They would be returned to the body inside a plastic bag before the incision was closed. A block under the back of the neck stretched out the throat, where the skin was neatly excised and peeled back to expose the underlying anatomical structure.

As they approached the table, Dr. Jones straightened. As usual, she got right to business.

"I'll start with where we stand on confirming this woman's identity as Holly Thorpe." The ME inclined her head toward the body. "Ms. Thorpe has no dental records that I could find."

"Her husband said she hadn't been to a dentist since she was a child," Bree said.

Dr. Jones continued with a nod. "Holly was thirty-four. If she hasn't seen a dentist since she was a child, it's possible that dentist is no longer in business or has purged their records. Dentists aren't required to keep records *that* long. According to her family doctor, she's never broken a bone. So, we could find no X-rays to compare. She has no tattoos or obvious scars. While the lack of those things matches this victim, it isn't enough. We still need scientific confirmation of her identification. Her hairbrush contained several strands with the root still attached. We're submitting those for DNA testing and will issue an official confirmation of ID as soon as those results are in."

"DNA tests can take months," Matt said. "That's a long time for the family to wait."

The ME wouldn't release the body to a funeral home until she was satisfied with the identification.

"I agree." Dr. Jones nodded. "Out of respect for the family, I contacted the lab to request a rush on the testing. I'm pushing to have results within the week." She gestured toward the body. "So, based on the information we *do* have." The ME ticked off the facts on her gloved finger. "Basic physical characteristics, the identification in her vehicle and purse, and Mr. Thorpe's recognition of his wife's wedding ring, we are prepared to issue a presumptive ID that this is Holly Thorpe."

Bree said, "I'd like to speak with her family before that information is made public."

Dr. Jones nodded. "If you would prefer to issue the press release, that's fine with me."

Matt was impressed with the ME's thoroughness and compassion. Dr. Jones treated the remains in her care like patients.

"Time of death?" Bree asked.

Dr. Jones frowned at the body. "My best estimate based on the condition of the body is that she's been dead at least three days but no more than five. I'm giving a time of death between noon Thursday and noon Saturday."

"Could you determine a cause of death?" Bree asked.

"Yes." Dr. Jones faced the body. "First of all, she did not drown. There was no froth in the mouth, nostrils, or trachea. No distension of the lungs. But more importantly, she was dead long before she went into the water."

Bree's posture stiffened. "How long?"

"Long enough for lividity to become fixed." Dr. Jones pointed to a purple stain that ran the length of the corpse's side. At the corpse's hip, a long, thin white mark was embedded in the dark purple. "Do you see this impression?"

When the heart stopped beating, gravity caused blood to pool in the lowest parts of the body. This process, known as lividity or livor mortis, usually became fixed around six to twelve hours after death, although being submerged in cold water would have slowed the process. Sharp, pale imprints were the result of dermal pressure and usually meant the body had been lying on an object in the hours immediately after death. The body's weight pressed down on the object and pushed the settling blood to the surrounding tissue.

Dr. Jones continued. "Normally, bodies that are submerged after death show lividity in the upper torso, head, and hands because of the position in which they tend to float." She demonstrated, curling her body forward and dangling her hands and head.

"So, the presence of a side-lying lividity pattern is atypical," Bree said.

"Yes. Now, it's possible she was lodged against a boulder or caught in an eddy." Dr. Jones waved a hand along the edge of the purple stain like Vanna White pointing out a vowel. She stopped with her fingertips a few inches away from the pale mark. "But the preciseness of the overall lividity pattern and the starkness and clarity of this mark suggests she was lying on her side on a hard surface for at least six hours after death."

Bree's shoulders dropped. "I think I know what made that mark. The handle of an ice scraper."

Dr. Jones tilted her head. "The size and shape would be about right. Yes. Do you have a specific ice scraper in mind?"

"There was one in the trunk of her car. I have a photo." Bree stepped away from the table, shifted her PPE gown, and pulled out her cell phone. She stripped off her glove and scrolled. After tapping on the screen, she showed the image to Dr. Jones and Matt.

In unison, they turned toward the body to compare the shape of the ice scraper handle to the white impression.

The ME nodded. "I'll need to confirm with measurements, but that looks like a good match."

Silence fell over them as they digested the implications.

After death, Holly probably had spent hours in the trunk of her own car.

Bree exhaled. "I'll have a deputy bring the ice scraper from the impound garage."

"Thank you," Dr. Jones said.

"How did she die?" Matt asked.

The ME crossed to a laptop on a table. Removing her glove, she scrolled and pulled up a photo of the victim's neck. "These scratches on the soft front of the neck aren't like the rest of the abrasions on the body."

Bree squinted. "They look like fingernail scratches."

"Yes, and they're deep," Dr. Jones agreed.

Matt stared at the photo. The scratches ran vertically from the soft flesh just under the chin to the hollow of the throat. Recognition swept through him. "She scratched her own neck."

"Yes." Dr. Jones motioned toward the victim's hands. "She has two broken nails. I took scrapings from underneath them and found some blood."

Bree said, "It must have been deeply embedded if the river didn't wash it away."

The ME nodded.

Matt pictured the victim clawing at her own neck. "Something was around her neck. She was trying to pull it off. I don't see any ligature marks."

"Correct." Dr. Jones moved toward the victim's head and pointed into the neck incision. "While all that was visible on the surface of the skin was slight redness, here you can see a band of hemorrhaging and deeper bruising. The pattern of ruptured blood vessels suggests pressure was applied by something rigid, like a forearm."

"A choke hold?" Matt asked.

"Probably." Dr. Jones pointed out specific structures. "But this was a poorly demonstrated technique. There's also slight damage to the windpipe and trachea. If the choke hold had been properly applied, there would be no damage to these structures."

"So, she was not strangled?" Bree craned her neck to see.

"Correct," Dr. Jones said. "The damage to the windpipe and trachea were not enough to compromise breathing. She died due to compression of the neck."

Matt's brother was a former MMA fighter, and Matt trained regularly at his gym. He was very well acquainted with choke holds. When a trained person applied a blood choke, the crook of the elbow was positioned over the windpipe so the airway wasn't compressed. The person could breathe. Pressure was applied to the sides of the neck, cutting off the blood supply to the brain and rendering the victim unconscious in seconds. A blood choke was also called a sleeper hold for this reason.

Dr. Jones stripped off her gloves. She set them on the table next to the body. "In normal grappling, like you see in mixed martial arts on TV, either the person submits before they're unconscious or their opponent releases the hold the instant they go limp. The blood supply returns to the brain, and the person wakes in a moment or so."

In reality, the referee watched closely and called the fight when one of the combatants lost consciousness.

"And if the hold isn't released?" Bree asked.

Dr. Jones gestured to the victim. "You die."

CHAPTER SEVEN

As she backed away from the table and Dr. Jones returned to her work, Bree digested the ME's information.

Holly Thorpe hadn't died by suicide.

So, who had killed her?

Bree walked to a nearby table covered with a white sheet. Holly's clothes had been spread out on the sheet to catch any trace evidence that could dislodge.

Each item of clothing was tagged, but each piece would be allowed to dry in a special drying cabinet before being bagged to prevent the growth of bacteria and mold that could degrade the fabrics and DNA. Bree would receive a list of items, but she noted the blouse was silk and a designer label. The jeans and boots were more common mall brands.

Bree led the way out of the autopsy suite. She and Matt stripped off their PPE and exited the office.

Outside, she turned her face to the spring sunshine. The warmth felt clean on her face but failed to eliminate the bone-deep chill of the autopsy suite.

Bree shivered. "Holly was murdered."

Next to her, Matt inhaled fresh air like he'd been underwater. "And her death was carefully and purposefully set up to look like a suicide, which makes it likely it was premeditated."

"Her killer even left a fake note." Anger sparked hot in Bree's chest.

"What now?" Matt asked. "Do you want to interview Owen Thorpe again now, or wait until we have more information?"

"We need a search warrant for their home." Bree pursed her mouth. She had volunteered to give Owen the ME's news about his wife's death. "I'll get Todd to fill out the paperwork. Let's visit her sister and verify Owen's bartender story while we wait."

Bree didn't want to give him any warning. Not that it would matter. If Owen had killed his wife, he'd already had days to dispose of the evidence.

Matt nodded. "Good plan. Don't give him time to shore up his alibi."

"Exactly." Bree phoned her chief deputy and brought him up to speed on the autopsy results. "Get a warrant for the Thorpe residence. We need background checks on Holly and Owen Thorpe and Shannon Phelps. Also, we'll want warrants to obtain financial statements for Holly Thorpe, Owen Thorpe, and Shannon Phelps. But first, call Holly Thorpe's employer, Beckett Construction, and see if she was at work on Friday. If we can trace her whereabouts, it'll help us narrow down the time of death."

"I'm on it." Todd ended the call. He hadn't had much investigation experience when Bree had taken over the department. The previous—corrupt—sheriff had preferred to keep his investigations close. But Todd was proving to be a quick study.

"Do you want to take Owen to the station to stew while we search his place?" Matt asked.

"No. I don't want to spook him into lawyering up. We'll talk to him first, then hit him with the warrant."

Bree and Matt dropped his Suburban at the sheriff's station, then climbed into her SUV.

Matt used the dashboard computer to retrieve Shannon Phelps's address. "Holly's sister lives on Rural Route 29." He entered the address into the GPS.

Bree headed away from town.

Fifteen minutes later, she turned into an upscale development of newer homes. Shannon lived in a gray, two-story, farmhouse-style home, complete with a front porch and hanging pots of flowers. "Nice house."

"A lot nicer than Holly and Owen's place," Matt said.

Bree's phone rang. She glanced at the screen. Todd. "You're on speakerphone, Todd. Matt is also here. What did you find out?"

Todd's voice echoed in the SUV. "I spoke with the secretary of Beckett Construction. Holly Thorpe worked a full day on Friday. She left at five o'clock. Paul Beckett, the owner, was not available."

"Do you have his number?" Bree asked.

"I'll text it to you," Todd said. "I'm working on the search warrant application now. I'll submit it electronically. So, it should come back soon."

Bree turned off the engine. "If Holly was at work on Friday, that narrows our time of death to five o'clock Friday night to noon Saturday. Thank you, Todd. I'll be back in the office in a couple of hours."

She ended the call. Todd's text came through with Paul Beckett's phone number. Bree called him but was transferred to a voice mail. After leaving a message asking him to return her call, she climbed out of the SUV and joined Matt in the driveway. They walked up the front steps onto the porch, and Bree knocked on the dark red door. Inside, a small dog erupted into yapping.

Footsteps inside approached. The door opened to reveal a petite woman with chin-length blonde curls. She held a small fluffy dog in one arm. The animal had a massive underbite, and its bottom teeth stuck out of its mouth like a piranha's.

"Can I"—she sniffed—"help you?" The family resemblance was strong between the sisters. Based off Holly's driver's license photo, Shannon carried ten or fifteen more pounds. The weight softened her face, where Holly's had been leaner and harder. Shannon pressed a wrinkled tissue to her eyes. Her eyes were red-rimmed and painful-looking. Her whole face was swollen from crying.

"Are you Shannon Phelps?" Bree asked.

Shannon glanced from Bree to Matt, where her gaze lingered for an extra second. Bree couldn't blame her. She introduced herself and Matt. Then Shannon's eyes widened as she seemed to take notice of Bree's uniform. "Oh, my God. You're here about Holly." Her face crumpled and fresh tears began to stream down her cheeks.

"May we come in?" Bree asked.

Shannon nodded, her face tight, as if she was unable to speak. She turned and gestured for them to follow her. They walked down a wood-floored hallway to a bright, modern kitchen decorated in shades of gray and white. Shannon set the dog on the floor and stood in the middle of the kitchen, as if she didn't know what to do. On the island, a tea bag's string trailed out of an empty mug.

"We're sorry for your loss," Bree said.

Shannon's head bobbed in a jerky nod.

"We'd like to ask you a few questions," Bree continued.

The dog at Shannon's feet growled, its beady black eyes locked on Bree.

Bree's fear of dogs was ingrained, but this one couldn't weigh ten pounds. Ignoring it, she faced Shannon.

"I'm sorry." Shannon slid onto a stool at the island. "He doesn't like strangers, but he's all bark. He won't bite."

The dog turned and walked, stiff-legged, toward Matt. He sniffed. Then for some inexplicable reason, his posture softened. His fluffy tail quivered, as if it was considering wagging.

Matt crouched and held out a hand. "Who's a good boy?" As usual, he showed zero self-consciousness using his high-pitched baby voice. Also, as usual, the dog fell for it and moved in for a scratch.

"Wow. He doesn't usually take to people." Shannon looked at Matt with new appreciation.

"He knows I like dogs." Matt rubbed the little pooch behind the ears. Then he straightened.

Bree gestured to the stool on the end of the island, diagonal to Shannon. He nodded, understanding that she wanted him to take the lead in the interview. Matt had clearly connected with Shannon through the dog. She would be more likely to open up to him.

Bree scanned the room. Her gaze stopped on a row of framed photos on a shelf. Most were of the dog, but Bree's eyes stopped on a photo of Shannon and Holly as little girls. She guessed they were eight and ten. They stood shoulder to shoulder, mirror images of each other, with softballs in the hands closest to each other and bats over opposite shoulders.

Shannon wrapped her fingers around her teacup and said to Matt, "I didn't believe Owen when he called last night. He said Holly killed herself, that she jumped off the bridge."

"Was Holly depressed?" Matt asked. "Do you have any reason to think she committed suicide?"

"We've both been sad about our mom. She has cancer. Stage four. Plus . . ." Shannon's breath trembled, and she paused to compose herself. One hand splayed on her chest. "That's the same place our daddy died."

Bree's attention sharpened to a knifepoint. That could not be a coincidence.

"When did that happen?" Matt asked.

Shannon nodded, and her voice softened. "It was a car accident. Holly and I were in high school. I still remember the deputy coming to the door to tell my mother. His car came down the hill and slid off the embankment right before the guardrail starts. Mom never was the same after that."

"I'm sorry that happened to you," Matt said.

"Thank you." Shannon blinked tear-filled eyes at him.

"I'm sorry for your loss." Bree exhaled and silently cursed Deputy Oscar for telling Owen his wife had died by suicide. Owen had spread the misinformation to Shannon, and now Bree would have to correct it. "I have some news. Your sister's death wasn't suicide."

Shock widened Shannon's eyes. "What do you mean?"

Bree knew there was no way to soften the blow. "She was murdered."

Shannon froze. "What? How?"

"We're trying to establish the timeline now," Bree said. "We're hoping you can help."

"But Owen said . . ." Shannon seemed confused.

Bree nodded. "It did appear as if suicide was a possibility last night, but the medical examiner issued a cause of death this afternoon."

"I can't believe it." Shannon bit a thumbnail, her attention turned inward.

Bree continued. "Owen said he thought Holly was here with you over the weekend."

Shannon's mouth split in a bitter frown. "She usually came here when they had a big fight. I kept telling her not to go back to him, but she wouldn't listen."

"Why did she?" Bree asked.

"She said she loved him." Shannon sighed. "They have—had—a volatile relationship. They were either lovey-dovey or fighting. There was no in-between with them." She looked away. "Last night I was so shocked I wasn't thinking straight, but all day I've felt like the news had to be wrong. Now Owen's voice keeps running through my head. He was too calm last night."

Bree gave her a few seconds to elaborate, but she didn't. "What do you think that means?"

Shannon lifted her gaze. Anger shone from her moist eyes. "That maybe he killed her."

"Do you have any reason to believe he killed her?" Bree asked.

Shannon lifted a shoulder. "Not on purpose, but maybe by accident. When they fought, they *fought*. They didn't have quiet, reasonable arguments. They had knock-down-drag-outs." Her eyes narrowed. "And I once heard Owen say that he wouldn't ever let her leave him. I'm not saying he's cold-blooded or anything, just that he has a bad temper. But then, so did Holly."

Matt leaned on his elbows. "Was Owen ever abusive toward your sister?"

Shannon flattened her lips in a thoughtful expression. "I don't know, but it wouldn't have surprised me, especially—" She stopped speaking suddenly.

"Especially what?" Bree asked.

"Nothing." Shannon's gaze dropped.

Was she holding back information?

"You don't know of any specific incident?" Bree asked. "Your sister never told you he hit her?"

"No." Shannon shook her head.

Frustrated, Bree switched gears. "When was the last time you talked to Holly?"

"She came here on Thursday night," Shannon said.

"What did you talk about?" Bree asked.

"We argued about Mom's care." Shannon closed her eyes.

"Was she particularly upset?" Bree shifted her position on the stool.

The dog growled at her, and Shannon stroked its ears. "We're both upset every time we talk about Mom."

"Who won this argument?" Matt asked.

"Neither of us. There is no win. Holly left still mad at me. She wants to transition Mom to hospice, and I don't." Shannon's face flushed. "Mom isn't ready to die." Despite her strong words, she didn't sound convinced.

Bree asked, "What does your mother want to do?"

"Mom's been fighting really hard. More treatments could give her another six months. Maybe more." Shannon didn't truly answer the question. "She needs in-home nursing. She used up all the days allotted by her insurance. Plus, there are copays, equipment, and medicine that isn't covered. Holly and I have been splitting the bills. Last month, the total was just over five thousand dollars."

"And Holly paid half of that?" Bree remembered Owen claiming they'd paid $1,000.

"Yes, but not before she complained forever about it." Shannon slapped a hand on the counter. The sudden noise startled the dog. "I'm sorry, Chicken." She kissed the dog on the head and set it on the floor. It ran to a small bed in the corner. Lying down, the dog rested its head on the bolster and stared at Bree as if it was planning her demise.

Shannon continued. "This fight between Holly and Owen was all his fault. I know it. He's been complaining about the cost, like money is more important than our mother's life. Though I guess he has what he wants now. He's off the hook for any more bills. There's no way he'll keep paying now that Holly is gone." Shannon sighed, bitterness souring her face.

"Where were *you* on Friday evening?" Bree glanced around the kitchen. Shannon's big house was substantially nicer than Holly and Owen's condo. Bree's gaze returned to Shannon.

"I was here, working late." Shannon got up and filled her mug with water at the tap. "I usually visit my mom in the evening, but I've had a cold. I haven't seen her in a couple of days. Her immune system is compromised. I can't risk giving her germs. Even a mild cold could kill her. Usually, if I can't visit, Holly does. It's going to be really hard to manage Mom by myself."

"What do you do for a living?" Bree asked.

Shannon put her mug in the microwave and pressed a button. "I run online marketing campaigns. Tea?" she asked automatically.

"No, thank you." Matt shook his head. "Do you have any proof you were working Friday night?"

"I don't know." Shannon's face creased. She looked toward the ceiling. "I waved to my neighbor as I brought in my mail and trash can around six o'clock or so, and I did paperwork most of the evening. I messaged back and forth with a client." She pursed her lips. "I have a security system that keeps track of when I turn it on and off."

"Which neighbor?" Bree opened a note on her phone.

"Across the street." Shannon pointed toward the front of her house. She sighed. "Frankly, I don't go out much. I don't have many friends. I prefer to be alone."

Bree noted the location of the neighbor's house. "Do you work for a company?"

"No." The microwave beeped, and Shannon took out her mug. "I work for myself. I have an office in the house."

"I'll need the contact information for the client," Bree said.

Shannon looked alarmed. "I'd rather not involve my client. I can't afford to lose business right now. With Holly gone, I'll have to pay all Mom's bills now."

"Thank you." Bree let it go for now. If she discovered information that implicated Shannon, she would revisit the client info. Until then, she couldn't force the woman to comply.

Matt gestured around the kitchen. "This is a nice house. Your business must be successful."

"I do all right." Shannon dunked a tea bag in her mug. "But just as importantly, I'm good with finances. I save. I invest. I'm frugal." Her chin lifted in a stubborn tilt. "You're implying that I have more money than my sister, and I should have just paid for more of Mom's care."

Bree said nothing, but that was exactly what she'd been thinking. She let the silence drag on for a few, uncomfortable seconds, knowing Shannon would likely want to fill it.

Shannon huffed. "Why should I have to foot the bill when my sister and her husband spend all their money? They have two salaries and can't manage to save a nickel." She sipped her tea, her face tight. "In December, they took a cruise. Six months before that, they flew to Vegas. Then they fought over the money Owen lost playing blackjack. Holly slept in my guest room for three days after that fight." She set down her mug. "All our lives, I've been the responsible one. As a reward, I've had to shoulder more of the responsibilities. That's not fair."

"No," Bree agreed. "Were you angry at her?"

Shannon didn't answer, but her eyes gleamed. *Self-righteousness?*

Matt said, "If my sister blew all her money on fun, then wanted to cut off my mom's nursing care, I'd be pissed."

Shannon's bitter glare agreed.

"How bad was your fight?" Bree asked.

"All sisters argue," Shannon said, but her tone was somber. "Especially in circumstances like ours." She shuddered. "But there's no way to take back the angry words I said to her. She's gone, and I have to live with the fact that the last thing she heard from me was how selfish, cruel, and irresponsible I thought she was."

"Please call me if you remember anything else that might be useful to our investigation." Bree left a business card on the table. The dog exploded into fresh barking as she and Matt walked toward the front door. As they left, Shannon watched them from her window, her face locked in a mask of thoughtful pain.

They walked across the street and knocked on the door. The neighbor answered and verified that when she'd returned home from work on Friday evening around six o'clock, she'd seen Shannon outside. Bree and Matt returned to the SUV.

Matt climbed into the passenger seat and closed his door. "Owen's looking better and better."

"Most murdered women are killed by their significant others." Bree started the engine, turned the vehicle around, and drove away from the house. "But Shannon also had motivation. Holly wanted to pull the plug on their mom. I can't imagine a more emotional subject for an argument."

"So, this was a crime of passion?"

Bree tapped a thumb on the steering wheel. "Blunt force trauma can be passionate. Strangulation feels passionate. Even a gunshot or knife attack can be fueled by emotions. But a blood choke feels more . . ."

"Calculated?"

"Yes," Bree said. "Even poorly executed, a blood choke takes knowledge and technique. If the ME is right, then the killer was behind her, with his arm around her throat. A real confrontation would be face-to-face. This feels sneaky."

"Dr. Jones said the technique wasn't great," Matt said. "But I wonder if our killer has studied martial arts."

"It's a possibility."

"Financially, Shannon is hurt by her sister's death," Matt pointed out.

"Yes, she is." Bree shifted the vehicle into gear. "But I also had the feeling she was holding something back."

"I caught that too. It was something to do with Owen and Holly's fights."

Bree checked her phone. "The search warrant for Holly's residence is in."

"Let's go see Owen," Matt said. "I find it interesting that he never mentioned Holly's father died at the same bridge."

"Me too." Bree called Todd and asked him to send a deputy to Owen's address with a copy of the search warrant in about thirty minutes.

"We'll stop at the bar on the way. I want to know how strong his alibi is before we question him again." Bree drove toward the Grey Fox, the bar located a few blocks from Holly and Owen's condo. The Grey Fox was a dive inside and out. A few men were lined up at the bar, sipping beer and watching sports on three TVs mounted from the ceiling. The bartender was about thirtyish and a scrawny five eight. The tattoo of a skull on his scalp showed through closely shorn dark hair. He was drying a wineglass with a suspiciously dirty rag. Bree crossed the Grey Fox off her list of possible hangouts.

The bartender spotted Bree's uniform and froze.

She walked up to the bar. "I'm looking for Billy."

"I'm Billy." But he looked like he'd rather be anyone else.

Bree introduced herself and Matt. "What's your full name?"

"Billy Zinke." He resumed drying the glass.

Bree said, "We'd like to ask you a few questions about Owen Thorpe."

Billy shot her a wary frown. "What do you want to know?"

Bree leaned her forearms on the bar. "When did you see him last?"

"He was here most of the weekend." Billy slid the dry glass stem up into an overhead rack and picked up another. "He showed up Friday night, pissed at his wife. Nothing new there."

"What time did he leave Friday night?" Matt asked.

Billy snorted. "He didn't. I had to pry him off his stool at closing and drive his ass home with me. If I let him walk, he'd have ended up in a ditch somewhere. Dude was hammered."

"What time is closing?" Bree asked.

"Four a.m." Billy tossed the rag over his shoulder.

"Why did you take him to your place?" Bree asked.

"Because he was so drunk, I was afraid he would fall and break something—like his head." Billy folded his arms across his chest. "Owen's been a regular here for years. Believe it or not, this place is not always busy. There have been plenty of nights that it's just me and a couple of customers watching the game." He nodded toward the TV overhead. "I've hung out with Owen plenty of nights."

"What time did he leave your place on Saturday?" Bree asked.

Billy shook his head. "I don't remember exactly, but neither one of us woke up before noon."

Bree glanced up at a surveillance camera mounted over the bar. "Do you have security feeds to back up that timeline?"

Billy followed her gaze. "We have security cameras on the front and back door. That's it."

"What about that one?" She nodded at the camera in the corner.

Billy lowered his voice. "Hasn't worked in years."

"Do you have a roommate?" Bree would have liked additional confirmation for Owen's alibi.

"No." Billy shook his head. "I live alone."

"I'd like the footage of the doors then, please," Bree said. "Also, I'll need you to come to the station and sign a statement."

"Sure." Billy disappeared through a doorway. He returned a few minutes later with a thumb drive. "Here."

"Thanks." Bree took the thumb drive.

If Owen had an alibi, then her job just got harder. Who else had wanted to murder his wife?

CHAPTER EIGHT

Shading her eyes from the afternoon sun, Cady pushed the hand truck across the parking lot and into the pet supply store. She'd spent the morning on her hands and knees, trying to lure a pit bull and her three puppies out of the crawl space of an abandoned house. Mud caked her sneakers. Sweat stained her ADOPT DON'T SHOP T-shirt, and dirt streaked her jeans—at least she hoped it was dirt. She desperately needed a shower, but she also needed a couple hundred pounds of dog food.

"Hey, Cady!" Russell called from the register as he scanned a leash for an elderly woman. A black French bulldog sat in her shopping cart. From its cloudy eyes and white muzzle, Cady assumed the dog was also a senior citizen.

"Hi, Russell." Cady waved on her way to the large cardboard box in the front of the store.

Russell handed the old woman her change and closed the register. "The box is full this week."

"That's great. We really appreciate the donations." Cady wheeled the cart to the front corner of the store. Inside, she found old towels, toys, and dog food. "Good score."

"Let me help you." Russell hurried over.

With his help, Cady maneuvered the hand truck under the edge of the box and tilted it backward. Then she wheeled it toward the door, which Russell held open. After she loaded the week's haul into the back of her van, she took a quick mental inventory. She needed additional dry dog food and some chew bones. She put the hand truck in the van and went back into the store.

Grabbing a cart, she hurried into the dog food aisle. She picked up a fifty-pound bag for her own four dogs. Then she selected additional bags for the dogs from Furever Friends that were boarding in Matt's kennel. Cady hefted a case of cans into the cart. The piled-high cart was heavy, and she had to lean into it to move it, so she left it at the end of the row to grab treats and chews. She rounded the end of the aisle and ran smack into a large male body.

She stumbled backward. "Excuse me." Recovering her balance, she looked up.

Shit.

Greg.

Her ex-husband stared at her. "Cady."

He was pale and his cheeks more pronounced than usual, but he was still the best-looking man she'd ever seen. His hair was jet black and wavy, and his eyes were bluer than a winter sky. He wore a black T-shirt and jeans that showed off the many hours he spent at the gym. She knew his abs were as sculpted as his cheekbones. He'd modeled underwear, among other things. The guy was built like a Greek statue.

Of course she would run into him today, when he looked like that, and she looked like . . . Why couldn't she have run into him last week, when she'd had a really good hair day? But then, the whole time they'd been together, she'd felt out of her league.

His looks were the reason she'd been enamored with him, but she'd learned her lesson. She'd paid a high price for being superficial, and she'd never be taken in by a pretty face again. Greg's head-to-toe handsomeness covered an ugly personality.

Memories flooded her, and her eyes turned misty. Her tears had nothing to do with Greg.

He coughed hard, the sound as deep and harsh as a seal's bark.

Despite the fact that she hadn't seen him in six years, and he seemed ill, she didn't inquire about his health. Instead, she remembered the bullshit he'd put her through, and she turned to get the hell away from him.

He shifted the bag of dog food he held under his arm. "You don't have to run away."

"I'm not running, but I have nothing to say to you." She grabbed her cart and spun it toward the front of the store. The weight nearly toppled it, and she rammed into a cardboard display of dog biscuits. Boxes tumbled to the floor.

Damn it.

More tears welled in her eyes as she remembered everything: the pain of her far-too-early labor, the doll-size baby wrapped in a hospital blanket, leaving the hospital with empty arms. She would always carry that hollow ache in her heart.

Now she was crying in a pet supply store.

In front of Greg.

Behind her, she heard Greg mutter, "Stupid bitch," under his breath. Louder, he said, "You're still crazy. I'm glad we broke up."

Anger gathered in her belly like a fireball. Greg didn't have an empathetic bone in his entire perfect body. He thought about only himself.

She whirled to face him. "You're *such* an ass."

His face reddened, and he stepped closer. "Don't talk to me like that."

"Or what?"

He glared but didn't respond.

Six years ago, Greg had been able to intimidate her. Not physically—she'd never been afraid of him. His intimidation had been psychological. He'd tormented her with guilt. She'd been an emotional and physical mess back then. She was neither of those things now. She straightened and lifted her chin. She and Greg were the same height. She couldn't believe she'd once worn only flats to protect his fragile ego. She'd been stupid to marry him simply because their short relationship had resulted in a surprise pregnancy. But buried deep under her grief was the joy that had blasted through her when she'd read the home test. She'd felt like a whole different person. At first, it seemed he'd changed too.

But he hadn't, not really.

She took one step closer and stabbed a finger toward his face. "Stay away from me, Greg. I'm not grieving the loss of my child this time around."

"Don't you mean *our* child, the one you killed with your careless-ness?" Greg's words sliced right through her.

She knew she hadn't been at fault, but guilt speared her in the heart anyway. She'd been five months along in a very healthy pregnancy. The doctor had told her she could continue with exercise she was comfort-able with until the last trimester. She'd been rowing since high school, but Greg had wanted her to stop. The fact that she was faster than him had always made him insecure. She'd been out on the river when the miscarriage started. She would carry that moment—and the nightmare that followed—for the rest of her life, like a scar on her soul.

Later, they'd learned the baby had had a heart abnormality, that he had died before she ever set out on the water that day, and even if he'd been born, he couldn't have survived. But right after his death, she hadn't known that. She'd blamed herself.

And Greg had blamed her too.

Instead of supporting her at the lowest moment of her life, he'd made everything worse.

But she would not argue about her son's cause of death with Greg. She didn't owe him anything.

"Leave me alone." Cady turned her back to him and pushed her cart toward the front register. She would not let him run her out of the store. She would not take his shit this time around.

"Sure," Greg called to her back. "Run away. That's what you do best."

The fingers of one hand curled around the handle of the shopping cart. With the other, she shot him the bird over her shoulder.

Russell appeared at the head of the aisle. He glanced between Cady and Greg and back to Cady. "Is everything OK?"

Cady forced a small smile. The muscles of her face were frozen. They felt like they might shatter. "Fine. Sorry about the mess."

Russell lifted one hand. "Don't worry about it." He frowned back at Greg, who was still standing in the same place, his face locked in an angry scowl.

Cady checked out and pushed her cart to the van. Across the parking lot, she saw Greg get into a small dark-gray SUV and drive out of the lot. Cursing at him, she heaved the heavy bags into the cargo area. The physical labor dispelled some of her anger.

Then she climbed behind the wheel and burst into tears.

CHAPTER NINE

Tuesday afternoon, Matt stood on the front step of the Thorpe condo. He leaned away from Owen and the waft of alcohol. The whiskey fumes coming off the man's body were overwhelming, as if he'd been marinated in booze. If someone lit a match within six feet of him, he was going up like a TIKI torch.

"What?" Owen swayed on his feet.

"We have news about your wife's death," Bree said.

Owen stared, glassy-eyed. "OK." With a *whatever* wave of his hand, he turned and staggered down the hallway. He clearly hadn't showered recently.

Matt and Bree followed him back to the kitchen. On top of the BO, the faint smell of vomit hit Matt hard. Someone—presumably Owen—had been sick somewhere. A nearly empty bottle of whiskey sat on the counter. A second bottle stood at the ready. A tumbler on the table held an inch of amber-colored liquid. Was Owen attempting suicide by alcohol poisoning?

"Wasn't your brother coming over last night?" Matt asked.

"He did." Owen pointed to the stairwell. "Steve is passed out upstairs."

He must be the puker.

"Who do you think brought me more whiskey?" Owen asked.

Not helpful.

Owen took a seat at the table and picked up the glass, the motion sure and smooth, as if he were operating on a professional level.

Bree sat on the other side of the table. Matt stood behind her chair.

"You haven't gone to work?" Her voice wasn't accusatory, just inquisitive.

"I called out sick." Owen sipped. "My boss cleared me to take the rest of the week off. First not-dickish thing he's ever done. I guess your wife has to die before you become a full-fledged human being to a bank."

Matt wanted to pour the rest of Owen's whiskey down the drain and shove Owen into a cold shower. He was killing himself, but what would Matt do if the love of his life were gone? He glanced at Bree. The way his thoughts automatically went to her unsettled him. It wasn't a bad feeling, just one that was strange to him. Did his feelings for Bree run deeper than he'd realized?

So, what if they do?

She was the whole package: smart, honorable, sexy, great sense of humor. Hell, she was literally a fucking hero. Yeah, he was totally fine with getting serious with her. The only sobering realization was that she might not feel the same way. But life was full of risks, right?

"Mr. Thorpe—" Bree began.

"Owen," he interrupted. "Mr. Thorpe sounds old."

Bree continued with a nod. "Owen, the medical examiner has issued a cause of death for your wife."

Owen paused with his glass halfway to his lips.

"Holly was murdered," Bree said.

He blinked several times in rapid succession, as if he couldn't comprehend the news. "What?"

"Your wife did not die by suicide," Bree explained in a patient voice.

Shock paralyzed Owen's face for a few seconds. "I don't understand."

Bree looked as if she was struggling to find the right words. But Owen was too drunk to understand any subtleties. Only the simple, brutal truth would penetrate his alcohol haze.

"Someone choked your wife to death," Matt said.

His statement was the virtual slap across the face that Owen needed. He startled. One hand went to his neck, and his face turned ashen. A range of emotions passed over his features, from grief to horror to confusion. He set his drink on the table. "Who would do that?"

"We were hoping you might have some information that will help us find whoever did this to her." Bree leaned forward. "Do you know anyone who was angry with your wife?"

"Maybe her sister." Owen jerked a shoulder. "They had a fight Thursday night. But I can't see Shannon killing Holly. They argue, but they're sisters."

"Holly told you about their fight?" Bree took out her pad and jotted down a note.

"Yeah." With a sigh, Owen picked up his whiskey and sipped it. "She came home crying."

Bree shifted her weight back. Her nose wrinkled, as if she was trying to ignore the smell. "Do you know what they fought about?"

"Money." Owen finished his drink. "Shannon wants to bleed us dry. She has tons of money, with her fancy house and nice car. But she was leaning on Holly for money for their mom's bills."

"According to Shannon, she's just better at saving," Bree said.

"Shannon's a bitch." Owen rolled his eyes. "It's easier to save more money when you make more money."

"You took a cruise a few months ago," Matt pointed out.

"So? We paid for that trip a long time ago, before Holly's mom got sick. We probably couldn't really afford it, but it was our first vacation since our honeymoon five years ago." He shoved his chair back and stood. "Shannon is right. Holly wasn't the best at saving. Neither am I. But weren't we entitled to *some* pleasure in life?" He carried his glass to the counter and refilled it. "I'm glad we took that trip." Tears shone in his eyes when he spun around. "At least I'll have the memories."

"What about the trip to Vegas?" Matt asked.

"Did Shannon tell you about that?" Owen gritted his teeth and walked back to his chair. "That was a business trip. A conference for community bankers. The bank paid for our hotel. We just had to spring for Holly's airfare. She flew on one of the bargain airlines. Cost us less than a hundred bucks."

Bree waited for Owen to ease into his seat. "Did you gamble while you were there?"

"A little," he admitted. "I lost a few hundred bucks. Holly was pissed. It was stupid. We ran out of money on the second day. The bank only covered my meals, so we ended up splitting meals for the second half of the trip." He toyed with his glass. "Look, just because Shannon is happy holed up in her house alone all the time doesn't mean the rest of us can stand it. Some of us actually need social interaction."

"When we spoke to you last night, you didn't mention that Holly's father died at the same bridge," Matt pointed out.

Owen shrugged. "I forgot. He died a long time before I met Holly."

"What about your wife's job?" Bree shifted topics. "Did she get along with her boss and coworkers?"

"For the most part," Owen said. "She didn't talk about her boss much, and the office is small. Other than Holly, he has a secretary and a few part-timers."

Bree pressed further. "And Holly never complained about anyone at work?"

"Everyone complains about work," Owen said. "And no one always gets along with their coworkers all the time, but I don't remember anything serious. The secretary is an old bitch who didn't like Holly. She was always making backhanded comments, but it seemed like she treated everybody in the office that way. Holly sometimes went out for happy-hour drinks with one of the part-timers. They went out last week, as a matter of fact. Her name is Deb."

"What night was that?" Bree asked.

"Tuesday," Owen said.

"What about her boss?" Matt asked. "Any tension there?"

"I don't think so. Paul isn't in the office much. He's hands-on with the business. Spends most of his time at jobsites." Owen raised the whiskey to his lips, then lowered it with a sigh. "I guess I can't stay drunk forever."

"You've met her boss?" Bree prodded.

Owen nodded. "A few times when I had to stop at the office for some reason. He isn't the kind of guy who hosts office Christmas parties or anything like that."

Bree stood, seemingly satisfied. "If you think of anything else you want to tell us, please call me." She set a business card on the table. "I'll need you to write down what you told me about your argument with Holly, the last time you saw her, and where you were between Friday at five p.m. and noon on Saturday."

"But I just told you all that," Owen said.

"I know," Bree said. "But I'd like it in your own words for my official records. I wouldn't want to get any details wrong."

Also, they would compare Owen's written statement with his verbal answers for discrepancies.

"OK. I will." Owen got up, dumped his whiskey, and filled the glass at the tap. "It still feels surreal. I keep expecting Holly to walk through the door." He stared at the water. "Can I see her?"

"You mean view her body?" Bree straightened.

Owen nodded.

Bree's brows knitted. "As soon as the DNA tests come back, the medical examiner will release your wife's body."

"How long will that take?" Owen's head swung back to Bree.

"The ME says she'll have the results within a week," she said.

He rubbed a hand across his scalp. "That long?"

Matt added, "You'll need to think about final arrangements. When Holly's ID is official, the medical examiner will call you to ask which funeral home you're going to use."

"Oh." Owen dropped into his chair again, as if the reality of choosing a funeral home brought the situation clarity.

A knock sounded on the door. Owen crossed the room and opened it. A deputy stood on the stoop.

"He's with me." Bree dropped the bomb. "He has a search warrant. We need to search your house."

"What?" Owen's voice rose with disbelief.

"Your wife is a murder victim," Bree explained. "We need to search her residence."

The deputy handed the warrant to Owen. He took it, not bothering to read it.

"Take Mr. Thorpe outside and wait with him," Bree said to the deputy. Then she waved a hand at Matt. "Let's start upstairs."

Owen glowered at the deputy but went out the front door without resistance.

Matt followed Bree. They tugged on gloves as they walked up the steps. Bree pulled a small digital camera from her pocket. On the left side of the landing were a full bath and a small bedroom currently being used as a combination guest room and home office. The main bedroom was on the right.

They veered into the guest room. A man lay sprawled, snoring, on a daybed. He smelled of vomit. Bree began photographing everything.

Matt tapped him on the leg. "Hey, buddy. Wake up."

The man startled awake with a loud snort. "What the fuck?"

"Sheriff's office," Matt said. "You need to go outside."

He belched and stumbled to his feet.

"I'll escort him out." Matt didn't want him to fall down the steps. He hauled the drunk down the stairs and out the front door, then left him with Owen and the deputy.

Back upstairs in the guest room, Matt walked past an open suitcase to the closet. Three polo shirts hung in a row.

Bree's camera clicked away as she photographed every drawer and surface. "We'll take the laptop and mail."

"There's only a couple of things in the closet." Matt jerked a thumb over his shoulder. "Probably the drunk brother's clothes."

He looked under the bed. Nothing. He turned to the desk, looking over Bree's shoulder. She was opening drawers. "Old bills, tax returns, large appliance booklets." She closed the bottom drawer. "Let's search the main bedroom. Keep an eye out for broken fingernails."

They had no idea where Holly had been killed.

Matt ducked into the hall bath as they passed. He turned on the light. A toiletry kit stood open on the vanity. Vomit was splattered on the toilet seat, and the room stank. Matt held his breath as he opened the linen closet, which was stocked with towels and toilet paper.

"Looks like it's kept for guests." He turned off the light.

The main bedroom had a large space for furniture. Walk-in closets flanked a short hallway that led to the en suite bathroom.

Bree walked straight through into the bath. Matt went into the first closet, which was clearly Owen's. Jeans, sweatshirts, and sweaters were stacked on shelves. Pants and button-up shirts hung on double poles. Six pairs of shoes were lined up under the hanging clothes. Matt looked between items and checked the pockets of Owen's jackets and inside his shoes. Boxes lined up on the top shelf held off-season clothes. Matt lifted the lid on the last box. Baseball cards. Unfortunately, they were wrinkled, stained, and otherwise damaged, unlikely to be worth any real money.

He emerged as Bree came out of the bathroom.

"Find anything?" She blew a stray hair off her face.

"No."

"Me neither." She stopped in the doorway to Holly's closet. "Wow."

Matt glanced in. Unlike Owen's neat space, Holly's looked like a department store had exploded. He counted forty purses.

"I'll start with the top half." Matt took down a plastic shoe-storage box and opened it. Silver high heels. He tried another. More heels, these bright red. "How many pairs of shoes can one woman wear?"

"Don't look at me. I hate shopping." Bree crouched to open a large shopping bag on the floor. She pulled out a square red purse. "This still has the tags on it." She set it aside and removed two shoeboxes. Pulling out another pair, Bree whistled softly. "OK. I have to admit. These are gorgeous."

Matt glanced down. The shoes were bright blue suede. They had a skinny heel and a red sole. He thought Bree looked amazing in her uniform or just jeans and boots. She was more of a simple woman. But he couldn't help picturing those sky-high heels on her.

Mind out of the gutter, Matt.

"They're Louboutins." Bree gently placed them back in the box.

The name was vaguely familiar to Matt. "Expensive, right?"

"Yes." Bree reached into the bag and pulled out a receipt. "These two pairs of shoes and the bag totaled eighteen hundred dollars."

"Seriously? When did she buy them?"

"Last week." Bree sat back on her heels. "She paid cash."

"Where was Holly getting all this cash?"

Bree took photos, then set the shopping bag aside. "We'll take these with us."

"Are they your size?" Matt joked.

Bree gave him a deadpan look. "As evidence."

He grinned down at her, and she couldn't hold her composure. Chuckling, she moved on to searching the rest of Holly's bags and boxes, opening every zippered compartment. "Those are the only items with a current receipt."

"Some of these other shoes look brand new." Matt turned a short boot over in his hand. The sole was perfectly clean and smooth.

"But we can't prove when she bought them without a receipt." Bree straightened.

Matt opened his phone and took a video of the entire closet.

They finished Holly's closet without finding anything else of note. The nightstands held the usual books, tissues, pens, and other odds and ends. They checked under the mattress and behind the headboard.

Bree opened a jewelry box on the dresser. "Damn."

Matt looked inside. Lots of shiny objects. "Some of that looks valuable."

She snapped pictures. "Let's ask Owen about all this."

Matt carried the shopping bag and laptop downstairs. The kitchen and family room didn't take as long to search. When they'd finished, Bree opened the front door. "You can come back inside now."

Owen went into the kitchen. His brother made a beeline for the stairs. He looked like a zombie, and Matt assumed he was going back to bed.

Owen stood in the middle of his kitchen, his face locked in a sullen frown. "What are you taking?"

"We'll give you a receipt for everything we take as evidence." Bree set the shopping bag on the table. She took out the receipt. "Where did Holly get the cash for these?"

Owen lifted a shoulder in a jerky movement. "I don't know."

"She bought them last week." Bree read off the total on the receipt. "With cash."

The color drained from Owen's face. "I don't know." This time his answer sounded less cocky and more unsure.

"What about her jewelry? Do you know where it came from?"

"No." He shrugged. "I don't pay attention to my wife's earrings." Owen spotted the computer in Matt's hands. "Hey, you can't take my computer!" he protested.

"Yes, we can." Bree nodded toward the folded warrant on the table. "It's listed on the warrant."

"Shit." Owen rubbed a hand down his face. "What am I supposed to use?"

"We'll get it back to you as soon as possible," Bree said. "We're almost done."

Bree and Matt went through the basement quickly. She wrote a receipt for the items they were collecting and handed it to Owen.

He snatched it from her. "I'm getting an attorney. I have an alibi."

Bree gave him a polite smile on the way out.

Matt headed for the door. "Thank you for your cooperation."

Owen looked angry enough to explode.

CHAPTER TEN

Outside, the fresh air wiped the stink of booze from Matt's nostrils. He followed Bree to the SUV and went around to the passenger side.

She stared at him over the hood. "Maybe Holly's source of cash killed her."

"Money is always a good motive for murder," he agreed.

Bree hesitated, one hand on her car door handle. "Let's talk to the neighbors."

They walked to the house next door. No one answered their knock. They had better luck at the unit on the other side.

A white-haired man of about sixty opened the door and gave Bree a hard stare. "You're here about the girl next door, right? How'd she die?"

"That's what we're trying to figure out." Bree introduced herself and Matt. "How well do you know the Thorpes?"

"Well enough to say hi. But I know one thing about them." He zipped his cardigan. "They fight all the time. Loudly. These walls are thin. I can't tell you how many times I went to bed with my noise-canceling headphones on." He shook his head.

"Did you hear them fighting last Friday night?" Matt asked.

"Yes. They screamed at each other for a good twenty minutes, then she stormed out with a suitcase." The older man rolled his eyes. "I also saw him drunk as a skunk the next morning. I was hoping they'd get a fucking divorce this time so I could get some sleep."

Bree pulled out her small notepad. "Do you know if Holly was close to any of the other neighbors?"

"No," he said. "I barely saw either her or her husband. Just when they were going out or coming home."

Bree took the neighbor's contact information. She and Matt tried several more doors in the same building. Two additional residents answered and confirmed the first neighbor's story: Owen and Holly kept to themselves and fought constantly.

Bree and Matt returned to her SUV.

"What next?" Matt asked from the passenger seat.

Bree blew out a hard breath. "What's next is even worse than meeting with the victim's husband and sister. We have to talk to Holly's mother." She checked in with Todd, who gave her the address for Penelope Phelps.

Mrs. Phelps lived in a senior-housing community of tiny, almost identical one-story homes. They went to the door and knocked. Nothing happened. Matt pressed the doorbell. The ringing echoed through the door. A minute later, something scraped inside the house, and the footsteps that sounded were slow and halting. What seemed like minutes passed before the door opened.

The woman in the foyer was probably about sixty, but she looked decades older. Frail and thin, she leaned heavily on a walker. Tennis balls capped the two nonwheeled feet. Petite like her daughters, Mrs. Phelps had clearly shrunk. She squinted hard through glasses thick enough to distort the size of her eyes.

Bree introduced them, showing her badge.

"You're here about Holly."

"Yes, ma'am." Bree folded her hands in front of her body.

Matt bowed his head.

With a labored breath, Mrs. Phelps stepped back. "Please, come in. I have some questions for you."

The door opened into the living room, where Mrs. Phelps shuffled to a chair. Easing into it, she reached for an oxygen cannula and arranged the tubing on her face. Wheezing, she gestured toward a blue sofa.

Matt and Bree sat next to each other. Matt rested his elbows on his knees and hung his clasped hands between them.

Bree perched on the edge of the cushion. "We're sorry for your loss."

"I never thought I'd outlive one of my girls." She met their gazes with rheumy eyes that didn't seem to focus well. "I don't care about much these days—except my children. It doesn't matter how old they get; your baby is your baby. If life wanted to kick me in the teeth one last time, this was the only way to do it."

Empathy flooded Matt. He couldn't imagine facing his own death and suffering the loss of a child.

Mrs. Phelps reached a shaky hand toward a shelf behind her. She selected a framed photo from among a dozen and brought it close to her face. "I still see them as little girls." She handed the picture to Bree, who tilted it so Matt could see.

Two girls sat across from each other at a table, drawing. Their postures were mirror images of each other. One was a little taller, with straight hair. The smaller girl had a head full of curls. Matt glanced at the adjoining kitchen and could see the same table.

"The girls were raised here in Grey's Hollow," Mrs. Phelps said. "We had a bigger house then."

Matt's heart squeezed at the innocent image. "How old are they in this picture?"

Mrs. Phelps touched the taller girl's face. "Holly was twelve. Shannon is two years younger." Her fingers fumbled as she opened the frame and removed the photo. She thrust it at Bree. "Take this with you."

"Oh, I couldn't," Bree protested.

"I want you to have it as a reminder that Holly was a real woman, not a case number or a statistic. She had people who loved her." Mrs. Phelps teared up, then wiped her face with her fingertips. "I can't hardly see good enough to make it out anyway."

Bree accepted the photo. "Thank you."

Mrs. Phelps took a deep breath and appeared to calm. "Up until this last chemo cycle, I was doing OK. But this one was rough. Even worse, it didn't even slow the cancer down." She leaned back in her chair and breathed. "I don't have the energy or appetite to eat. Shannon wants me to get a feeding tube. She says it's a minor procedure." She placed a hand protectively over her belly. Her chin dropped with defeat. "Shannon wants me to keep fighting, but my body is done. I'm done. I can't hold out much longer. I don't want to. Not after this. Losing a daughter is just too much. It's all just too much. I've decided to go into hospice."

"Have you told Shannon?" Bree asked.

Mrs. Phelps shook her head. "It wouldn't be fair to do it over the phone. I'll wait until I can tell her in person."

Bree cleared her throat. "When did you last talk to her?"

"She called late last night. I was asleep when the phone rang. At first, I thought I was having a nightmare." She ran her tongue over her dry lips. Covering her mouth, she coughed, a dry, hacking sound.

"Can I get you anything, ma'am?" Matt asked. "Water?"

She nodded and gestured toward a doorway. Matt went into the tiny kitchen, found a glass in the cabinet, and filled it at the tap. He brought the glass back and handed it to her. She took it with both hands.

"No disrespect intended, ma'am, but are you all right being here by yourself?" Bree asked.

"The nurse will be here soon," Mrs. Phelps said. "Usually Shannon or Holly come in the evening."

"When did you last see Holly?" Bree asked.

"I think it was last Wednesday or Thursday. I can't keep track of the days." Mrs. Phelps paused to catch her breath. "And I can't believe Holly killed herself." She tried to lift her glass to set it on the table, but her arm sagged.

Matt took the water and set it down for her.

"Holly didn't die by suicide," Bree said in a gentle voice. "She was killed."

"I knew she wouldn't have done it. I knew it." Mrs. Phelps's voice weakened. She seemed to deflate even more. Her eyes drooped and closed. Her breathing grew shallow. Alarmed, Matt watched her for a few seconds, relieved to see her chest rising and falling.

He leaned closer to Bree and whispered, "Is she asleep?"

He was hoping she wasn't dying. But then, given her physical discomfort, maybe dying would be merciful. He and Bree crept from the room.

In the car, Matt glanced back at the house. "I sure as hell don't want to die like that."

"She can't opt to not have cancer."

"That's not what I mean." He struggled for the words. "Maybe Shannon is being selfish in wanting to drag out her mom's death. You could make a case that asking her to keep fighting is cruel. Having a tube surgically placed in your stomach doesn't sound pleasant."

"She said it was considered a minor procedure."

Matt snorted. "My definition of *minor* is a procedure performed on someone else."

After he'd been shot, he'd had enough *minor procedures* on his hand to know.

"Or, Shannon just wants to keep her mother around as long as possible." Bree reached for the key, then stopped and leaned back in her seat. "I know how hard it is to lose your mother. If I was Shannon, I might be fighting for every last second that I could spend with my mom too."

"I'm sorry. I wasn't thinking . . ." Guilt swamped Matt. "I haven't experienced the same losses that you have."

"You still have a right to your opinion." Bree reached for the key and started the engine. "But Mrs. Phelps seems like she's running out of fight after losing Holly."

"Cancer sucks."

"On that we agree," Bree said. "But does the argument between Holly and Shannon give Shannon adequate motivation to kill her sister?"

Matt had once responded to a call and found a man who'd shot his brother for drinking the last can of his favorite beer. "People find all sorts of reasons to kill each other."

CHAPTER ELEVEN

Bree drove back to the sheriff's station, a headache throbbing in the back of her skull. She shouldn't have skipped lunch, but the morgue wasn't a great place to visit on a full stomach. She hadn't had time to eat since. She checked her messages.

"Paul Beckett called me back," she said. "He'll be available at his office tomorrow morning at eight o'clock if we want to talk to him."

"Big of him." Matt's voice dripped with sarcasm. "I wouldn't want to interrupt his business talking about his dead employee."

Bree scratched her forehead. "We'll need to issue a statement identifying Holly as a murder victim. Controlled information is better than wild speculation."

"What do we do now?" Matt asked, reaching for the door handle.

"We check in with Todd and see if the warrants are in yet. I'd like to go home before the kids go to bed, even if I have to come back." Bree stepped out of her vehicle. She would likely miss dinner, but she could be home in time to read a bedtime story to Kayla. They were on the third Harry Potter book. Seeing Bree come home at the end of every day helped ease the little girl's fears, as did sticking to their normal routine.

Bree used the back door to enter the station. Todd was at his desk. As soon as he spotted Bree and Matt, he hurried toward them.

"Do you have background information?" Bree asked.

"I do," he said.

"My office. Five minutes," she said.

She and Matt stopped in the break room. Matt made a cup of coffee. Bree grabbed water and a pack of Peanut M&M's from the vending machine.

In her office, she sat at her desk and typed a brief statement for the press, which she gave to Marge to pass on to their media contacts. By the time she'd finished, Matt and Todd had joined her.

Todd took a guest chair and set a manila folder, a three-ring binder, and his laptop on the front edge of Bree's desk. He tapped on the cover of the binder. "I've already organized the case book."

The case book, also called a murder book, would hold a copy of every report, interview, and photo they collected on the case. Anyone who worked on the investigation would have ready access to all pieces of information.

Bree sat in her chair and opened her bag of candy. Matt paced the narrow space behind Todd.

"Let's start with Holly." Todd opened the folder and pulled out a photo of her. "She has no criminal record. She's been married to Owen for five years and has worked as a bookkeeper at Beckett Construction for seven. I confirmed the story about her father. Walden Phelps died in a single-vehicle accident on Dead Horse Road sixteen years ago." He slid a police report across the table toward Bree.

She skimmed. "No questions about the accident not being an accident?"

"No," Todd said. "According to the report, he was coming down the hill too fast and hit black ice. The toxicology screen showed his blood alcohol level was elevated to 0.11."

"Impaired but still walking around," Matt said.

"Yes," Todd agreed.

Bree set the report aside. "What about her financial situation?"

Todd shuffled through some papers. "They're broke. No savings in the bank. They're behind on all their bills, including the mortgage.

Their credit card debt has been steadily increasing. They're only making the minimum payments."

"What about paying a home health aide service?" Bree craned her neck to see the folder.

Todd shuffled through his papers. "I see about a thousand a month going toward health-related companies. Some of that was charged to their credit cards. Seems like when they approach a card's maximum, they open a new one."

"What about payments to Shannon Phelps?"

Todd shook his head. "I don't see any checks to Shannon or any significant cash withdrawals."

"Shannon said Holly was paying a couple of thousand a month. Owen said a thousand, which agrees with their statements. Where did the rest of the money come from?" Bree's question was rhetorical. "Moving on to phone records."

Todd continued. "I reviewed her calls for the week before her death but didn't see anything that stood out. She mostly called and texted with Owen, her sister, and her mother. There were several calls to Beckett Construction and her boss, Paul Beckett, including one on Thursday. She made a very brief call to her sister at 5:05 Thursday evening. The last use of the phone is a text message chain with Owen late Friday afternoon discussing what they were having for dinner. The phone shows no use after that point."

"Makes sense. She died between five p.m. Friday and noon Saturday," Bree said.

Todd nodded. "Moving along to Owen. He's employed by Randolph Savings and Loan. He doesn't use his phone as much as his wife did. Most of his texts are with Holly and three additional numbers. One of those numbers belongs to Steve Thorpe."

"That's Owen's brother," Bree said.

Todd nodded. "The remaining few calls are businesses: an insurance company, an auto shop, a pharmacy, et cetera."

"Have a deputy call Owen and ask him to identify the three additional numbers, including his brother's," Bree said. "Then verify his information."

Todd made a note. "Onward to Shannon Phelps. Never married, started her marketing company six years ago. Seems to be moderately successful. She's not rich, but she pays her bills on time and has a small amount of savings."

Bree updated her chief deputy on the interviews she and Matt had conducted. "The bartender at the Grey Fox has provided Owen with an alibi for Friday night. Let's get a background check on him. His name is Billy Zinke."

Todd scribbled on a piece of paper.

Bree handed him the thumb drive she'd collected from the Grey Fox. "Here's the surveillance video from the front entrance to the bar Owen says he was in all night. Have a deputy review it and confirm any sightings of Owen."

Matt scrubbed a hand over his face. "What's the plan for the evening?"

Bree checked her watch. "Let's call it a day and start fresh in the morning with a visit to Beckett Construction. Hopefully we'll have more data at that point."

"OK." Matt got up and left the room.

Todd stood.

Bree held up a hand. "Is Deputy Oscar in yet?"

Todd nodded. "Just."

"Please send him in when you leave," Bree said.

"Yes, ma'am." Todd slipped out the door.

Oscar appeared a minute later. He adjusted his duty belt and swaggered into her office.

"Please close the door." Bree folded her hands on her desk and waited for him to shut the door and sit facing her desk.

His mouth was flat and his eyes dark. "If this is about the other night . . ."

Bree responded with a lift of both eyebrows. "It is."

He squirmed and clenched his hands into fists on his thighs.

"This is not the first time I've had to reprimand you for not following procedures. We have those procedures for a reason."

Oscar's gaze dropped to study his hands.

Bree continued. "In this case, you told a man that his wife had died by suicide. Not only had her remains not yet been identified by the medical examiner, but suicide was not the ME's finding."

Oscar's chin jerked up. "What?"

"She was murdered."

"But she jumped off the bridge." Oscar blinked.

"Why do you think that?" Bree asked.

Oscar was silent for a moment. "That's what I heard."

"From who?"

His jaw tightened and he looked away again.

Propped on her elbows, Bree massaged her temples for a few seconds. She didn't want to pressure Oscar to reveal who had told him. Cops stood by each other. One should be forced to rat out another in only an emergency or very important situation. Oscar had been with Owen Thorpe. The information must have come from one of the deputies at the scene. It didn't matter who, she decided. Deputies talking among themselves wasn't the problem. Making assumptions and relaying those assumptions to victims' families were the real issues.

Bree lifted her head. "The victim was already dead when she went into the water."

The deputy looked confused.

"Today, I had to tell Mr. Thorpe that his wife's death wasn't a result of suicide. That she'd been killed. As you can imagine, this came as quite the shock to him after your pronouncement." Bree sat back in her chair. "Last time you didn't follow procedure, you lost control of a violent suspect. I gave you a break, even though your sloppy technique endangered everyone in the station." She let that statement sink in for a few seconds. "We were all lucky no one was seriously injured."

Oscar swallowed. A few months before, he'd unintentionally allowed a dangerous suspect to slip out of his restraints.

"This time, a written warning will go in your personnel file."

"That's not fair!" Oscar jumped to his feet.

Bree stared him down. "Procedures are in place for reasons. I expect you to follow them. Do not fail to follow proper procedure a third time."

"Is that all?" Oscar's face reddened.

Bree waited three heartbeats to answer. "Yes."

"Can I go out on patrol?"

She nodded, and he stormed out of her office.

Her headache crescendoed. She glanced at her watch, packed her briefcase, and locked her office. Todd was still working at a computer station.

She stopped in front of the desk. "Don't stay too late. You need sleep too."

"Yes, ma'am." His gaze slid to the door Oscar had just exited.

Bree shook her head. She didn't want to talk about Oscar. She wanted to shower, eat, and read to Kayla. When had her wants become so simple?

Todd lowered his voice. "With all due respect, ma'am, watch your back."

◆ ◆ ◆

Bree jerked awake with her phone vibrating on her hip. She was sitting up in Kayla's bed, the book they'd been reading open in her lap. Kayla's head rested on Bree's shoulder. The little girl's breathing was deep and even, her eyes closed. Bree's foot was numb. Ladybug was stretched out, her head on Bree's ankle, cutting off the circulation. Bree wiggled her foot free and flexed her ankle. A pins-and-needles sensation rushed into her toes.

After closing the book and setting it on the nightstand, Bree extricated herself from under the child and set her head gently on her pillow. Kayla snuggled deeper under her blanket and sighed. The dog's eyes followed Bree to the door.

Bree's phone vibrated again. She hurried into the hallway and pulled Kayla's door almost shut. Closing her own bedroom door behind her, Bree answered the call. "Sheriff Taggert."

The voice on the other end of the line whispered, "This is Shannon Phelps. I think there's someone outside my house."

"Are your doors locked?" Bree checked the time. Eleven thirty.

"Yes," Shannon said in a low voice. "And my alarm is on."

"Stay put. I'm on my way, and I'm sending a car. Do *not* go outside."

"OK. Oh, no!" Shannon's voice dropped to a whisper. "I hear something downstairs. I don't want them to hear me." The line went dead.

Bree phoned dispatch and requested a patrol vehicle be sent to Shannon's address. As she spoke, she grabbed her gun from the safe. After fastening the hip holster to her belt, she put on her backup piece and ankle holster. Without bothering to change clothes, she hurried downstairs.

Dana had fallen asleep on the living room sofa with a book in her lap. She blinked awake and looked up as Bree hit the landing. "Something wrong?"

"Shannon Phelps, the victim's sister, thinks someone is breaking into her house." Bree went to the kitchen. At the back door, she shoved her feet into her black athletic shoes and tugged the hem of her jeans over the baby Glock on her ankle.

Dana followed. "Be careful."

"I will. Don't wait up." Grabbing a jacket that read SHERIFF on the back, Bree opened the door. "I'll text you."

She jogged to her SUV, slid behind the wheel, and drove onto the main road. She stepped on the gas pedal and called Matt. When he answered, she explained what was happening.

"I'll meet you there," he said.

Bree drove to Shannon's address and parked at the curb. Using the radio, she called in her arrival to dispatch. "What is the ETA on the responding units?"

"Four minutes," dispatch answered. "No units were close by."

Randolph County encompassed a large chunk of mostly rural land, including several unincorporated towns with no police departments. The sheriff was responsible for all policing within those jurisdictions. It was impossible for Bree's small force to adequately cover the area. Having a unit nearby when it was needed was largely a matter of luck.

"Roger that." Bree didn't wait. Too much could happen in four minutes. "Responding units, be advised Sheriff Taggert is on scene in plain clothes."

Don't shoot me was implied.

Grabbing her Kevlar vest, she shrugged into it and fastened the Velcro straps. Then she drew her weapon, pulled a flashlight from the glove compartment, and slid from the SUV.

The neighborhood was dark and quiet. Bree heard the distant bark of a dog. She approached the gray farmhouse. No lights shone in the windows. Even the porch light was out. Bree eased up the front walk, her sneakers silent on the concrete. She cut across the lawn, staying in the shadow of a huge oak tree in the center of the front yard.

Overhead, the wind whistled in the big oak. Bree put one shoulder to the tree and glanced around it. She saw no one. She jogged up the front porch, stood to one side of the door, and knocked. Keeping her back to the siding, Bree scanned the front lawn.

Shannon didn't answer the door. Nothing moved. The house sat in eerie silence.

Bree left the porch and started around the side of the house. She peered around the corner. The side yard was empty. Sweat dripped between her shoulder blades, and her heart thudded behind her breastbone.

A siren approached in the distance. Bree exhaled. Backup was on the way but sounded as if it was still a few minutes away.

Barking sounded from inside the house. Bree ran back toward the porch. She leaped up the front steps. She tried the doorknob, but it was locked. Using the butt of her gun, she broke a narrow window next to the door, reached in, and turned the dead bolt. Standing off to the side, she shoved open the door.

Bree held her weapon in front of her and stepped across the threshold. In the shadowed hallway, she paused to listen, but the sound of her own heartbeat drowned out the small noises. Adrenaline surged through her bloodstream. She drew in a deep breath and held it for a few seconds to control her heart rate and blood pressure. Then she grounded herself in her physical surroundings so she didn't get tunnel vision. Living room on the left. Wood floor underfoot. A hallway led to the kitchen.

When she let out her breath, her hearing improved. A door banged. Bree moved toward it. She reached the end of the hall. Moonlight streamed in the window, highlighting the kitchen island and stools. Bree eased through the room, sweeping her gun as she checked each corner. The kitchen and family room were clear.

Gun in hand, nerves standing on end, she headed toward the sound. She opened the pantry. Clear.

An eerie silence blanketed the house. There was no hum of appliances. No air moved through the vents.

She crept through the darkness to a short hall off the kitchen. There were no windows, and the corridor was pitch-black. Bree raised her flashlight. Holding it away from her body, she turned it on and illuminated a closed door. She eased closer and reached for the knob. It turned in her hand. She pulled it open and swept the beam of her flashlight around an empty powder room. Bree exhaled hard.

She checked the attached laundry room. There was no space big enough for an adult to hide. She backtracked to the kitchen. A light wind ruffled her hair. She stopped short, looking for the source of fresh air. Then she saw it. The french door leading to the deck wasn't completely closed.

Did the intruder leave through that door?

Or is that how they got in?

She crept toward the open door, out onto the deck, and scanned the yard. A six-foot wooden fence enclosed the yard. A few trees cast shadows on a large expanse of grass. On the side of the yard, the gate swung in the wind.

The breeze passed over Bree's skin. Goose bumps lifted on her arms. He or she could have just left the house when he heard Bree arrive. *Damn it.* She wanted to give chase. But she couldn't leave Shannon alone.

Bree went back into the house, returned to the foyer, then went up the stairs. She stepped onto the landing. A floorboard creaked, and she held her breath, listening. But all was quiet.

Too quiet.

Moving as swiftly as possible, she turned. The first bedroom on the left of the landing was empty. Bree opened the closet and shined her flashlight inside. Nothing. The second was a home office, with a desk and a built-in wall unit. The third room was outfitted as a guest room. Bree ducked out. The hall bath was clear.

Which left the main bedroom.

She clicked off her flashlight. Moonlight lit the hall, and she didn't want the beam to make her a clear target to someone hiding in a dark corner. She crossed the landing and put a shoulder to the doorframe. Angling her body for the best cover, she peered inside. Her eyes had adjusted to the dimness, and she could see half the room. Clear.

Simultaneously stepping through the doorway and turning, she cleared the blind spot. A closet door stood open, and Bree used her flashlight to check inside. Grateful that Shannon's closet was neat, she shined the beam along the floor to make sure no one was hiding under the hanging clothes.

Only one closed door remained, which she assumed was the en suite bath.

Bree stood on one side of the door, her shoulder to the wall, her gun braced in front of her body. "Shannon?"

The dog barked, followed by Shannon's voice, high-pitched and frantic. "Oh, my God. Oh, my God. Who's there?"

Bree called out, "Shannon, it's Sheriff Taggert. Are you all right?"

"Yes," came the shaky response.

The siren came closer.

"You can come out now." Bree moved back and waited. What if the intruder was in the bathroom with Shannon, forcing her to answer? "Please keep your hands where I can see them."

The door opened slowly. Bree's breath caught in her throat as she waited, gun in hand.

"I have a gun." Shannon stepped out. She clutched her little dog against her chest with one hand. In her other, she carried a small revolver.

"Put the gun on the floor and step away from it." Bree motioned her to step aside. "Is the weapon registered?"

"Yes." Shannon followed Bree's instructions.

Bree approached, picking up the revolver and putting it in her pocket. Then she checked in the bathroom. The large shower, garden tub, and linen closet were all clear.

"A couple of minutes after I talked to you, the dog started barking. Then the lights went out, and I heard someone moving around downstairs." Shannon's words tumbled over each other. She wore yoga pants and a T-shirt. Her feet were bare. Without the revolver, she looked vulnerable. The dog growled. "I was afraid to use my phone. I didn't want them to hear. I locked us in the bathroom."

"That was smart." Bree holstered her gun. "Let's go outside."

Bree herded Shannon to the front of the house. Red and blue lights swirled as a sheriff's car parked at the base of the driveway. Bree opened the front door and led the way onto the porch. She lifted a hand to acknowledge the deputy getting out of his vehicle, then turned to Shannon. "Do you keep your gate open or closed?"

"Closed and locked." Shannon moved quietly on bare feet.

The intruder was probably long gone. Why was Shannon a target, and was tonight's break-in related to Holly's murder?

Chapter Twelve

Matt brought his SUV to a short stop behind a deputy's vehicle. He saw Bree standing on the porch of Shannon's house, in jeans and a Kevlar vest. The air rushed from his lungs.

She's OK.

He'd known she wouldn't wait for him or backup, not when Shannon's life could be in danger. Bree wasn't reckless, but she would always put the safety of others before her own.

He grabbed his large metal flashlight from the door compartment and leaped out.

His eyes met Bree's. "Are you all right?"

"Fine." But the set of her shoulders was tense. Bree waved the deputy and Matt closer. They met in the driveway. "Deputy, please stay with Ms. Phelps. Matt, you're with me."

Matt fell into step beside her. "You're not giving me a gun, so you think the intruder is gone?"

She nodded. "The house is clear. I suspect the intruder went out the back door when he or she heard me arrive."

They walked along the side of the house. Matt stopped and pointed to a window. The glass had been cut away. The extracted pane sat on the grass leaning against the house.

Matt rose onto his toes to look through the window into the garage. Inside, a lawn mower stood next to a black Ford Escape. Other tools and supplies were stacked in the corner. "Looks like he or she went in this way."

They moved through the side yard. Bree pointed to Shannon's gate, which stood open. Shannon's neighbors didn't have fences. Matt and Bree jogged along the fence line. At the end of Shannon's property, Matt shined his flashlight on the ground. A path of crushed grass led through the neighbor's lawn. "The vegetation is too thick to show actual footprints."

The rear neighbor's yard was wide open. Bree could see the street on the other side of the property. "The intruder could have parked over there and walked across the grass to Shannon's house."

They walked from Shannon's yard to the street but saw no footprints. The rear neighbor's house was dark and empty-looking. Bree and Matt walked back to Shannon's house. She stood in the driveway with the deputy.

"Is the neighbor behind you home?" Bree jerked a thumb in the direction of the house.

"No," Shannon said. "There's usually a boat parked next to the house. It's not there, so I think they must be on vacation."

So, no one was home to report a strange car parked there.

"I want to check something," Bree said.

Matt followed her to Shannon's garage. They passed a hedge trimmer and other yard tools. Some two-by-fours and sheets of plywood were stacked next to a toolbox, some small gardening tools, and a box of random junk. Bree went to the breaker box in the corner and opened the door.

Matt aimed his flashlight on the box. The main breaker had been thrown.

"They turned off the power." He flipped the switch, and the power came back on with the hum of appliances. The alarm system began to blare. They went back into the house and confirmed the lights were on. They returned to the driveway, where Shannon was scrolling on her phone. "As soon as the Wi-Fi resets, I can turn it off." She tapped on the screen. The alarm went silent.

"I need a better alarm system." She wrapped her arms around her waist. "It was the cheapest one. My budget was tight when I bought the house."

"Does it have battery backup?" Matt asked.

Shannon lifted a shoulder. "I don't know."

So, that's probably a no.

Matt glanced back at the house. "Is the door between the house and the garage alarmed?"

Shannon shook her head. "No, I was trying to save some money. It seemed redundant since they put contacts on the window and the overhead door has an electric opener."

"Overhead doors are not that hard to break into." Bree holstered her gun. "But it looks like the intruder entered through the garage window."

Shannon looked confused.

"The contacts are magnets," Matt explained. "They are placed on the frame and window to line up when the window is closed. The alarm goes off if the contact between those magnets is broken. So, they only work if a window is forced open. Your intruder cut out the whole pane of glass. He didn't open the window frame or disturb the contact between the two magnets."

Shannon's jaw dropped. "I never thought of that."

Matt didn't believe security systems were something that should be purchased with a Groupon. Whoever had sold her the security system should have explained it better. Criminals were very resourceful.

He continued. "You should ask your alarm company about adding battery backup and cellular monitoring to protect you in case of power outages. Also, you should have the door between the house and the garage alarmed."

"OK." Shannon's voice was weak. "I didn't even keep that door locked before tonight, but I will from now on."

Bree turned toward her deputy. "Dust the garage windowsill and glass for prints. Then come inside and dust the door handles to the interior garage door and the french doors off the kitchen." She turned back to Shannon. "I need you to walk through the house and tell us if anything is missing. Please don't touch anything. I don't want you to disturb any fingerprints."

Shannon shoved her hair back with shaking hands. "Yes, of course."

Her steps were hesitant as she led the way into the house. Matt and Bree flanked her. Shannon toured the living and dining rooms, then moved toward the kitchen at the back of the house. She stopped in the middle of the room, turning and scanning her surroundings. "So far, everything looks normal."

"Did anything else unusual happen tonight?" Bree asked.

Shannon brushed a curl off her forehead. "I got a phone call from a reporter wanting to interview me about Holly's death. I told him no."

"Unless you recognize a caller, you should let your voice mail pick up for a while," Matt suggested. "Reporters can be relentless."

"OK." Shannon stared at the kitchen island. Her hands went to her face, and her mouth opened in a short, shocked gasp.

Bree's hand shot to the weapon on her hip. "What is it?"

Shannon pointed toward the sink, her hand trembling.

The sink was full of water. In it, a six-inch doll floated facedown.

Matt's gut twisted. He walked closer and inspected the small blonde doll. Its straight hair looked like it had been roughly snipped to shoulder length.

Both the position and hair matched how they'd found Holly Thorpe's body in the river.

Sick.

Shannon stared at the sink, her face drawn. Her legs looked wobbly, and she reached for the corner of the island to steady herself. She drew in a sharp breath.

Bree took her elbow and steered her toward the couch. "Breathe."

Shannon gasped. "Why would anyone *do* that?"

To terrorize you.

Bree crouched in front of her. "Do you know why anyone would want to scare you?"

Shannon shook her head hard. Her face was pale. "What am I going to do? I can't go to my mom's house until I get rid of this stupid cold, and I wouldn't want to draw any danger to her anyway. Without Holly's help with Mom's bills, I can't afford a hotel."

Bree said, "I'm going to have a deputy park out front for the rest of the night. Tomorrow, you should call your alarm company and have your security system beefed up."

"I will," Shannon said.

The deputy came into the house with his fingerprint kit. "No clear prints on the windowsill or glass." He went to the french doors, knelt, and set down his kit.

"Do the kitchen faucet too." Bree moved toward the front door.

Matt thought that anyone smart enough to circumvent Shannon's alarm system was also smart enough to wear gloves, but procedure needed to be followed.

"I'll be right back." Bree disappeared down the hallway and returned a minute later carrying the small point-and-shoot camera she kept in her glove compartment. She began taking pictures of the doll in the sink.

"I'll board up your garage window. I saw some plywood out there." Matt returned to the garage and secured the window.

He went back inside the house. The deputy was finishing dusting for prints. Matt toured the house, checking every window and door to make sure it was locked. When he walked into the family room, Shannon was still on the sofa. She hadn't even changed position.

Bree sat on an ottoman, a small notepad balanced on her knee. "Do you have any idea why someone would break into your house?"

"No." Shannon chewed on her thumbnail.

"Could Holly have left something here?" Bree asked.

Shannon lowered her hand and picked at her cuticle. "I don't think so. I cleaned the guest room after she stayed with me last. I didn't find anything."

"Do you mind if I look?" Bree stood.

Shannon shook her head. "Go ahead."

Bree strode down the hall. As Matt checked the french doors, he heard her footsteps overhead. She returned in just a couple of minutes. Their eyes met. She shook her head. "There's nothing up there. Dresser and closet are empty."

"I don't even use that room for storage," Shannon said. "Holly was the only one who used it."

"I have one more question for you." Bree stopped in front of Shannon. "How did Holly pay for your mother's medical bills?"

"She paid the nursing service about a thousand a month directly. She reimbursed me the remaining fifteen hundred in cash." Shannon folded her hands in her lap.

Matt double-checked a window lock and turned toward her. "She gave you cash? She didn't write a check or use an app?"

Shannon's face went blank. "No."

"You didn't think that was odd that your sister gave you fifteen hundred dollars in cash?" Bree asked.

Shannon shrugged. "Holly said she sold some of her designer clothes and purses. I didn't think much of it. She liked to shop, even when she couldn't afford it."

Matt and Bree shared a look. It was doubtful that Holly had made that much money selling secondhand clothes, even designer labels.

Shannon raised teary eyes and waved a hand in the vague direction of her kitchen. "Who would want to scare me like this? I've never hurt anybody."

"I don't know. *Yet.*" Bree folded her notepad and stuffed it into her back pocket.

"OK." Shannon's voice trembled. She brought her legs onto the couch and wrapped her arms around her knees. She didn't look reassured.

Bree returned her revolver and bullets. "How long have you owned your gun?"

"About ten years," Shannon said, pocketing the ammunition.

"How often do you go to the range?" Bree asked.

"Not as often as I should," Shannon admitted. "It's been a few months."

"It's not much good to you unless you practice," Bree said.

"I'll go soon," Shannon promised.

Bree and Matt left. The deputy settled into his vehicle to keep watch. Outside, Bree got into her SUV and lowered her window. She lifted the evidence bag that contained the doll. Its face was scraped and faded. "It looks old. I doubt we'll be able to trace its purchase."

Matt leaned on the open window. The doll was creepy. "Anyone who has or ever had kids could have one of those lying around."

"Easy enough to find them at garage sales too." Bree set the bag aside. "I'll drop it off at the forensics lab and see if the techs can pull trace evidence or fingerprints. Since it was floating in water, I suspect not. But it's worth a try. You never know what will cling to an object." She looked up from the doll. "I'll pick you up in the morning for our meeting with Paul."

"OK." Matt didn't like the circles under her eyes. He would help her however he could. But there was nothing else to be done tonight. He stepped back and gestured toward the house. "This is clearly related to Holly's murder. Until we find her killer, Shannon isn't safe."

CHAPTER THIRTEEN

Matt threw the ball across his backyard. Greta, a black German shepherd he was currently fostering for Cady, tore across the yard like a cannonball. She scooped up the ball midstride, whirled, and raced back to Matt. She dropped it at his feet, backed up, and barked.

"Aren't you demanding?" Matt snagged the ball from the ground with a lacrosse stick and sent it flying again. Greta streaked after it.

Matt looked down at the tan-and-black German shepherd stretched out behind him in a patch of morning sun. "How long before she tires out?"

Brody yawned and rested his big head on his paws.

"You're probably right," Matt said to his dog. "You used to have that much energy."

Brody rolled onto his side and closed his eyes. Despite his lazy attitude, he missed the work as much as Matt did.

Greta dropped the ball at Matt's feet and barked. He repeated the lacrosse-stick maneuver, and she raced after the ball again.

"Is she always this energetic?" Bree's voice sounded behind him.

Matt spun around. Bree was leaning on the fence, her gaze tracking the black blur racing on the grass.

"Yes," he said.

Greta returned. Matt scooped up the ball and commanded her to sit in German. One hundred percent focused on him, the lean black dog obeyed.

"Is that normal?" Bree looked wary, but then, she always did around the big dogs.

Brody stood and stretched. He ambled over to the gate and wagged his tail at Bree. Hesitantly, she reached over the gate and touched his head. Brody sat politely.

"She's a young and very driven dog, which is why she'll make a great K-9," Matt said.

"I can't get the county commissioners to even talk about money for K-9 training. They keep putting off our budget meeting."

Matt sighed. "So? You knew this would happen. You planned on it. Cady is determined to place Greta with the sheriff's department. She'll make it happen. The fundraiser will be a success." Ladybug and Greta had both come from Cady's rescue. "She suggested we host a black-tie casino night. She's done that in the past, and it worked well for her. Big donors like the publicity. I'll bring Greta in and show her off."

Bree gave Greta a doubtful look. "Will she be ready for her performance?"

"She's gorgeous and smart." Matt gave the dog a hand signal, and she dropped to her belly. He commanded her to stay.

"She's impressive," Bree admitted.

Since they were alone, Matt walked over to Bree and leaned down to give her a proper hello kiss. He lifted his head. "Hi."

"Hi." She blinked up at him, her hazel eyes softer and more vulnerable than usual.

"I've missed you." As he said the words, it struck him how true they were.

She rose on her toes and kissed him back. "I've missed us."

Warmth spread through Matt. Bree wasn't demonstrative. Small gestures and words meant more coming from her than most people. A tragic childhood had taught her to hold her feelings close. But he was chiseling through those walls.

She cleared her throat and stepped back. "When will Greta be ready for training?"

"She'll be ready for the academy by the time you have the money."

"Then I'll cross my fingers the fundraiser is enough."

"You need to be more optimistic. Tickets will sell out." Next to Matt's leg, Greta wiggled, bored. "Do you want to pet her?"

"Not really," Bree said. "I wish I did, though."

"She's not vicious, just excitable." Matt glanced down at Greta. Her attention hadn't left his face. "And focused. Very focused."

"Honestly, her size and intensity are intimidating." Bree had been mauled as a child and had a lifelong fear of dogs. "Ladybug is about all I can handle at this time."

"How is she?"

"Pretty good." Bree smiled. "I know I was mad at you for tricking me into adopting her, but now I'm really glad. I never thought I'd say it, but she's good company. Kayla has been sad with Mother's Day coming up, and Ladybug won't leave her side."

"Dogs know." Matt commanded Greta to heel and headed for the house. "Let me put the dogs away, and we can go."

Bree stepped backward as Greta passed. Her response seemed automatic. Bree might have adjusted to having the completely unintimidating chubby rescue dog in her life, and she was even warming up to Brody. But a hardwired, energetic young German shepherd was clearly a totally different animal. Matt put the dogs in the kitchen and closed the metal gate he'd bolted into the wall.

"Will that hold her?" Bree eyed the gate doubtfully.

"Not if she wanted to get out, but she'll stay with Brody. And he can't jump over anymore." The thought of his dog aging saddened Matt. He and Brody had been through so much together. There were only a handful of people he was closer to than his dog. Bree was on that short list. In the brief time he'd known her, they'd faced multiple crises. She'd always had his back. Maybe she also had his heart.

Brody stretched out on his orthopedic bed. Greta stretched out next to him and licked his face. He sighed.

"I'll see you later," Matt said to the dogs. "Cady will come at lunchtime to let you out. Be good."

He and Bree went outside and climbed into the SUV.

Behind the wheel, she chuckled.

"What's so funny?" he asked.

"I used to think the way you talk to the dogs like they're children was weird. Now I'm doing it."

"Don't you talk to your cat?"

"Yes, but like he's my equal—or superior."

Matt laughed. "Your cat is an asshat."

"Yeah. But he's my asshat."

They rode in silence for a few miles. Then Bree turned toward town. "Todd did a little research on the company last night. Beckett Construction has been in business for more than thirty years. The business was started by Paul's father, who died years ago. Considering the nature of their business, they've only had a few minor lawsuits over the years, and they have an excellent reputation."

"What type of construction do they do?"

"High-end kitchens, including new construction, renovations, and additions," Bree said. "Paul Beckett is married to Angela Beckett. They have twin nineteen-year-old boys."

A short time later, she pulled into an industrial complex. Beckett Construction occupied a small office building and an adjoining warehouse. Bree parked and they went inside. The office was bare bones, with drop-ceiling tiles and flat, commercial-grade carpet. Beckett Construction clearly didn't waste money on overhead.

The secretary had obviously just arrived. She was a tall, robust woman in her late fifties with short, ash-blonde hair. She was stowing her purse and brown-bag lunch in her desk drawers as the pair approached.

Bree introduced them. "We're here to see Paul Beckett."

The secretary glanced at the closed door behind her and frowned. "Mr. Beckett isn't in yet. Did you have an appointment?"

"Yes," Bree said.

"Then he'll be here." The secretary typed on her phone with both thumbs. "Usually, he stops at our current jobs first thing. I texted him to let him know you were here. This is about Holly, isn't it?" Her eyes misted.

"Yes," Bree said.

"I can't believe she killed herself. I worked with her every day, and I didn't see that coming." She plucked a tissue from a box on her desk and blotted her eyes.

Bree's statement about the murder had gone out to the press, but the secretary clearly hadn't seen it.

"She didn't die by suicide," Bree said. "She was murdered."

"Oh." The secretary froze. "That's horrible." She inhaled a few times and, with effort, composed herself.

"I'd like to ask you a few questions," Bree said.

Paul's lateness for their meeting was annoying, but it was also an opportunity to question his employees without the boss's presence.

The secretary gave Bree a wary look. "All right."

Bree began. "Was there any animosity between Holly and the other employees?"

"Not that I'm aware," she said.

"What about with the boss?" Bree asked.

"Animosity?" the secretary asked. "No."

"No one was mad at her?" Matt asked. "Most offices have their share of personal drama."

"I didn't say we had no drama." The secretary gave him a wry smile. "But there's nothing serious. Our part-time help is young. One of them is always late, and she dresses very inappropriately for a place of business." She sighed with disapproval. "The other one is pretty reliable, but she has an attitude." The secretary rolled her eyes. "But all we have is typical office drama, mostly petty squabbles over who ate whose yogurt, if you know what I mean."

"I do," Bree said. "Did you and Holly ever spend time together outside of work?"

The secretary picked up a pair of readers on her desk and toyed with them. "No, but Holly is more than twenty years younger than me. We got along fine here. She did her job. I do mine. Holly was usually on time and fairly conscientious about her work. Sometimes she liked to go out for happy-hour drinks. I'm tired at the end of the day. I go home."

"I'll need the names and contact information for the part-time employees," Bree said.

The secretary wrote the information on a piece of paper. She tapped the point of her pen next to one of the names. "Deb has a second job as a waitress at the diner. If she's not home, try there."

The door opened and a college-age woman entered. She wore jeans with holes in the thighs, a cropped sweater that showed off a belly ring, and Converse sneakers. The secretary's irritated glance at the clock pegged the newcomer as the *always late and inappropriately dressed* employee. As much as he didn't want to, Matt had to agree with the secretary, which made him feel really old. The girl looked like a hot mess.

Her eyes opened wide as she took in Bree's uniform. "You're here about Holly." She burst into tears, her whole chest heaving.

The secretary picked up the box of tissues and carried it to the girl. She made some soothing *there, there* noises.

When the girl had calmed down, the secretary introduced Bree and Matt. "This is Connie, one of our part-timers."

Not Deb, then. Matt was disappointed. He wanted to question the part-timer Owen had claimed hung out with Holly after work.

"I'd like to ask you a few questions about Holly." Bree glanced around. "Is there somewhere we can speak in private?"

"Sure." The girl gave a nervous shrug. "I guess we could go in there." She walked toward a doorway. They went into a larger room. A long table occupied the middle, and a computer station was set up at each end. Connie set her bag on a filing cabinet.

Bree asked Connie the same questions about Holly, but the interview yielded no new information. She'd had drinks with Holly once or twice after work, but said, "She's kind of old, ya know? I'd rather hang out with my friends, but I didn't want to hurt her feelings."

Matt had never heard of pity drinks.

By the time they'd finished with Connie, it was eight thirty, and Paul still hadn't arrived. They returned to the outer office. While the secretary called Paul again, Matt walked the office perimeter, stopping to look at framed photos of gleaming new kitchens that hung on the walls.

The secretary lowered the phone. "He's not answering."

"Is that normal?" Matt asked.

Seemingly unconcerned, the secretary set down her phone. "He's not very good about returning calls, and I don't usually call him this early in the morning. He visits whatever jobsites he wants, then stops in the office when he can. Some days, he doesn't even make it here at all. It can be frustrating."

Bree stopped in front of the desk. "Do you know where he was going this morning?"

The secretary wrote a list of addresses on a sticky note. "We have three crews. These are the jobs they're scheduled to work on today. We also have additional jobs in various stages of completion. Some are waiting on materials. Others need inspections before the work can proceed. Paul is most likely at the first address, the one on Bleeker Street. They uncovered major structural issues this week." She handed the note to

Bree. "Paul has been in this business most of his life. He can do the job of every man under him, from laying tile to carpentry. If there's a problem, he'll get it fixed. But sometimes he ignores the administrative side of the business. He might have forgotten about your meeting. His brain tends to be highly focused."

"Thank you." Bree accepted the slip of paper. She gave the secretary her card. "If you think of anything that might help us in our investigation, please call me."

"I will." The secretary opened an old-fashioned Rolodex and filed Bree's card under the letter *S*, presumably for *Sheriff*.

The door banged open, and a tall, heavyset man stalked through the door. He turned angry eyes on Bree and Matt. "You have ten minutes." He continued into his office, leaving the door open.

Some greeting.

Bree lifted a brow at Matt. He shrugged and followed her into the office.

Sifting through a stack of papers on his old metal desk, Paul nodded at the two plastic chairs facing it. "Don't get too comfortable. I don't have much time for bullshit this morning."

Bree sat. "Mr. Beckett, we're here to ask you some questions about your employee Holly Thorpe. You're aware that Ms. Thorpe was murdered."

Paul froze for a split second before setting down the stack of papers. "I heard she committed suicide."

"You heard wrong." Matt eased into a chair without taking his eyes off Paul's face. "Holly was murdered."

Paul scowled, but he'd reset his poker face. "I don't see what this has to do with me."

"Holly worked for you." Bree pulled out her tiny notepad and a pen. "When was the last time you saw her?"

Paul scanned a paper and set it aside. "Friday. She was working on the computer when I went in to grab something off the printer."

Bree clicked her pen. "What time was that?"

"Around nine in the morning, I think. I can't swear to the time. I only stopped in for a few minutes before heading out to check on jobs." He picked up another paper.

Bree cleared her throat. "This is a serious matter, Mr. Beckett. I'd appreciate your full attention."

He glowered. "I don't have to talk to you at all."

Irritation rose in Matt's throat like heartburn. *Arrogant prick.* This was why he preferred his dogs to most humans.

But Bree had better people skills. "Mr. Beckett, we're talking about the murder of your employee." Her tone was serious and just mildly chastising.

Paul threw down the papers on the desk, leaned back, and crossed his arms. *Oh, yeah. Much better.* Matt fought the urge to roll his eyes.

"Are you aware of any problems Holly was having?" Bree asked.

Paul frowned. "Like what kind of problems?"

Bree rolled a hand in the air. "Did she get along with her coworkers? Was she dealing with personal issues?"

"I don't care about any of that." He exhaled loudly through his nose, like an irritated bull.

"Holly worked for you for seven years," Bree pointed out.

"In the *office*," he emphasized. "I spend most of my time at jobsites."

Matt felt his eyebrows crawl up his forehead. "But seven years is a long time."

"What's your point?" Paul's tone sharpened.

"There's no point, Mr. Beckett." A muscle in Bree's jaw tightened. Normally, she had great patience, but Beckett's attitude was clearly frustrating her. "Was Holly late to work recently? Did you have any problems with her work lately? Was she making unusual mistakes, or did she seem distracted?"

"If she was fucking up on the job, I would have fired her." Paul shifted forward, dropping his hands to his desktop. "I don't put up with a lot of bullshit. People do their damned jobs, or they find another place to work."

"So, you don't know if Holly was late or was having work issues?"

"Ask my secretary." Paul waved an angry hand toward his door. "She keeps track of employee records."

Bree leaned forward, placing her hands on her knees. "Did *you* have any issues with Holly?"

"Her work seemed the same as usual." He enunciated each word.

Bree didn't break eye contact. "Where were you on Friday evening?"

He hesitated for only a second before biting off the words. "I don't remember. Let me check my calendar." He picked up his phone and tapped the screen. "There's nothing scheduled. I probably went home."

"But you don't remember?" Matt asked. "It's not like we're asking where you were six months ago. Last Friday doesn't seem that unreasonable."

Paul ignored him, but a muscle in the side of his face twitched. He was hiding something.

"Were you here alone?" Bree asked.

Paul's nostrils flared. "My wife and I are separated."

Interesting. He'd managed to not answer yet another question.

"When did you separate?" Bree asked.

Paul didn't blink. "She moved out a couple of months ago," he continued, his face tight enough to crack. "If I had known I would need an alibi, I would have made plans. Now, if you'll excuse me, I have work to do. My carpenter didn't show today. I have to go cut molding."

Bree leaned forward. "You spoke to Holly last Thursday on the phone."

"Did I?" Paul's eyes narrowed.

Bree's head tilted. "What was the nature of that conversation?"

"I don't recall exactly." His face went blank. "She was my book-keeper. Sometimes she had a question or two about the accounts." Paul pushed up from his desk. Opening his top drawer, he brushed through a loose pile of business cards. Selecting one, he tossed it on the desk in front of Bree. "If you want to ask me any more questions, call and make an appointment with my lawyer." He straightened, then folded his arms across his chest.

Bree collected the attorney's business card. "Thank you."

Her tone wasn't even sarcastic. Matt was impressed.

"You can show yourselves out," Paul said in a *don't let the door hit you in the ass on your way out* tone. He dropped back into his chair and stared at them with angry eyes.

Bree led the way out of the office. She gave the secretary a *thanks* and a wave on their way to the door.

Outside, they climbed into the SUV.

"That was interesting." She started the engine.

Matt fastened his seat belt, shoving the buckle together harder than necessary. "What a jerk. Did he answer a single question?"

"No. He did not." Bree thumped a finger on the steering wheel. "Now the big question is why not? *Is* he just a jerk, or was he purposefully evading our questions for a reason?"

She grabbed her phone, called Todd, and asked him to do a deep background dive on Paul Beckett and Beckett Construction.

"Now what?" Matt asked.

"We need to track down the other part-time employee, Deb, and we need to find out what Paul Beckett is hiding."

Chapter Fourteen

Bree led the way up the concrete ramp in front of the diner. Matt held the door for her, and they went inside. The diner was split into two sections: a counter area with two rows of booths overlooked the front parking lot, and a dining room with tables and chairs stretched along the back of the restaurant. Between the breakfast and lunch rushes, the diner was quiet. A few customers sat on stools at the counter, but most of the booths were empty. The dining room was blocked off with a sign on a metal stand.

She spotted the manager, a white-haired man carrying an armload of menus. He looked like Colonel Sanders without the goatee. She caught his eye, and he hurried over and slipped behind the counter, tucking the menus into a slot. "How can I help you, Sheriff?"

Bree introduced Matt. "We need to speak with Deb Munchin."

The manager's bushy white eyebrows rose. "I hope she's not in trouble."

"No," Bree assured him. "But we're hoping she can help us with a case."

"Of course." He turned toward a waitress in black slacks and a white blouse. "Would you ask Deb to come to the front? She's in the stockroom."

The waitress eyed Bree's uniform with interest, but she nodded and walked away. She went behind the counter and disappeared through a set of swinging doors.

"I'm Roger." He leaned both hands on the counter. "Can I bring you coffee or something to eat while you wait?"

"No, thank you." Bree never accepted free food or any other service from local businesses. The sheriff shouldn't owe anyone a favor.

A minute later, a young woman with long dark hair tied up in a neat bun approached them. She was in her late twenties. Like the other waitresses, she wore black slacks and black athletic shoes. Just below the short, hemmed sleeve of her white blouse was a tattoo of a unicorn.

Roger bowed and turned away. "Take your time, Sheriff."

Bree stepped into the empty lobby. "I need to ask you a few questions."

"Is this about Holly?" Deb's mouth went grim.

"Yes," Bree said.

Deb looked over Bree's shoulder and frowned. She cleared her throat while covering her mouth, then whispered, "Can we go outside?"

Bree glanced back. The manager was watching them.

"Let's get some fresh air," Matt said in a louder voice, then motioned toward the door. He held it open for Bree and Deb, and the three of them walked onto the concrete walkway and around the corner to the side parking lot.

"Thanks." Deb pulled a pack of cigarettes from her pocket. "Roger is an OK guy, but he can't keep his nose out of other people's business. He's the last person you want to tell something personal."

Was she going to share some personal information?

But Deb was quiet for a few seconds as she lit a cigarette.

Bree blinked as a plume of smoke blew directly in her face. "When was the last time you saw Holly?"

Deb drew on her cigarette. "Friday. I only work two days a week at Beckett, usually Thursdays and Fridays, but sometimes they ask me to switch. It all depends on what needs to be done."

"What do you do there?" Bree asked.

Deb blew a smoke ring. "Whatever they need. Mostly payroll, but every quarter they also need help with tax docs."

"Was Holly acting normally?" Bree took her notepad from her pocket.

Deb shrugged. "I guess."

The wind shifted, and the smoke trailed into Bree's nose. "How well do you know her?"

"I dunno." Deb's shoulder jerked.

"Would you consider yourself Holly's friend?" Matt asked.

"Just a work friend." Deb flicked ashes from her cigarette. "We might grab a drink after work to bitch about stuff, but we don't hang out other than that. We haven't even done the happy-hour thing in ages."

Bree lifted her pen. "You didn't go out with her last week?"

"No." Deb's brows knitted. "It's been at least a month, probably more. She keeps blowing me off." She sounded a little hurt and went quiet again.

Bree tried another angle. "Do you like your job at Beckett Construction?"

"No." Deb snorted. "I'm probably gonna quit. I was trying to get out of waitressing. Working in an office doesn't make my feet hurt, but it's just not worth it. I asked Roger today if I could get more hours here."

"Why?" Matt asked.

"Because Paul Beckett is a fucking octopus." Deb made a disgusted face. "Handsy as hell. He's so old. It's gross."

Bree was not surprised. Paul acted like a man who thought the rules didn't apply to him.

"What do you mean *handsy*?" Anger brightened Matt's eyes. Like most good men, he was always offended by men who used their power to abuse women.

Deb frowned. "I mean, he'll go out of his way to rub up against me, and he's grabbed my ass a couple of times. And then he smirks, like there's nothing I can do about it." She dragged on her smoke, then nodded toward the restaurant. "Roger's as gossipy as an old lady, but he's decent and keeps his hands to himself."

Matt's mouth flattened. "Did he proposition you or threaten to fire you if you didn't have sex with him?"

"No. He never took it any further." Bitterness dripped from Deb's words. "He just likes to show me that he can do whatever he wants. Not that everyone minds," she added, her voice huffy.

"Who doesn't mind?" Bree asked.

"Holly." Deb dropped her cigarette and ground it under the toe of her shoe.

Bree's brain clicked as a piece of the puzzle fell into place. "Did she say that?"

"No." Deb gave Bree an *are you stupid?* look. "But I know she was fucking him."

"Holly was having sex with Paul?" Bree clarified.

"That's what *fucking* generally means." Deb lit another cigarette, as if she was trying to inhale as much nicotine as possible while on her unscheduled break.

"How do you know?" Bree asked.

"I saw them together." Deb dragged hard on her second cigarette. She glanced toward the front of the restaurant. "Look, I was attracted to Holly." She stared at Bree, then Matt in challenge, as if daring them to judge her. "I knew nothing would ever happen between us. She didn't go that way, but seeing her with Paul . . ." She shook her head. "Her marriage was intense. She was always bitching about wicked fights she'd have with her husband, but she always said she loved him too. After I saw her with Paul, I thought she was mostly just full of shit."

Bree tried to make sense of her rambling. "Where did you see them together?"

Deb flushed. "Last Tuesday—I asked Holly to go out for drinks. She said she had to get home, but she was acting really weird." The woman glanced away. "I followed her." She flicked more ash. "She drove to Paul's house. He answered the door and let her in."

Interesting.

"Do you have any proof?" Bree asked.

"Like pictures?" Deb's voice rose.

Bree nodded.

"Hell no. That's creepy. I got the hell out of there before either of them saw me." Deb smashed her second cigarette, the gesture both angry and final. "What kind of a weirdo do you think I am?"

Bree assumed the question was rhetorical because Deb had been jealous enough to follow Holly, and that was strange enough.

Stalkerish, even.

Which prompted Bree to ask, "Where were you last Friday night?"

Deb jerked. "What?"

Bree rephrased her question to be more specific. "Where were you between five o'clock Friday evening and noon on Saturday?"

Deb drew in a small gasp. "That's when Holly was killed, isn't it?"

"Yes," Bree said.

Deb pressed a hand to the base of her throat. "What the hell? I give you information, and you turn it back on me?"

"We're ruling everyone out who was in Holly's life," Bree lied.

Deb squinted, her expression becoming more guarded. "I worked the breakfast shift on Saturday morning." She inclined her head toward the diner. "Had to be in at five, so I stayed home Friday night and went to bed early."

"Can you prove you were home?" Bree prodded. Deb was impulsive and temperamental. Anger might make her drop her guard.

She lowered her hand and clenched it into a fist. "I live alone."

"Did you order pizza or see any neighbors?" Matt asked.

"No." Deb evened her weight between both feet. "You can't pin this on me." Anger deepened her voice.

"We're not trying to *pin* this on anyone." Bree faced her squarely. "But we will find who killed Holly."

Deb glanced at the diner. "You should talk to Paul's wife, Angela."

"But Paul and his wife have been separated for months," Bree said. "Why would she care?"

Deb's eyes went a little mean, and she lowered her voice. "For one, Holly was fucking her husband. Two, Paul was heading for bankruptcy. The company was bleeding cash and posting losses every month."

"What do you mean?" Bree asked.

Deb shook her head. "I shouldn't have said anything. I could get into trouble." She shrugged. "Fuck it. I'm quitting anyway. Paul is up to something. When I ask him about unusual transactions, he gets all mad and refuses to answer my questions." She gave her head a frustrated shake. "He's such an asshole. It is my actual frigging job to reconcile the accounts, which I can't do if I can't categorize expenses." She huffed. "And he's been acting just generally weird."

"In what way?"

"Jumpy and even more cranky than usual." She pursed her lips. "One night a few weeks ago, I stayed late to work on the first-quarter statements with Holly. Paul came in. I'm not sure he knew I was there. He went into his office and left the door open. I saw him take a thick envelope out of his safe. It was full of cash. He counted it, put it in his pocket, and left."

"Do you remember what day this was?"

Deb's eyebrows dropped into a V. She pulled out her phone and opened her calendar. "It was three or four weeks ago, on a Wednesday.

I didn't put it on my calendar because they called me in at the last minute."

Someone knocked on the glass, and they all turned to look. Roger gestured to his watch, then pointed at Deb and mouthed, "Sorry."

She waved back at him. "The lunch rush will start soon. I really have to go."

"Thank you for your help." Bree watched Deb disappear into the diner.

Matt stroked his beard. "I can't decide if she's angrier because Paul grabbed her or more jealous that Holly slept with him and not her."

"I suspect both. Emotionally, she was all over the place." Bree started toward her vehicle. "We have a solid reason to officially make Paul Beckett a suspect—and request additional warrants." She called Todd. "In addition to the background info on Paul and his company, I want personal bank and credit card statements and business financials as well."

"Yes, ma'am," Todd said. "We've fielded a dozen calls from news outlets."

Bree sighed. "OK. Call a press conference for this afternoon. I'll give an update on the case and take questions." She ended the call.

"Don't look so annoyed," Matt said.

"You know press conferences are one of my least favorite activities."

"Look on the bright side. We have two new suspects to investigate."

But Bree had been hoping this case would wrap up quickly. Instead, it was getting more complicated.

Chapter Fifteen

Matt settled at one of the deputy cubicles and spent the next few hours typing reports, summarizing interviews, and doing basic research on their suspects. Todd requested subpoenas and phone and financial records, while Bree was tied up with the press conference and paperwork. The regular duties of being a sheriff didn't go away because of a fresh homicide case. Todd and Matt reviewed reports as they came in. Shannon Phelps called to report her alarm company had sent a tech to her house, and he was currently making the changes Matt had suggested to her security system, along with a few additional upgrades.

It was four o'clock before Bree met Matt and Todd in the conference room. Matt brought his folders and laptop with him.

Bree sat at the head of the table and stretched. "Where are we?"

Todd closed the door behind him and dropped into a chair.

Matt started. "I have the background report on Paul Beckett. No criminal record, just a bunch of speeding tickets he's accumulated over the past year." He turned to the page on Beckett Construction. "His construction company was started by his father over thirty years ago. Paul has been working there since the beginning. He became president eight years ago after his father had a massive fatal heart attack at a jobsite." Matt pinched the bridge of his nose. A headache had formed behind it. "We're still waiting on his financial statements."

"Anything on Holly's laptop?" Bree asked.

Todd shook his head. "The tech at the lab is working on it now." He opened his own laptop. "I checked out Deb Munchin. No criminal record, but she was arrested for stalking and harassing a coworker at a dollar store two years ago."

Matt perked up. That sounded promising. "Did the arrest report contain any specifics?"

Todd nodded. "A female coworker claimed Deb followed her home from work and sat outside her apartment, watching her."

"Creepy." Bree made a note. "And Deb admitted to doing just that with Holly."

"Yeah," Todd agreed. "But the charges were dropped when Deb agreed to leave her alone. She quit the job, and there were no more complaints. So, I assume she complied."

"Still." Bree drummed her fingers on the table. "Stalking is a very personal crime."

"Like choking," Matt added. "And we already know that Deb had a thing for Holly."

"And Deb admitted to following Holly to Paul's house. Jealousy is a potential motivation for the murder." Bree straightened. "Let's dig deeper into Deb's background and contact the victim for more information."

Todd typed on his keyboard. "Background information on Billy Zinke shows no criminal record. I found nothing on him more serious than a few parking tickets."

Bree looked thoughtful. "Can we think of other ways to poke holes in Owen's alibi? He's not at the top of my list right now, but I don't want to leave clues unturned."

"I could go to the Grey Fox to talk to the regulars," Todd suggested. "If Owen is a regular, then people might remember him being there last Friday night."

Bree nodded. "Not a bad idea. Go in plain clothes. Take Collins with you. Female patrons will feel more comfortable talking to a woman."

"Yes, ma'am. What about Shannon?" Todd asked. "Is she still a suspect?"

Bree nodded. "Yes. It's too early to rule anyone completely out. On one hand, she doesn't have an alibi, and she has motivation to kill Holly. On the other, she will suffer financially because Holly is no longer around to share the cost of their mother's medical bills."

Matt scrolled on his computer. "The preliminary autopsy report is in. No surprises." The final autopsy report wouldn't be complete until all the tox screens came in, which would take weeks. "There's a trace-evidence report from forensics. Traces of something called metabasalt was found in the trunk of Holly's car."

"Metabasalt?" Bree looked up.

Matt skimmed the report. "A billion-year-old stone from the Blue Ridge Mountains of West Virginia, blah blah blah. It's ground into a green clay that's used in making Har-Tru tennis courts."

"No one has mentioned Holly playing tennis," Bree said.

"Maybe she didn't, but maybe her killer does," Matt said.

Bree stood. "We'll do a follow-up interview with Shannon."

"I'd also like to talk to Paul again." Matt couldn't decide if he was difficult—or guilty.

"Not sure what we'll learn from him. He's uncooperative." Bree frowned.

Exactly, thought Matt. "And I want to know why."

"Let's set up an appointment to talk to him." Bree reached for her phone.

Matt stopped her with a raised hand. "Or, we could follow him tonight and see where he goes after work."

"A stakeout?" Bree groaned.

"I know they suck," Matt said.

Stakeouts were not as exciting as they were portrayed on TV. They were mostly sitting in your vehicle eating fast food and trying not to fall asleep.

"It could take days to catch Paul doing anything at all, let alone something illegal."

"I know," he agreed. "But Deb said Paul took a bunch of cash out of his safe on a Wednesday night. Tonight is also a Wednesday night. Also, he won't talk to us, and we both thought he was hiding something. We need to find out what he's up to. We could get lucky."

"You're right. We'll try a stakeout." She checked the time on her phone. "Let's break for dinner. I'll pick you up afterward."

Matt grabbed his files and drove home. Cady's van was in the driveway. Matt collected his mail, then went into the house.

His sister was unsnapping Greta's leash. "I just had them outside. I was here anyway, and I didn't know what time you'd be home."

Matt gave her a quick one-armed hug. "Thanks." His sister's eyes were red, and she looked tired. "Are you OK?"

Cady nodded, then sighed. "I saw Greg yesterday."

Matt stiffened. "Was he bothering you?"

"No." She shook her head. "It was an accidental encounter. He seemed as surprised to see me as I was to see him."

"But?" Anger flared in Matt's chest.

Cady gave him a jerky shrug. "He's still an ass."

But the incident had upset her. Matt wanted to drive to her ex's house and *upset* him.

"Want me to kill him for you?" He was joking. Mostly.

"No." She put a hand on his forearm. "I'm a little sad, but I'll be OK. In a way, it was good to see that he hasn't changed. It confirms that I made the right call divorcing him."

"Did you honestly ever question that?"

Cady let out a long breath through her mouth. "I wasn't thinking straight back then."

"You were grieving," Matt corrected.

She nodded. "I'll be OK in a couple of days. I just need to keep busy."

Matt assessed her with a frown. He'd been wrong when he'd assumed that she'd gotten over it. She was still grieving. If she'd had a partner who'd worked through their shared grief with her, like a team, would she still be this unhappy? Equating marriage with teamwork brought Bree to mind.

"It's not like I don't ever think about him," she said in a sad voice.

Matt knew the *him* she was referring to was not her ex but the baby who'd never had a chance. His heart broke for her. He gave her a hard hug. "I'm always here for you."

"I know, and thanks." Cady hugged him back. "Now, let's talk about something else."

Brody and Greta crowded Matt for pets. He knelt down and tried to give both dogs equal attention. Greta lost interest and chased after a tennis ball, but Brody leaned on Matt, who stroked his side. "There's my boy."

Matt set his files on the table.

"Dad sent pot roast." Cady pointed to the fridge. "He knows you're working an investigation and didn't want you to starve to death. You should probably call the 'rents. They worry."

"I will." Matt laughed. "They really know how to pile on the guilt."

"At least they also pile on the mashed potatoes and gravy."

"Good point." Matt's stomach rumbled. "It's a price I'm willing to pay. There's nothing like Dad's pot roast."

A retired family doctor, Matt's dad was the cook in the family. Their mom was a retired teacher who couldn't make edible toast.

Cady tapped the closed folder on the top of Matt's stack. "I know Shannon Phelps."

"You do?" Matt went to the fridge and took out a glass container. His dad had separated meat, mashed potatoes, and carrots into three piles and smothered everything with gravy. Practically drooling, Matt put the container in the microwave.

Cady nodded. "She adopted a dog from us a couple of months ago."

"What do you remember about her?" He punched in two minutes on the keypad and hit "Start." The microwaved hummed.

"Blonde. Short. About this tall." Cady indicated a height with her hand level with her shoulder. "She was shy, almost introverted, but I liked her. She was sweet with the dog."

The microwave beeped, and Matt removed his dinner. The scent of his dad's gravy filled the kitchen.

"I matched her with a little dog, a super nervous type. We named him Chicken because he was so scared. I thought Shannon would be a good fit for him because her house would be quiet. She said she didn't get much company and worked from home. Their personalities matched. She was skittish too."

Matt carried the steaming dish to the table. His sister sat across from him.

"Want some?" He gestured to the food.

"Are you kidding?" Cady rubbed her stomach. "Dad already fed me."

Matt dug in. "What else do you remember about Shannon?"

"I felt really awful for her. Someone in her family was sick." Cady lifted a finger and cocked her head, trying to remember.

"Her mother." Fork in hand, Matt stared at his food. Shannon Phelps would never have a homecooked meal prepared by her parent again.

"What's wrong?" Cady asked.

"Shannon's sister was killed."

"What?" Realization lit in Cady's eyes. "The woman found at the Dead Horse Road bridge."

"Yeah. Keep her identity to yourself, OK?" Matt sighed and picked at his food. He needed to eat regardless of his appetite. "Shannon doesn't need extra gossip on top of media attention."

"Sure. That's horrible. She wanted the dog for company. I hope he helped."

"Me too," Matt said.

Soon, Shannon would have no family left in the world. She'd already lost her father and her sister. Her mother was dying. And someone had broken into her house to leave her a nasty message.

Why? Matt could not think of a motivation to frighten Shannon.

For one second, he considered what he'd do if someone hurt a member of his family. Then he pushed the thought away. It was too painful to even contemplate. While Bree was working hard to reconnect with her family, Matt had always had the support and love of his. When he'd been shot and his career abruptly cut off, it was his family who'd gotten him through the ordeal.

"How was the dog adjusting?" Cady asked.

"He was still nervous," Matt said. "I doubt that's going to change."

"I hope he isn't too much for her to handle." She frowned. "It can take months for a rescue's true personality to come out. I'll reach out to her and check up on him."

Cady took animal rescue seriously. She worried about every animal she placed. Adopters had to sign a form promising to return dogs to the organization if the placement didn't work out.

"I suspect she's overwhelmed by her situation, not by the dog."

Cady pressed her lips together into an angry line. "I hope you find her sister's killer."

Determination and empathy flooded Matt. Already damaged, Shannon's life was in free fall because someone had murdered Holly. The sisters might not have seen eye to eye on their mother's care, but they'd still had each other. There was nothing like family. Now Shannon was alone and facing another bout with grief.

He stabbed a piece of meat. "Don't worry. I will."

CHAPTER SIXTEEN

Bree parked her SUV next to the house. From there, she could see through the kitchen window. Dana opened the oven to check on dinner. Bree's brother, Adam, pulled dishes from the upper cabinet, while Kayla gathered utensils from the drawer. Luke sat at the table, writing in a spiral notebook.

The domestic scene punched Bree in the heart. She'd never had this in her entire life. She'd been separated from her siblings after their parents' deaths and raised alone by a cousin. The absence of Adam and Erin in her childhood had been profound, and the isolation had left a mark. Bree had to work hard at maintaining personal relationships. She often had to force herself not to make quick decisions, but to step back and evaluate situations. Her instinct to withdraw from any relationship that could render her vulnerable was pure self-preservation, born of a lonely and traumatic childhood. Before her parents' murder-suicide, she'd lived in an abusive and terrifying home. For most of her life, she'd had no one to rely on but herself.

But she was an adult now, and she was determined to put the past behind her. Her own sister's murder had taught her the importance of family. If only she'd learned that lesson before Erin had died.

With tears gathering in the corners of her eyes, she slid out of the SUV and veered toward the barn. She rolled open the heavy door and turned on the light. Three heads greeted her. Riot, Luke's bay gelding, nickered and kicked his stall door. Pumpkin bobbed his head, begging for a scratch or a treat. The sturdy little horse was definitely spoiled. She scratched him under his flaxen forelock on her way by. She grabbed a brush and slipped into Cowboy's stall. The paint was a calm, patient beast. He didn't move as Bree swept the brush over his coat in long strokes. "Your white patches are looking dingy. Did you roll in the mud today?"

He shifted his weight. His eyelids drooped.

"Maybe it'll be warm enough for a bath this weekend." Bree worked on a crusted patch of dried mud on his rump. Cowboy had excellent ground manners. He was unflappable on the trail. He wasn't fancy, but he was a sound, sensible horse all around. Bree hadn't been on a horse since she was a kid, but when she rode Cowboy for the first time after her sister's death, she felt safe. He—and the other two horses—had been slaughter-bound when Erin had pulled them from the kill buyer's pen. Bree stopped brushing and rested her forehead on Cowboy's neck. "She loved you, you know. Erin was one of the kindest people I knew."

Cowboy wrapped his neck around Bree.

She laughed. "I know you're just checking my pocket for treats, but I'm going to pretend this is a hug."

The horse dropped his head and picked at his hay.

Bree gave his shoulder a rub before leaving his stall, her heart just a little lighter. On the way to the house, she shook off her grief. Tonight, she would enjoy her family and savor the bonds forming between them. Shannon Phelps's sorrow was a reminder that happiness could be ripped out from under one's feet at any time. Nothing should be taken for granted. Every moment of happiness was a gift to be appreciated.

Guilt prodded her. She owed her brother an apology. He'd asked one thing of her since she'd moved back to Grey's Hollow: to go with him to the old Taggert place, the house where their father had shot their mother and then himself. And Bree had been putting it off for months, while Adam had done everything she'd asked of him.

Bree walked in the door, shed her boots, and braced herself for Ladybug's greeting. The big dog galloped over and slid on the tile. Bree caught the ungainly mutt before she slammed into the wall. Unfazed, the dog wagged her tail stump and snorted like a pig as Bree rubbed her ribs with both hands.

Kayla waited until the dog bounced away, then moved in for a hug. Bree kissed her on the top of her head. She went to the table and did the same to Luke. On the outside, he seemed to tolerate her affection, but she knew that deep down, he needed it. Though Bree often felt like she floundered in her new parenting role, she was the best person for the job. She knew better than anyone else what it was like to live with the kind of sorrow Kayla and Luke had experienced.

And she was determined to do right by them. They would not be cast off, isolated, and further damaged as she had been.

Releasing Luke, Bree gave her brother a peck on the cheek. Adam wore ripped jeans and a faded old T-shirt, both liberally streaked with paint. He was a very successful artist, but you'd never know it from his clothes. He had no interest in fancy anything. He'd driven the same ancient Ford Bronco for decades and lived in a converted barn he'd purchased solely for the light. Instead, he'd spent his money on Erin and her kids. He'd bought and maintained the farm Erin had wanted but never could have afforded on her income as a hairstylist. In that way, Adam had been a better sibling than Bree. But then, he and Erin had grown up together. They'd had a bond that Bree had been shut out of.

Which also meant he'd probably felt Erin's loss more acutely than Bree, something she had never considered before. Life was all about learning, she supposed. But she needed to learn faster. Some lessons always felt as if they came too late.

"Wash up. Dinner's almost ready." Dana slid two homemade pizzas out of the oven. She took a cutter from the drawer and rolled it across the pies like a pro.

Bree crossed to the sink and washed her hands. She glanced at Dana's black silk blouse, bootcut jeans, and heeled shoes. "You look nice."

"I have a date." Dana used a spatula to transfer slices to a platter.

Bree took a can of seltzer from the fridge. "Deets now, please."

"It's just coffee." She shrugged. "We connected through a dating app."

"Seriously?" Bree felt her brows climb her forehead. "An app?"

Dana deadpanned. "Believe it or not, Grey's Hollow is not a hotbed of dating activity." She tossed the cutter in the sink. "Not everyone meets a total hottie on her first day in town."

"I'll give you that one." Bree snorted. Her relationship with Matt had been a complete surprise. "Be careful. Text me his picture and contact info."

"I'm meeting him at a coffee shop. I'll go early, so he doesn't know where I park." Dana tugged on her jeans at the thigh, lifting the hem so Bree could see the handgun strapped to her ankle. "And I'm fully accessorized. I've got this."

"OK. I believe you." Bree joined the kids and Adam at the table.

Dana had said she enjoyed her new life with Bree and the kids after two and a half decades of dealing with criminals all day long. But sometimes Bree forgot how much her friend had given up to help the Taggert family. She must be lonely.

Dana frowned at Bree. "You haven't changed clothes. Does this mean you're going back to work tonight?"

"Matt and I are staking out a suspect's house." Bree thought about leaving Luke to babysit Kayla. At sixteen, he'd be old enough in any normal household, but she hesitated. They all had experienced too much violence to have a completely normal life.

"I can cancel my date," Dana offered.

"I don't want you to do that—" Bree said. She should have asked Dana before she'd arranged this stakeout. But she'd assumed her friend would be home, which was selfish.

"No need," Adam interrupted. "I'll hang with the kids."

Bree smiled at her brother. "Thanks, Adam. I can get Kayla ready for bed before I go."

"But I want to stay up with Adam and Luke!" Kayla protested.

Bree stifled the urge to say no. It was a school night, but exceptions had to be made. Kayla had suffered so much loss in her short life. She needed the opportunities to experience joy, even for something as simple as staying up past her bedtime once in a while.

"OK," Bree said. The little girl would probably fall asleep on the couch anyway.

Happy, Kayla chattered through the meal, while Bree interrogated Luke about his day. At least that's how it felt. As usual, the teen was reluctant to provide many details, and Bree had to drag the information out of him. When dinner was over, Bree and Adam cleaned up the kitchen. Dana fluffed her hair, freshened her makeup, and left for her date.

Bree grabbed a windbreaker and said goodbye to the kids.

"Pick a movie," Adam called over his shoulder as he followed her out onto the porch. The sun hung low in the sky, casting long shadows. Dark clouds hovered in the distance.

"There's a storm coming." He stuffed his hands into his jeans pockets and squinted at the sky.

"Thanks again, Adam."

"You don't have to thank me. We're family, right?"

"Yeah. We are." Bree faced him. "Which brings me to my apology. It's been two months since you asked me to go back to the house with you. I've been avoiding it. I'm sorry."

Back in March, Adam had floored her by announcing he'd purchased their run-down, needing-to-be-condemned childhood home.

The same home in which their entire lives had been shattered twenty-seven years before.

The place where their father had killed their mother.

Bree looked away, then realized that was just another avoidance. She forced herself to meet her brother's gaze.

"I understand, Bree." Adam's hazel eyes, the exact color of her own, didn't blink. "I won't make you go there. I'm sorry I even asked. It was selfish of me. I didn't fully realize how difficult it would be for you. You remember everything." And she knew he was desperate to remember anything at all about the parents who had died when he was an infant.

"You have no reason to apologize. I *need* to face that house. I just wish it wasn't taking me so long to work up the nerve." Bree felt her face heat, even as dread pooled cold in her belly. As much as she recoiled at the thought of returning there, her own cowardice embarrassed her.

Adam put a hand on her arm. "It's OK. The house will still be there whenever you're ready."

They had both grown over the past four months. Adam had been emotionally distant, a defense mechanism like Bree's need to control everything. But when she'd demanded a place in his life and help raising their sister's kids, he'd stepped up without a single complaint.

"I promise we'll go soon."

"That's good enough for me." He turned and walked back into the house.

Bree slid behind the wheel of her SUV. She drove toward Matt's house and the thickening clouds, mentally preparing to stake out the home of a potential killer.

CHAPTER SEVENTEEN

Matt drove his Suburban toward Paul's house. Bree's marked vehicle was not suitable for a stakeout, especially if they might need to follow Paul at some point. Through the windshield, the sun dipped low, and Matt lowered his visor to counter the glare. In the rearview mirror, dark clouds gathered behind them.

"Can you believe Dana is having coffee with a guy she met on a dating app?" Bree asked from the passenger seat.

"Those apps are popular."

"I guess." Her phone buzzed, and she glanced at the screen. "Did you ever date someone from an app?"

"No."

Bree was the first person he'd dated in three years—since the shooting.

"Beckett's bank statements are in," Bree said. "Todd reviewed them."

Matt sipped coffee from a stainless-steel mug. "What's his financial situation?"

"That's the interesting thing." She scrolled. "Deb was right—his bank balances are down across the board. Don't get me wrong. He's still rich. But it's not clear where the money is going."

Matt set his mug in the console. "He said he and his wife were separated. Could he be paying an attorney?"

"This has been happening for the last two years. His wife only left a couple of months ago." Bree tapped her phone screen. "Todd says some of the withdrawals were cash."

"Cash? Maybe he's making payments to his wife?"

"But why cash?" Bree asked. "Surely, if he was giving his estranged wife or his lawyer money, he'd want a record of it."

"You're right. It doesn't make sense." Matt put both hands on the steering wheel and tapped it with his thumbs.

The GPS told them that their destination was ahead on the right. Matt checked the map on the dashboard screen. The Beckett house was around the next bend in the road. "I'd better pull over here."

Bree fished into a duffel bag at her feet for a camera with a telephoto lens. "Nice little country estate." Her radio squawked on her duty belt, and dispatch relayed information about a minor car accident. She lowered the volume.

Matt steered toward the shoulder of the road, concealing the SUV in the shadow of the roadside trees. He squinted through the windshield. "Do you see what I see?"

With a solid, square front, the big stone home stood at the end of the driveway like an English manor. The blacktop formed a circle in front of the house, then curved around to a detached garage.

Behind the garage, tall fencing surrounded a tennis court.

"Bingo. A tennis court." Bree raised her camera. The lens whirred as it focused. "I don't see any sign of life in the house."

The landscape lights were on, but the house sat dark.

Matt scanned the front of the property. "His truck is probably in the garage."

He turned off the engine, and they settled in to watch and wait. Bree lowered her camera into her lap. The wind gusted, shaking leaves off surrounding trees. Matt drank his coffee, grateful to be inside the vehicle. He watched Paul's house and scanned the property for movement.

"There." Bree raised her camera again. She snapped a picture. "It's Paul. He's leaving the house."

Matt straightened in his seat. He watched Paul enter his detached garage through a side door. Matt started the engine. The overhead garage door rolled up, and a Maserati sedan backed out. "That's not going to be hard to follow."

The car turned onto the road in the opposite direction, but Matt still waited to pull out. He followed far enough behind Paul that his taillights were just visible. They drove for about fifteen minutes before Paul turned into the entrance for a small office complex. Matt killed the headlights before following his vehicle.

Most of the buildings were dark as Paul drove toward the back of the complex. Matt cruised to a stop, the end of his Suburban hidden behind the corner of a building. He kept a football field of asphalt between his SUV and Paul's car. "Can you see him? I don't want to get closer. We're too conspicuous in this empty lot."

Bree took out her camera and raised it. "Yes. He's approaching the dumpster. There's a minivan there, nose out. Paul is parking next to it. He just lowered his window and passed a white envelope into the minivan."

"Can you read the license plate of the minivan?" Matt asked.

"No." Bree's camera clicked away. Thunder boomed in the distance, and a gust of wind kicked leaves across the blacktop.

"How about the driver?"

"I can see that there's a man in the van, but there isn't enough light to see his face." Bree took more pictures. "I'm using the night-scene setting, but the pictures are going to be dark." She lowered the camera. "He's leaving."

The transaction had lasted less than two minutes. Paul backed out of the space and drove toward the exit of the complex.

"Follow Paul or the minivan?" Matt asked.

"We'll stick with Paul. He's our suspect." Bree held up her camera. "Here's hoping forensics can brighten these pictures so we can read the minivan's plate."

Matt and Bree both slid down in their seats as Paul drove around the corner and away from them. After Paul's car turned onto the main road, Matt started the engine and followed. He waited until they were on the road before he turned on the headlights.

Lightning snaked across the sky, and light rain pelted the windshield, obscuring the view. Matt turned on the wipers and increased his speed until he could just see Paul's taillights on the road ahead.

"He's going home," Bree said.

Thunder rumbled, and the rain picked up. Paul's taillights turned into his driveway. The overhead door rolled up. Paul drove into the garage, and the door rolled back down. A light glowed in the windows that flanked the four bays. Matt returned to the same observation spot they'd used before and turned off the headlights.

Bree watched through her camera lens. She frowned. "He hasn't come out of the garage."

"Maybe he's waiting for the storm to pass."

"Did you hear that?"

"Hear what?" All Matt could hear was the drum of rain on the vehicle's roof.

Bree tilted her head and closed her eyes. "I don't know. I thought I heard three cracks."

"Like thunder or gunshots?" The hairs on the back of Matt's neck quivered.

The rain stopped, and Matt listened intently. He heard nothing but the distant rumble of thunder as the storm moved away. The garage windows went dark, probably the automatic light going off. He scanned

Paul's property. Landscape lighting brightened the front yard to near daylight. "He's still in the garage, right? In the dark."

"Yep." Bree lowered her camera. "I don't like it. I have a bad feeling."

"Then let's check it out."

"Let me try to call him first." She tapped on her phone.

Matt heard the line ring several times, then switch to voice mail.

"Mr. Beckett, this is Sheriff Taggert. I'd like to make arrangements for you to come to the station for additional questioning. You are welcome to bring your attorney." She left her number and ended the call. "Let's go." She reached behind the seats and pulled out their body armor vests. "Just in case."

She handed one to Matt and put on her own. Then she turned off the volume on her radio. Matt slipped into the vest and fastened the Velcro straps. They grabbed flashlights and climbed out of the vehicle. Bree met him behind the Suburban. He opened his cargo hatch and retrieved his rifle. "Just in case."

Water dripped from trees as they jogged along the shoulder of the road and down the driveway.

They approached the dark garage. Sweat gathered under Matt's vest.

The long building had four overhead doors, one side door, and two windows on either side of the four bays. Matt jogged to the first window and put his back to the siding next to it. He carefully peered around the window frame. Despite the darkness, he could make out the rough shapes of three vehicles, including Paul's truck and the Maserati. There wasn't enough light to see inside the vehicles or into the corners.

"Do you see Paul?" Bree asked.

"No." Matt scanned the building. Nothing moved. Yet goose bumps rose on his arms as a cool, damp breeze swept across the yard.

"Let me check the other window." Bree jogged toward the other end of the garage. "Maybe I can get a better view."

Pop pop pop.

The sound of glass shards hitting the concrete followed the gunshots. Matt dropped to the ground behind a landscape boulder. He lifted his rifle but couldn't shoot back without knowing where his bullets would go or who they could strike. Fifteen feet away, Bree hit the grass. When Matt looked over, she wasn't moving.

Chapter Eighteen

Where is Matt?

Pain roared through Bree's left arm. She lay still, playing dead, moving only her eyeballs as she searched for him. In her peripheral vision, she saw him hunkered down behind a big rock. He had the rifle pointed at the garage.

He's all right.

Bree scanned the garage but saw no signs of the shooter. Without moving, she looked for cover. She didn't want the shooter to know she was alive until she found a barrier. About ten feet away, a big oak tree blotted out the night sky. The trunk was two or three feet in diameter.

That'll do.

She exhaled hard. Her heart kicked against her ribs, her pulse rushing in her ears. She needed to move. Her position out in the open was too vulnerable. She took a deep breath, cradled her injured arm to her ribs, and rolled behind the tree. To protect the majority of her body, she scrambled into a sitting position and put her back to the trunk. She drew her gun and waited for gunshots in response to her movement. When the night remained silent, she reached for her phone with her left hand. More pain shot through her arm, and the wet warmth of fresh blood soaked her sleeve. She froze. After setting her gun in her lap, she used her right hand to turn on her radio, report shots fired, and request backup.

Thankfully, a unit was nearby. ETA five minutes.

Call complete, she exchanged the radio for her gun again. Weapon in hand, she peered around the tree and scanned the building. The shots had come through the window from inside the garage. Was he—or she—still inside?

Or had the shooter moved into a new position—one with a better shot at Bree or Matt?

She looked for movement but saw nothing. The broken window was dark and empty. She checked her watch. Four minutes until backup arrived. The flood of adrenaline had dulled the pain. Sweat rolled down the middle of her back and soaked her shirt under her duty belt. Cool air gusted over her, and she shivered. Hopefully she was just cold and not going into shock. While she'd been lying on the ground, water from the rain had soaked through her uniform pants.

The shooter could still be in the building.

She glanced at her phone, then returned her attention to the building.

ETA three minutes.

Still no sign of the shooter.

Bree kept watch. She marked off the seconds by the echo of her heartbeat in her wound. As long as she and Matt kept their heads down, they'd be OK until backup arrived.

Matt zigzagged across the grass, the movement startling her.

Her heart punched into her throat.

"What are you doing?" she whispered.

He scrambled up next to her. He stayed low and kept the tree between him and the shooter, but he was partially exposed. He held his rifle across his lap and kept it aimed at the garage.

"You should have stayed where you were!" she said in a harsh whisper.

"You're shot."

"I know. I don't want you to be shot too." Bree glanced at her arm. Blood saturated her sleeve to the elbow. Her arm continued to pulse with an adrenaline-dulled throb. She looked him over. "You're OK?"

"Yes." Matt's face was pale and drawn. "Can you watch the building?"

"Yes." She craned her head around the tree. "Did you see the shooter?"

"No." He set down the rifle and ripped open her sleeve.

Bree kept her eye on the garage, but she saw nothing. Then again, she hadn't seen the shooter before he shot her either. "He could be anywhere."

"I don't have anything to bandage this with." He ripped off the rest of her sleeve, folded it, and pressed it to the wound. "Hold this." He removed one of his bootlaces and tied it around her arm. "The wound isn't that deep—a straight furrow—but you need to hold still. You're making it bleed more."

"Backup should be here in a minute. Until then, we have to sit tight. I won't bleed to death in the next couple of minutes." But Bree felt a fresh rush of blood from her wound soak the makeshift bandage.

"You might if you don't keep still." Matt's voice was grim.

Bree tucked her thumb into her duty belt to immobilize her arm.

They couldn't retreat. There was no cover between them and their vehicle.

The seconds ticked by. Bree's wound pulsed.

Thrum. Thrum. Thrum.

It seemed longer than a minute before sirens approached. The first sheriff's department vehicle pulled into the driveway. Deputy Oscar was behind the wheel. He caught sight of Bree and Matt and drove his vehicle across the grass toward them. He angled his car between them and the garage. Crouching, Matt opened the rear vehicle door and helped Bree inside. Then Oscar drove them back to Matt's SUV.

Bree summed up the shooting while Matt retrieved his first aid kit. He covered her wound with gauze and applied a proper bandage. "That should keep you from dripping on the crime scene." As soon as Matt tied off the bandage, he picked up his rifle.

Another deputy arrived.

"Oscar, do you have binoculars?" Bree asked.

"Yes, ma'am." Oscar brought them from his vehicle.

Bree looked through them at the garage. She saw no sign of movement.

Is the shooter still in there?

She pointed to Matt. "We'll circle around the garage." She turned to the deputies. "You two take the front entrance."

They split up.

Matt and Bree jogged in an arc, giving the garage a wide berth.

"You probably shouldn't be running," he said.

"Probably not." Bree shrugged. She wasn't accustomed to being in a leadership position. Sending others to do the more dangerous tasks while she waited in a safe place felt unnatural. It was her instinct to take on the riskier jobs herself.

They moved from tree to tree until they rounded the side of the building. No motion or sound came from inside. Bree lifted the binoculars again and spotted a pane of glass leaning against the siding. "Shooter went into the garage through the side window."

"Let me guess," Matt said. "The glass is removed."

"Yep." Bree lowered the binoculars.

She used her radio to check in with the deputies. "All still clear out front?"

Oscar answered, "Affirmative."

"Let's get closer." Matt led the way, zigzagging through the trees to the corner of the building.

Bree gave her deputies the command to advance, pocketed the binoculars, and pulled out her weapon.

Matt put his back to the wall while Bree crouched under the window, the cut-away glass at her feet. He led with the rifle and peered around the window frame. He swept the beam of a flashlight around the garage. "I don't see anyone."

"The shooter probably took off right after he shot me." Sweat dripped down Bree's spine. White pain radiated through her arm, and nausea swirled in her belly. Adrenaline overload was leaving her shaky and sweating.

"You all right?" Matt asked.

"Yeah." She swallowed.

"Hold on. I do see something. There's a man lying on the floor."

"Beckett?"

"Don't know," Matt said. "I can't see his face."

She rose onto her toes and looked over the windowsill. Exchanging her weapon for her flashlight, she scanned the garage. Nothing moved in the two beams sweeping around the area. The Maserati sedan and a Porsche 911 Carrera shared the space with Paul's pickup. Bree moved her flashlight. A shadow on the ground caught her attention.

"I see him." She squinted. "Next to the Maserati."

She relayed their location and gave the command for her deputies to enter through the front door. The door opened and two more lights appeared in the garage. One deputy reached for the wall and flipped a switch. Overhead lights brightened the darkness. The two deputies worked as a team to check in and around each vehicle.

"Clear," Oscar called out as he holstered his weapon.

Bree led the way around to the front of the building. The garage was one big open space. Beckett's vehicles filled three bays. In the remaining quarter of the garage, a workbench lined the wall.

Matt walked around the Maserati. "It's Paul Beckett."

Bree went around the front of the vehicle.

On the other side of the sleek sedan, Paul Beckett lay sprawled next to the driver's door in a small puddle of blood.

Bree almost rushed to the man's side and stopped short. There was no need to check his pulse. He was clearly gone, and she couldn't risk contaminating the scene with her own blood. Paul's empty blue eyes stared up at the ceiling. In the center of his blue polo shirt with a Beckett Construction logo were three large red splotches.

Bree studied the puddle of blood. Still wet, it glistened. "He was shot while we were watching the house from down the road."

She scanned the concrete and workbench, looking for a gun. The surfaces were clear. Beckett hadn't shot himself. Nor had he shot Bree.

Where did the shooter go?

CHAPTER NINETEEN

"We need to clear the rest of the property," Bree said.

Matt pointed to her crudely bandaged arm. "You need to get that taken care of."

"I will." But first she'd assess the scene.

They went outside and surveyed their surroundings. The parking area spanned the distance between the house and garage. At least an acre of lush, tree-dotted lawn surrounded the two buildings. The grass faded to a meadow with thicker woods in the distance. She saw nothing alive other than a couple of bats flying over the tennis court. An owl hooted in the distance. Tires grated as another deputy's vehicle arrived.

"Not many places to hide out here," Bree said. "Not until you hit the woods."

She assessed the distance. A shooter would need a sniper rifle to be a threat from there. "We didn't see the shooter come or go. They must have come through the meadow."

Matt pulled out his cell phone. "Looking at my map app, I see a road on the other side of those woods."

Bree examined the ground. "No footprints."

She turned and sized up the house. It had to be six thousand square feet. Paul's wife had left him, and their kids were at college. But she couldn't assume the house was empty.

Bree assigned one deputy to secure the garage and begin a crime scene log, making a record of everyone who entered the scene. She, Matt, and the two additional deputies went to the front of the house. The door was locked. She could see through a narrow pane of glass next to the door. There was no one in the foyer.

Bree pressed the doorbell. A chime sounded inside.

No answer. She rang the bell again, then knocked hard on the door and called out, "Sheriff's department!"

Nothing.

"We're coming in," Bree yelled.

She broke one of the panes with the butt of her gun, reached in, and unlocked the dead bolt. Weapons drawn, they filed into the house. A staircase curved up one side of the foyer. Bree motioned for the deputies to take the second floor.

Bree and Matt moved left into a formal living room. They went through the doorway and swept their weapons from corner to corner.

"Clear." Bree pivoted on her heel.

They crossed the foyer into the dining room and repeated the process.

Matt put his back to the wall. "Clear."

Bree led the way down the hall to a kitchen and great room bigger than the entire first floor of her house. Sleek and modern, the rooms were light on furniture and knickknacks. A marble fireplace took center stage. Across the back of the house, wide windows and two french doors showcased the views of the lawn, meadow, and woods behind the house. The kitchen island was a white marble slab the size of Bree's barn door.

She opened a door and found a massive pantry. Matt checked a closet. They made their way through the kitchen to the laundry room and a half bath. Retreating from the kitchen, they went down a short hallway on the other side of the great room. On one side, a home office held a desk and a wall of bookcases. Farther down the hall were a bedroom and a full bath. No one was hiding in the closets.

Footsteps on the stairs brought them back to the foyer.

"Upstairs is clear," the deputy said.

"Let's go outside." Bree led the way back out into the warm evening.

Paul's death allowed them to conduct a search for a killer or a potential additional victim, but proper procedure needed to be followed in order to look for and collect evidence.

Two more sheriff's vehicles arrived. Todd stepped out of his cruiser. Matt returned the AR-15 to his Suburban and retrieved Bree's camera. She assigned two deputies to search the perimeter of the property and waved for Todd to follow her to the garage. On the way, she phoned the medical examiner's office and the county forensics department.

Bree gave Todd a quick update. "We need a search warrant for the Beckett residence."

Typing with both thumbs, he took notes on his phone. "No offense, ma'am, but maybe you should go to the ER?"

"I will as soon as I speak with the ME." Bree swallowed another rush of nausea. With the adrenaline fading, she was moving on sheer stubbornness at this point. "She's on the way."

Todd can handle the scene after that, right?

They reached the garage door. Bree stopped in the doorway and surveyed the room while Matt went inside. Careful not to step in the blood, he crouched next to the body. With some maneuvering, he worked Paul's wallet from the rear pocket of his jeans and opened the billfold. "There's money in his wallet. A few hundred dollars, and his credit cards are still here too."

"Not a robbery then," Bree said.

"Why did the killer want him dead?"

She scanned the scene with new perspective. Beckett was lying next to his Maserati. "From the position of the body, it looks like he was shot as he got out of his car."

Matt put on gloves. "The only place the shooter could have hidden is behind one of the other vehicles."

Bree pictured Beckett climbing out of his Maserati. "He got out of his car and closed the vehicle door." She studied the body. Paul's hands were flung out toward the overhead doors. "Maybe the shooter stepped out from around the front of the truck and confronted him."

Matt assessed the position. "The angle seems right. The Porsche is too small to hide behind."

"Paul is separated, likely with an impending divorce." Bree backed away from the body. "We need to talk to Mrs. Beckett."

"On it." Todd headed for the door. "Someone's here."

Bree walked out of the garage.

A Mercedes sedan pulled up to the curb, and a woman emerged. She was in her early fifties. Her short blonde hair looked expensively tousled. Lean and tall, she wore dark jeans, ankle boots, and a trench coat like a fashion model. As she took in the sheriff's vehicles, her gaze focused on Bree.

The wife? What a coincidence.

"Ma'am." Bree introduced herself. "What is your name?"

"Angela Beckett," she said in a halting voice. "What's going on?"

Instead of answering, Bree asked, "What is your relationship to Paul Beckett?"

"His wife." Angela seemed like the sort of woman who always looked put together. Her appearance was her armor. Her clothes were pressed and her makeup perfectly applied. Delicate diamond studs decorated her earlobes, and a skinny bracelet winked in the light of the garage fixture. "What's going on here?"

Bree looked for a place to talk to the woman privately, but there wasn't one.

"What is going on?" Angela's voice rose as she pointed a finger at Bree, and bright spots of color splotched her cheeks.

Bree knew there was no way to soft-pedal the news. "We found Mr. Beckett inside the garage. He's dead. I'm sorry for your loss."

The woman's face froze in stunned disbelief. "Paul is dead?"

"Yes, ma'am."

"How?"

"He was shot," Bree said.

Angela's hand dropped to her side. Her perfect posture slumped. "I can't believe it."

Bree waited, sensing there was more.

"We didn't get along very well, but Paul was . . . larger than life, to be cliché." Angela's brows knitted. "It doesn't seem possible that he's gone."

"Where were you this evening?" Bree asked.

"Paul and I separated months ago." Angela sighed. "I'm staying with a friend. I came here to get more of my things." She stared at her ankle boots. "He changed the locks, so I can't get in when he's not here."

"Where are your kids?"

"The boys are both away at college. One is in North Carolina. The other is in Michigan." She chewed on her lip, smearing her lipstick onto her teeth. "I'll have to call them."

"Why did you and Paul separate?" Bree asked.

Angela's mouth flattened. "It sounds stupid, but he was having a totally predictable midlife crisis. He bleached his hair. He bought cars. He chased younger women." She humphed, seemingly exasperated. "He cheated throughout our marriage, but he never flaunted it in my face. I could ignore it as long as no one knew. He was always discreet until recently. I told him he was going to get old no matter what he did, but he continued to chase youth like he had nothing to lose."

But he had had something to lose—his life.

"Though he no longer cared if he lost me," Angela said. "Can I go inside and get my things?"

"No, ma'am." Bree checked the woman's left hand for a wedding band. It was still there. "You'll have to wait until the scene is released."

The ME's van pulled into the parking area, interrupting the interview. Angela's eyes widened. "This just happened? Paul is still in there?"

"Yes, ma'am."

Angela blinked several times, then her eyes refocused as she comprehended that her husband's body was still on the premises. She started toward the garage. Bree stepped in front of her.

"I want to see him." Angela's eyes filled with tears.

No, you don't.

But since people rarely took Bree's word on that, she said, "I'm sorry, ma'am. This is a crime scene. I can't let you in."

Angela's eyes widened as her gaze dropped to Bree's arm. A large spot of blood was now visible as it began to soak through the bandage. "Oh, my God. What happened to your arm? You were shot too, weren't you?"

"I have to talk to the medical examiner now." Bree signaled for a deputy. "Take Mrs. Beckett to the station."

"What?" Her mouth dropped open. "You can't do that! Am I a suspect?"

Of course you're a suspect.

Angela frowned at the patrol vehicle like it was a petri dish. But then, that was probably a fair comparison.

"Mrs. Beckett," Bree began. "I need to ask you some questions. There's too much I don't know about your husband's death. You could be in danger. I'd feel much better if you would wait at the sheriff's station while I get a handle on what happened here. I'll come and talk with you later tonight. At this moment, everyone and no one is a suspect."

Angela's forehead creased. "I won't answer any questions without my lawyer present."

Did all rich people have a lawyer on speed dial? Bree reconsidered her night. She'd be spending part of it at the ER. There was no getting around that. She probably wouldn't have the time or energy to conduct a proper interview tonight anyway. "I need your contact information to set up an interview for tomorrow morning."

"You can't come to my friend's house. She'll be sleeping. She's an ER nurse who works the night shift."

Frustrated, Bree forced her jaw to unclench. She preferred to question people in their own surroundings, where they were more relaxed and less wary. But she couldn't force the issue. "We can do the interview at the sheriff's station."

Angela pulled a cell phone from her pocket. "I'll let you know if and when my attorney is available."

Short of arresting her, Bree could not force Angela to agree to an interview. Speaking to the police was voluntary. Most people just didn't know that. Most people also wanted to appear cooperative because avoiding questions made them look guilty. Angela Beckett either thought she was better than most people, or she actually had something to hide.

Paul had been uncooperative as well. Were the Becketts involved in something less than legal?

Bree handed her a card. "Let my office know what time you'll arrive."

Angela snatched the card and turned back toward her vehicle.

"And be careful, Mrs. Beckett," Bree called.

Angela's sure stride hesitated just for a second, then she strode on with slightly less confidence.

Bree walked over to the ME's van.

"I'm seeing too much of you, Sheriff. Again." The ME grabbed booties from her PPE container. She turned to face Bree, her gaze dropping to Bree's arm. "What happened?"

"It's minor," Bree said.

Dr. Jones raised one eyebrow. "I didn't ask you to assess your own injury. I asked you what happened."

Bree had only ever heard two tones to the ME's deep voice. One was soothing and compassionate, used to address the families of victims.

The other was confident professional. But tonight, the doctor sounded like a pissed-off mother calling a teenager to the carpet.

"I was . . . sort of . . . shot," Bree admitted.

Dr. Jones exhaled hard. "How long ago?"

"I don't know exactly."

"I assume it was before you called me?"

"Yes."

Dr. Jones muttered something under her breath. Bree caught the word *stupid* among the mumbling. Then the ME jabbed a finger in Bree's face. "You have five minutes. If you're not on your way to the ER at that time, I will call an ambulance myself."

"OK. OK." Bree lifted her good hand in surrender.

With a quick nod of agreement, the ME and her assistant followed Bree into the garage, where Matt was examining the pickup truck.

Bree filled Dr. Jones in on the discovery of the body while the ME's assistant took photographs, beginning at a distance and spiraling in for close-ups.

Dr. Jones halted a few yards away and scanned the scene for a minute before moving closer and crouching next to the body. Bree showed her Paul's wallet in the evidence bag, still open to show his driver's license.

Dr. Jones glanced at it. "No question as to his ID then."

"No." Bree stood back and watched the ME work.

Dr. Jones took temperature readings in the air, then cut open the corpse's shirt. Without disturbing the gunshot wounds, she made an incision over the liver and inserted a thermometer to record core body temperature. A corpse loses heat at a rate of approximately 1.5 degrees Fahrenheit per hour until it reaches ambient temperature. The ME always needed to consider environmental conditions, but the fresher the corpse, the more accurate the estimated time of death.

Bree already knew that Paul Beckett's body was very fresh, but the ME had to confirm his time of death with scientific methods.

Dr. Jones grasped the corpse's head. It turned easily. "Rigor mortis hasn't begun." Chemical reactions in the body caused the muscles to contract or stiffen, a process that normally began about two to four hours after death and first presented in the jaw and neck. She pointed to the torso, the skin nearest the contact with the floor. "Lividity isn't visible yet either." Lividity started about thirty minutes after death and was generally visible within an hour or two. She rocked back on her heels. "Considering these factors, along with loss of body heat, he's been dead thirty minutes to an hour."

Bree checked the time on her phone. Eight forty. She did the math. "I thought I heard gunshots at approximately eight o'clock."

The ME agreed with a nod, then glanced at Bree's arm and tilted her head expectantly.

Bree nodded. "I'll head to the ER now."

She didn't ask about cause of death. The ME wouldn't comment, but it was pretty clear what had killed Paul: three bullet wounds in his chest.

Bree headed for the door. She looked down at a dusty green smear on the concrete. "What's that?"

Matt crouched over it. "That looks like green clay."

CHAPTER TWENTY

"Paul has a tennis court, so finding green clay here does not seem unusual, but it's still a strong link between this crime scene and Holly's." Matt straightened. He noticed marks on Paul's truck and walked closer to inspect them. Scratches marred the black paint between the front and rear windows.

Bree approached, her expression pained. "Did you find something?"

Matt pointed to the marks. "Looks like someone tried to break into the vehicle. If you insert a long instrument behind the rubber seal right here, you can manipulate the door handle."

Bree dropped her hands to her sides. "We don't know where or when that happened."

"True." Matt stepped away.

"Sheriff," Todd called from the garage doorway. "The forensics team is here."

"Did you take photos?" Bree asked Matt.

"I did." He pointed out the scratches on the truck to Todd. Then Matt handed over the camera. "There are also photos of Paul's activities earlier this evening that need to be brightened."

"I'll send the pics to forensics and have the truck fingerprinted." Todd pulled his notepad out of his pocket and wrote in it.

The medical examiner's assistant wheeled a gurney loaded with a body bag into the garage. They were preparing to transport Paul's body to the morgue.

"Then let's leave the scene to the forensics team." Bree led the way out of the garage and took a few minutes to speak with the crime scene techs as they suited up.

"Let's go." Matt gestured toward his vehicle.

"All right." She looked reluctant to leave the scene, but she was also pale as chalk. Blood saturated the bandage.

"Todd can handle the scene." Matt herded Bree away without touching her.

"You're right." She walked toward the SUV. Her body curled over her cradled arm. She was hurting much more than she would admit. "Or you could stay and supervise."

"No." Matt was *not* leaving her side.

She didn't argue, another sign she was faking being OK. Yet she managed to sum up her quick talk with Angela Beckett while they walked.

On the road, a news crew was setting up. The cameraman turned toward Bree, and the reporter called, "Sheriff Taggert."

Nick West.

Matt wanted to hustle her by. "Keep walking. Ignore him."

"I can't. The camera is on." She paused, and he watched her lower her arm to her side and force her body upright. She stepped sideways to hide her arm behind Matt as she turned to the reporter. "Mr. West."

"We're live with Sheriff Bree Taggert. What can you tell us about the shooting?" Nick West was young and local and had a good reputation.

But right now, Matt had to resist punching him as he shoved the microphone in Bree's face.

"I can't comment yet, not before the family has been notified," she said.

"The medical examiner is here, so this was a fatal shooting?" West craned his head around Matt. The reporter's eyes tracked to Bree's arm and widened. "What happened to your arm, Sheriff?"

"Just a minor injury. I'm fine." Bree shifted her feet in a wider stance, as if her balance was off. "One person died, and we are investigating the shooting. We believe the shooter is still at large. After family members have been notified, the sheriff's department will issue an official statement."

"The man who lives at this address is the employer of the woman whose body was found on Monday. Are the two crimes related?" Nick had done his homework—and fast.

"We cannot assume that this early in the investigation, but it is possible," Bree said.

"Is the public at risk?" the reporter asked.

"At this time, we have no reason to believe there is any increased risk to the general public." The muscles of Bree's jaw tensed, like she was grinding her molars.

"The crime was personal?"

"I'll issue a statement in the morning." Bree turned away, her *I'm fine* mask dissolving as soon as the camera was on her back.

Matt resisted taking her elbow. She wouldn't like to appear weak. He glanced over his shoulder. The reporter was doing a sound bite with the house and law enforcement vehicles as a backdrop. Matt helped her remove her Kevlar vest. Then he tugged off his own and tossed them both into the back of the SUV. He opened the passenger door and helped Bree into the vehicle. When she settled into the seat, she closed her eyes.

"You OK?"

"Please drive," she said through clenched teeth.

He started the engine and drove onto the road. "Damned reporters."

"West is all right. He's just doing his job, and you have to admit, he's good. He connected Holly's death and Beckett's address together faster than I would have expected."

"Or someone leaked the connection." Matt turned at an intersection.

"Doesn't matter. Are we out of sight?"

Matt glanced in the rearview mirror. The flashing lights of emergency vehicles disappeared as he drove through a bend in the road. "Yes."

"Pull over."

He guided the SUV onto the shoulder.

As soon as the vehicle came to a stop, she threw open the door, slid out, and vomited.

Matt jumped out and ran around to her side.

She held up a hand. "It's OK. All done."

"Stop saying you're OK. You're not. Know why? Because you were shot." Matt found a bottle of water in the vehicle. "Rinse your mouth but don't drink any."

She obeyed, spitting water into the roadside grass. "I'm sorry."

"For what? Being human? Bree, you need to relax with the hero complex."

"Do I have a hero complex?" She tried to smile, but the twitch of her mouth was more of a grimace. "I thought I was just a control freak."

He snorted. "That too."

She turned toward the SUV. Wobbly, she stumbled. Matt caught her elbow. She paused and leaned into him for a minute. A shudder passed through her. He wrapped his arms around her, careful of her injury, and held her close. Protectiveness rushed through him, and Matt scanned the road to make sure they were alone. Bree didn't deserve to have a moment of vulnerability recorded.

A minute later, she lifted her head. "Thanks."

"You're not going to apologize, are you?"

"No."

Progress.

She walked toward the SUV, and Matt helped her back into the vehicle. Then he slid behind the wheel.

"I have to call home. That was a live report. I don't want the family to see it before I tell them I'm injured." She pulled out her phone. "Adam? First of all, go out onto the porch." A minute later, she said, "I was injured at the scene. But I'm OK. Probably just need a few stitches. Matt is taking me to the ER. Please keep the news off. There was a reporter there, and I don't want the kids to see the segment before I get home and they see with their own eyes that I'm fine."

Matt bit back a retort. *You are not fine!*

He couldn't hear Adam's response.

"I'll call you back a little later," Bree said. "Just tell the kids I'm going to be home later than I thought. I'll explain everything in the morning." She lowered the phone to her lap.

"You could have told him the truth," Matt suggested.

"I don't want him to worry, and I didn't lie."

"You omitted." In this case, Matt didn't see much difference. But he didn't point that out. Tonight, Bree had leaned on him. Maybe someday she'd learn she could lean on other people as well.

She was silent as he drove the rest of the way to the hospital. He left his vehicle at the curb and helped Bree inside. A nurse hurried over.

"The sheriff has been shot," Matt said in a quiet voice.

The nurse hustled them through a set of double doors. She opened the last curtain in a row of triage bays. "This is the most private spot we have."

"Thank you." Bree sat on the gurney and leaned back, handing Matt her phone.

The nurse lifted the bandage, frowned at the wound, then lowered the bandage back into place. "I'll grab a doctor, the paperwork, and something for the pain."

She returned a minute later with a youngish doctor. The nurse took scissors and began to cut Bree's shirt.

"I'll be in the hallway." Matt turned away.

"Wait." Bree unclipped her duty belt and handed it to him. "Take my backup piece too."

Matt tugged up her pant leg and removed her ankle holster. Then he went outside, locked the guns in the vault in his SUV, and parked the vehicle in the lot. As he walked across the asphalt toward the ER entrance, Bree's phone rang. Dana's name appeared on the screen.

Matt answered the call. "It's Matt."

"Is she really OK?"

"Yes. We're at the ER. A doctor is checking her out now."

Dana's sigh of relief was audible. "I just saw her answering questions on the news. The reporter came back on saying he couldn't believe the sheriff had talked to him so calmly when apparently she'd been shot."

"To be cliché, it's just a flesh wound."

"You can't bullshit me. I've actually seen bullet wounds."

"Sorry. I know that." Matt winced. He should have been honest. Instead, he'd minimized the situation the same way Bree had. "It's a straight furrow through her left triceps. Messy, but not terribly deep. She walked into the ER on her own two feet, and I expect she'll walk out again later tonight."

"That's better."

"I thought you were on a date." Matt stopped on the concrete outside the sliding doors.

"Not a date. A disaster. Guy did nothing but talk about himself for an hour straight. I'm on my way home now. Does Adam know?"

"Yep. Bree called him."

"OK." Dana sounded partially mollified. "She should have called me too."

"I know. I'll tell her."

"Please do. Call me if anything changes or if she needs anything."

"Will do." Matt ended the call and went inside. He walked into the ER hallway just as the doctor emerged from behind Bree's curtain.

"You can go back in," the doctor said.

Matt pulled the curtain aside. Bree was curled on her right side, her back to him. She wore a tank top. Her bloody uniform shirt sat in a plastic bag at the foot of the bed. The nurse had started an IV and, from the blurry look in Bree's eyes, given her pain meds.

"Feeling better?" he asked.

"Uh-huh." She sounded sleepy.

"We're giving her something for the pain and nausea," the nurse said. "The doctor is coming back with a local anesthetic. Then he'll clean and stitch the wound." She pushed a plastic chair next to the bed, then walked out.

Bree's breathing had evened out, and the muscles of her face had softened. But it was the tattoo on the back of her shoulder that held Matt's attention. He'd seen the one on her ankle and thought it nicely done, but this . . .

This was something else.

It was a stunning piece. Delicate dark green vines draped over her shoulder. A dragonfly in flight, larger than Matt's splayed hand, perched on her shoulder blade, its wings fully spread. Its body of brilliant blue and pale green was almost iridescent in the overhead light. He had to look closely to see the huge scar he knew the tattoo covered. The artist had cleverly incorporated the raised scar tissue into the tattoo as texture. But if Matt looked closely, he could see the ugliness under the beauty. The scar had stretched as she'd grown, but he could still see its outline. It didn't take much to imagine a large dog with its jaws clamped around a child's shoulder. The dog would have shaken its head, trying to break the child's neck—Bree's neck—like Greta shook a stuffed toy. He could almost hear the terrified screams. She'd been five years old.

How had she survived?

The doctor returned, and the nurse directed Matt to the hallway again. As he left, he glanced back at Bree, curled up like a child. The dragonfly seemed to stare back at him. From a distance, the creature's posture challenged him to dare its ability to overcome—to transform an ugly experience into a work of art.

Bree had told him the story, but seeing the scar brought a fresh wave of anger and empathy rolling through him. A burst of respect followed. It was no wonder she was terrified of dogs. Who wouldn't be after a vicious, nearly fatal attack? Her true courage shone in her determination to overcome her fear. In short, she had survived because she didn't know how to quit. She kept going, no matter the stakes, in every situation. He'd seen her plow headfirst into situations that would freeze most in their tracks. She was smart and skilled—but she'd also been lucky.

At some point, her sheer bullheadedness might get her killed.

CHAPTER
TWENTY-ONE

After the doctor had finished cleaning, stitching, and bandaging her wound, Bree's arm was blissfully numb. As much as she resisted the use of drugs, she was also appreciating their existence. She heard the squeak of the nurse's shoes as she moved around the cubicle.

"You rest," the nurse said. "I'll be right back." She left the room.

Bree closed her eyes. Her body felt heavy. She heard footsteps in the doorway but assumed it was either the nurse or Matt. She didn't open her eyes.

"Bree."

Her brother's voice startled her. She opened her eyes and rolled to her back. Dizziness from the sudden movement and the drugs rolled through her.

Her brother stood in the doorway, his hazel eyes grim and devastated.

"Adam." She didn't know what else to say.

He rushed forward, then stopped abruptly at the side of her bed. "I want to hug you, but I don't want to hurt you."

"I'm OK, Adam. Just a little woozy from the meds. It was just a few stitches." Bree shifted over a few inches and patted the gurney next to her. She lifted her good arm. "Hug away."

He perched on the edge of the gurney and wrapped his arms around her. As she pressed her forehead into his shoulder, she was transported back to a cold January night when she'd huddled under the porch with baby Adam in her arms and their four-year-old sister, Erin, at her side. Bree could feel the cold dirt under her bare feet. Feel the baby shaking in the freezing night. She remembered holding her breath and hoping the hiding spot she'd picked was the right one. At the age of eight, she'd known that if she'd chosen wrong or if she couldn't keep the baby quiet, their father would find them—and he'd kill them all.

Hot tears rushed from her eyes. She tried to stop but ended up hiccuping, her body jerking in embarrassing shudders.

Adam rubbed her uninjured arm. "It's OK."

Tonight, her world felt backward. Adam was the strong one.

She didn't know how much time went by until the torrent passed and she caught her breath. She lifted her head and swiped under her eyes. "I'm sorry."

"What for?" Adam released her and brushed a hair off her face.

"I don't even know." Bree sighed. She needed to stop apologizing for being human, but it was a hard habit to break. "Why are you here? I told you on the phone I was OK."

Anger flashed in Adam's eyes. It was not an emotion he often exhibited. "I watched your interview at the crime scene. Then a few minutes later, the reporter said you'd been shot."

"Ugh." Bree barely remembered the exchange with Nick West. At the time, she'd been concentrating on not throwing up. "Did I sound like an idiot?"

"You looked and sounded like a badass, as usual." He frowned. "I understand the persona you need to portray to the public, but you should have told *me* the truth. All of it. You have to stop trying to protect me from everything. I've been a functioning adult for a long time."

"I know, but it's hard for me. You'll always be my little brother."

"I'm six inches taller than you."

"And you've turned into a good man." She touched his hand. "I'm proud of you."

"I know before Erin died, I let my art consume me. I didn't connect with her or the kids—or you—as much as I should have. I will always have those regrets."

"I'm just as guilty—"

"Let me finish." A sigh rolled through him. "But since Erin died, and you asked me to help with the kids, I've tried really hard to do better. At first it was a struggle, but now that I realize what was missing from my life, it's not hard at all. So, stop apologizing every time you need me to help with something. Stop feeling like you have to do it all yourself. You want us to have a real relationship, but it can't be one-sided, with you doing all the supporting. You can lean on me now. That's how this family thing is supposed to work, I think."

"You're right." Emotions welled up in Bree's throat. From sorrow to gratitude, they hit her faster than she could fully process them. Treating Adam like a child was arrogant on her part, as if she were the only person who could be strong or make a good decision. If she wanted respect and love and trust from him, then she had to give the same back. "I'll do better, and if I slip, promise to call me out on it. Don't let me be a bossy bitch."

"You're never a bitch, but I promise to call you out on the bossy." Adam nodded. "You must be exhausted. When can you get out of here?"

The nurse walked back in. "I have your discharge papers. The local should last a few hours. Expect the wound to hurt more tomorrow." She set a plastic bag of paperwork in front of Bree. "Prescriptions for antibiotics and pain meds are in the bag, along with wound care instructions.

You need to keep it still for a few days. Is there any chance you're going to sit on the couch and watch TV for the next week?"

"No," Matt said from the doorway. "She won't."

"Didn't think so." The nurse pulled a sling out of its plastic wrapper. "Please wear this. You do not want to rip out those stitches."

Fifteen minutes later, Bree was ready to go. She slid to her feet slowly, testing her balance. Adam took off his zippered hoodie and wrapped it around her shoulders.

"She needs two prescriptions filled." Adam slid them out of the plastic bag.

"I'll take care of those." Matt took the papers. "There's a twenty-four-hour pharmacy in Scarlet Falls."

"I can wait until morning," Bree said.

Matt shook his head. "But there's no reason for you to do that. I'll drop off the meds later. Take care of her, Adam."

"I will." Adam took her elbow and held it all the way to his truck. He put her in the passenger seat. Bree fell asleep on the way home and jolted when Adam touched her arm. "We're home," he said.

Adam helped her into the house and up the stairs. Dana took over getting Bree out of her uniform and into pajama bottoms and a clean tank top. Then Bree stretched out, and Dana elevated her bandaged arm on a pillow.

"Do you want me to lock the animals out of the bedroom?" Dana asked.

"No. Who knows what that cat will do if he doesn't get his way?"

Dana laughed. "OK. You asked for it." She opened the bedroom door. Ladybug jumped onto the bed and curled up next to Bree's legs. Vader took his usual place on the second pillow.

Despite her exhaustion, Bree fell into a fitful sleep. She dreamed of something unseen chasing her. No matter how fast she ran, it stayed right on her heels. She woke breathless in her dim room. Pain throbbed through her arm. Her mouth was dry, and her head felt as heavy as a bowling ball.

Dana had fallen asleep in a chair next to the bed. She sat upright and blinked bleary eyes. "I'll get you some water and a pain pill." She left the room without waiting for Bree's response.

"Aunt Bree?" Kayla stood in the doorway. "I heard you cry. Did you have a bad dream?"

"I did." Bree struggled to sit up. She touched her face. Her cheeks were wet.

Kayla walked closer. "You're hurt."

Bree's heart thumped. "Just a little, like when you fell roller-skating a few weeks ago."

"I can make you feel better." Kayla turned and ran out of the room. She came back a minute later with the Harry Potter book they'd been reading. The mattress tipped and rolled as she scrambled into the bed, each movement sending fresh bursts of pain through Bree's arm.

Dana came back in. "Oh, baby. You probably don't want to disturb—"

"She's fine," Bree said. She took the pill and washed it down with water. Then she settled back onto her pillows.

Kayla knelt to turn on the bedside light. The cat reluctantly shared his pillow as the little girl leaned back and began to read. Bree closed her eyes. She heard Dana easing back into her chair. Bree focused on the child's voice, as if it could keep her demons at bay until daylight.

CHAPTER TWENTY-TWO

Morning was still dark as Cady led her dogs down the street. She untangled the four leashes in her hand. Her Great Dane mix, Harley, walked obediently at her side. Ahead, a neighbor walked her Australian shepherd. As the pair approached on the opposite side of the street, Cady's two pitties wagged their tails, eager to play. Taz, the Chihuahua, lunged and barked at the end of his leash. Sighing, Cady scooped him into her arms. He continued to growl.

"Sorry." She waved to her neighbor.

The neighbor laughed and waved back. "He's a fierce little bugger."

"You have no idea."

Taz trembled, not with fear but with the desire to chase away the Aussie. At six pounds after a full meal, Taz was the self-appointed pack leader and the only dog Cady had ever owned who refused to be trained. Luckily, he was small and fragile, with teeth the size of Tic Tacs and legs as skinny as pencils. But he was convinced he was a mastiff.

Ten minutes later, she returned her dogs to the house and gated them in the kitchen and family room. Taz's house training was not reliable, and the pit bulls were both young. They chewed on everything. Fed and walked, the dogs stretched out for a nap, and Cady headed to her brother's house to feed the rescues. Alone in the car, she fought the well of sadness in her chest.

Damn Greg.

Seeing him had brought back too many memories. Since then, she'd slept poorly and lost her appetite. She rubbed a tired eye.

Keep busy.

She left her neighborhood. A few miles later, she turned onto the rural highway that led toward her brother's place. She glanced in her rearview mirror. A set of headlights turned onto the road behind her. She rarely saw much traffic this early in the morning. She stopped at an intersection. The car behind her fell back. She looked both ways and turned right. A minute later, headlights shone in her rearview mirror again. She made another turn. The car didn't get any closer, but those headlights stayed in her wake.

The hairs on the back of her neck lifted.

Was someone following her?

She pictured Greg's angry face at the pet supply store. Had he decided to torment her again? It was exactly what he'd done the last time he wanted to punish her. Part of her wanted to stop the car and confront him.

Don't be stupid.

She was well trained in martial arts, but what if Greg had a weapon? As she taught in her classes, physical self-defense was a last resort and not a substitute for common sense.

She pressed her gas pedal to the floor. Her van leaped forward, and the car fell back again. Ten minutes later, she turned into Matt's driveway and parked next to her brother's truck. She twisted in her seat and watched the road through the rear window. The vehicle drove past without slowing. She couldn't read the license plate, and it was too dark to see the make and model, but it appeared to be a dark-colored SUV, like the one Greg had been driving.

The entrance to the interstate was farther up the highway. Had it been a coincidence that the car had been behind her the whole way here?

Or had it been Greg?

Chapter Twenty-Three

Matt's phone rang as he was feeding his dogs their breakfast. It was barely seven o'clock. He read Bree's name on the screen and sighed as he answered the call. "Shouldn't you still be asleep?"

"Probably." She sounded tired. "What time are we interviewing Mrs. Beckett?"

"Eleven o'clock." He gave up. Bree was going to do whatever she wanted. There was no stopping her.

"OK. I already spoke with Todd. The warrants are in. I want you to go to the Beckett residence with him and the forensic techs this morning."

Wait. Was she delegating? Normally she liked to run point on key elements of an investigation.

"I'd planned on it," he said.

"Todd's investigative skills have come a long way in the last few months, but I'd still like you on board."

But Matt had assumed Bree would want to come along, even if she had to drag her sorry, injured self. "How did he get the warrants so fast?"

"He submitted everything electronically last night, and the judge came in early this morning. I'll meet you at the station before eleven."

"OK," Matt said. "What are you going to do this morning?"

"Nothing." She sighed.

"Wow."

"I know," she said in a wry tone. "I promised Kayla I'd rest this morning. I'm only allowed to go into the office, and I have to sit down the whole time I'm there."

Matt held back a laugh. The only person who could control Bree was eight years old.

"I'm glad," he said when he could trust his voice. "Do you need a ride?"

"Adam will drop me off at the station. I'll see you at eleven. Would you bring my vehicle to the station?" She had left it at his house the night before when they'd decided to use his Suburban for the stakeout at Paul's.

"I will. Take it easy."

"I don't have much of a choice." Bree didn't sound happy about that.

Matt called Todd and arranged to meet him at Paul Beckett's house. When he left, his sister's minivan was parked near the kennel, and the lights were on. Matt drove to Beckett's place, where Todd was waiting in his vehicle in the driveway. He climbed out as Matt pulled in.

"How's the sheriff?" Todd squeezed the bridge of his nose.

"Doing OK. She'll be in later this morning."

"I'm surprised she isn't here already."

"So is she," Matt said.

On the other side of the parking area, crime scene tape barred entrance to the garage and cordoned off the area where Bree had been shot.

"Forensic techs are on the way," Todd said. "Interesting piece of info: Paul Beckett has a Sig Sauer P226 registered in his name."

"Let's see if we find it."

"I sent the pictures of Paul handing off that envelope in the parking lot over to forensics. They're going to brighten the photos and see if they can get the license plate of the other vehicle."

"Great," Matt said.

The forensic team arrived. Everyone put on gloves and shoe covers before going in through the front door.

Matt and Bree had already toured the inside of the house the previous evening, but they'd been focused on finding a potentially armed suspect and/or additional victims, not evidence. This time, Matt made his way through the rooms slowly, taking pictures and making notes of things he wanted seized as evidence. The forensic techs started with photos.

Todd opened the fridge. "Not much in here but beer and Chinese takeout. There are four half-eaten containers, though. Seems like a lot of food for one guy."

"Maybe he planned to eat it for multiple nights." Matt peered in the sink. "But then, there are two wineglasses in the sink, so maybe he had company."

Todd checked a recycling container. "A half dozen beer bottles and an empty bottle of wine."

An undercounter wine cooler held a few dozen bottles. Portraits of twin boys from infancy to high school graduation lined the hallway. A framed snapshot of Paul and the boys on a fishing boat sat on a table behind the sofa. In the photo, the boys looked to be about ten. Matt scanned the soft gray walls. There were empty places where it seemed pictures had been removed. He walked closer. Small holes in the drywall confirmed his suspicion.

Todd joined him. "Someone took down a bunch of photos."

"I haven't seen a single picture of Angela Beckett."

"They *were* separated." Todd turned toward a short hallway.

"Now she doesn't need one." Matt followed him into the home office.

Todd thumbed through a pile of mail stacked on the credenza. "Looks like household bills."

"We'll take them." The desktop was clear except for a laptop perfectly centered on the leather desk protector. Matt used a pen to open the desk drawers. Surfaces were free of clutter and dust. "Everything looks pretty normal. We'll take the computer and iPad too."

He walked out of the office. The guest room looked as if it hadn't been used in some time. They finished searching the downstairs before heading for the stairway.

"The place is so clean. It almost looks like no one lived here." Todd followed Matt upstairs. Two kids' bedrooms were on one side of the landing. Half-empty closets held neat rows of hanging pants and shirts. Shelves held stacks of folded jeans and sweaters. Every item in the drawers was precisely organized, even the socks and underwear. Soccer and tennis trophies lined the bookshelves in the first room. They went into the second room, where they found lacrosse and tennis trophies.

"Both boys played tennis. Remember the green clay from both Holly's and Paul's crime scenes?"

"Yes." Matt dropped to his knees to check under a twin bed. Standing, he scanned the walls. "There are pennants from a school in North Carolina in here and ones from Michigan in the other room. I'll get the boys' cell phone numbers from Paul's phone. We'll verify the boys were at their respective schools yesterday."

"You can drive here from either North Carolina or Michigan in ten or twelve hours." Todd closed a closet door. "Why would one of the sons kill his own dad?"

"Anger at the way Paul treated his mother? We don't know anything about the boys' relationships with their father."

"True." Todd pivoted one hundred eighty degrees, his gaze sweeping over the room. "Nothing in either of their rooms looks like it's been touched in months."

"Doesn't mean much," Matt said. "Beckett clearly has a regular cleaning service. This is a big house, and it's spotless."

"I can't see a man like Paul Beckett mopping floors and scrubbing toilets after work," Todd agreed.

"We'll get the contact information for the cleaning service. The people who empty trash cans and clean bathrooms know a lot about their employers' private life."

They moved on. A huge bedroom suite occupied the rest of the second floor.

Matt paused in the doorway. "At least it looks like someone has actually been in this room."

A king-size bed stood between two windows, and two matching chairs faced a wall-mounted TV. One nightstand held only a bedside lamp. On the other, earbuds and an iPad sat next to an alarm clock and an empty coffee cup on a coaster.

"I live alone," Todd said. "The only room that looks occupied is my bedroom. I rarely use the kitchen. Most nights, I eat takeout standing over the sink, shower, sleep, and go back to work. I watch football in my recliner Sunday afternoons and Monday nights." The chief deputy glanced at Matt. "It's not as pathetic as it sounds."

Matt raised his gloved hands. "I'm not judging. Replace watching football with training dogs and add Sunday brunch with my parents to that mix, and you have my life." At least that had been his life before Bree returned to Grey's Hollow. Now, Matt spent at least one night a week with her. Most of the time, they had dinner with her family. Occasionally, they managed a real date. He had to admit that he liked the change.

He went to the nightstand that clearly belonged to the victim and opened it with his pen. A framed photo lay facedown next to an economy box of condoms. He turned over the frame. "He removed his wedding photo from view and stocked up on condoms."

"Not surprising." Todd walked into the bathroom. A few minutes later, he emerged. "There are several used condoms in the trash can and a recently filled bottle of Viagra in the medicine chest." He walked closer and eyed the sheets. "I see a long dark hair on that extra pillow."

"We'll get a forensic tech to collect the biological evidence for possible DNA comparisons. I don't want any chain-of-command issues that can be challenged in court." Matt checked the other drawers in the nightstand and found another full box of condoms. He pulled a camera out of his pocket and took photos.

"Mrs. Beckett hasn't lived here for a couple of months." Todd straightened. "Did the cheating drive their separation, or did the separation prompt the cheating?"

"She told the sheriff he always cheated, but he recently stopped being discreet."

"That's fucked up."

"Yep. But anger, jealousy, and social humiliation all give Mrs. Beckett motive to kill him." Matt moved to the nightstand on the other side of the bed. Empty. He opened a walk-in closet. Two-thirds of the hanging space and shelves were empty. He checked the pockets of pants and jackets and looked inside shoes and handbags. He spotted several large cardboard boxes on the top shelf. Glass rattled as he took one down. He opened the lid. It was full of framed photos of the whole family, the glass broken as if someone had thrown the photos into the box with force. Careful of the shards, he set down the box and began lifting the pictures to view each one.

Todd peered in the doorway. "What did you find?"

"The missing photos." Matt turned one so Todd could see it. "Mrs. Beckett on the tennis court with the boys." A short white skirt and sleeveless blue shirt showed muscled arms and legs. Both sons looked very much like Angela, tall and naturally lean. Their father was heavyset. "Do you remember seeing any pictures of Paul playing tennis?"

"No."

"Me neither." Matt replaced the lid and reached for a second box. It was filled with tennis trophies engraved with Angela Beckett's name. He added the photos and trophies to his list of evidence. "I have to get back to the station to review with the sheriff before Angela Beckett's interview."

"I'll bag and tag the evidence and secure the scene after the forensic team leaves."

"Keep looking for Paul's gun."

"I will," Todd said. "But we've looked in every place large enough to hold a handgun. Unless he had some kind of super-secret hidey-hole, it isn't here."

Matt made a few calls on his way back to the station. One was to the deputy who'd been assigned to examine Paul's cell phone. From him, Matt obtained the phone numbers for the Beckett twins.

Then he called Timothy Beckett and introduced himself.

"This is about my father, isn't it?" Timothy's voice was sharp, almost angry.

"Yes. Do you know what happened?"

"My mom called last night and said someone killed him."

"That's correct. Where are you right now?" Matt asked.

"I'm still in Michigan. My last exam is scheduled for next week, but my professor agreed to let me take it later today. I'll pack tonight and leave early tomorrow. Should be there by dinnertime."

"Do you intend to go to the house?"

"No." Timothy's response was immediate. "Mom said he was killed there. I'll stay with a friend."

"Where were you yesterday evening?"

"I was taking an exam from four to six. I had to sign in with my ID. There'll be a record, if you want confirmation."

"I do. Thanks," Matt said. "Were you aware of the difficulties in your parents' marriage?"

Timothy hesitated, then said in a guarded tone, "You'd better ask my mom about that."

"But you were aware they had problems."

"Doesn't everyone?" Timothy replied.

"Were you close to your dad?" Matt thought about the number of pics of the boys with their mom and the single photograph of the twins with their dad.

"Dad was always working." Timothy evaded the actual question and said in a final tone, "Look, I have to go."

"I'm sorry for your loss." Matt let him go. Timothy had an alibi, and Matt could follow up with an in-person interview when he'd returned.

"Yeah. Thanks."

The line went dead.

Matt called Noah Beckett next. "I'm Matt Flynn, a criminal investigator with the Randolph County Sheriff's Department."

"I assume this is about my dad." Noah's voice sounded shaky. "My mom called last night."

"I'm sorry for your loss," Matt said. "Are you at school?"

Noah sighed. "I didn't tell my mom when I talked to her, but I finished the term early. I'm in Grey's Hollow."

Chapter Twenty-Four

Bree stared out the passenger window of her brother's ancient Bronco. Several news crews clustered in the sheriff's station parking lot. "Drive around the building and drop me at the back door."

Adam followed her instructions, driving into the fenced rear lot. He pulled to the curb.

Bree slid out of the vehicle. "Thanks, Adam."

"Let me know if you need a ride home."

"I will, but I intend to drive my own unit home tonight," Bree said. Then she closed the passenger door.

Adam waited until she had the back door open before he pulled away.

She entered the station, headed into her office, and settled at her desk. Despite her tough words, she felt like she'd been beaten with a stick. She also felt partially naked without the weapons she'd left with Matt the night before. But weapons and pain meds did not mix. She would not carry guns if she was incapacitated.

A knock sounded on her doorframe. She looked up to see Matt and was glad no one else was there to see the automatic smile she couldn't suppress. "Come in."

He set her duty belt and backup piece on her desk. "I thought you'd be missing these."

"Definitely." With her arm in a sling, Bree struggled to strap on the belt one-handed.

"Let me help." Matt stood in front of her. He fastened the belt around her waist. "The parking lot is full of press."

"I'm giving a statement this afternoon." Bree adjusted the belt, then sat in her chair and lifted her foot onto the desk. Resigned to not being able to dress herself, she asked, "Would you help me?"

"Sure." Matt tugged up the hem of her cargo pants and wrapped her second holster around her ankle. He adjusted her pant leg back into place over her black athletic shoe.

She swung her foot under the desk. "Thank you."

"You're welcome." He leaned over her for a few seconds before settling into one of the two chairs that faced her desk. He smelled nice, like citrus and cedar.

She rolled her eyes at herself. The heavy ache weighting her arm told her the drugs had fully worn off, yet she was still punchy. Normally, she was all business in the office. But then, she hadn't slept well. Maybe exhaustion and pain had weakened her normal barriers. Feeling extraordinarily vulnerable, she did what she always did: returned to the case. "How was the search of Paul Beckett's residence?"

"We took the usual electronics and paperwork. A few interesting notes." Matt ticked off the items on his fingers. "Mrs. Beckett is a serious tennis player, as are both of their sons. We found signs that suggest Paul had recent female companionship—someone with long dark hair. Paul owns a handgun, which we did not find. This morning, forensics confirmed that the green smear from the garage floor is the same green clay found in Holly Thorpe's trunk. The clay also matched the type used on the Becketts' tennis court. Last, I spoke with the twins, Timothy and Noah. Timothy is still in Michigan. I assigned a deputy to verify his alibi, but it seems strong."

"I sense a *but* coming." Bree settled back in her chair.

Matt's eyes gleamed, not unlike a cat that had spotted a mouse. "Noah is here in Grey's Hollow."

"Angela Beckett thinks he's in North Carolina."

"He says he finished the term early. He didn't want to get in the middle of his parents' separation, so he's staying with a friend. He has no alibi."

"Interesting." Bree hated to think of a son killing his own father, but she'd seen family kill family many times before. High emotions, personal histories, and conflicting loyalties often blurred the line between love and hate. "Did you get any sense of the boys' relationship with their dad?"

"Paul worked a lot. They both seem closer to their mother, but neither one would talk about their parents' relationship over the phone."

"Let's get Noah in for an interview."

"He's on his way." Matt grinned. "I wanted to get a statement from him ASAP. Once his mother finds out he was in town and has no alibi for his father's death, she'll lawyer him up and shut us down."

"I'm sure you're right. She'll do whatever it takes to protect her kids."

Marge buzzed in with an armload of paperwork. Sharp eyes assessed Bree. "You look awful."

"Thanks," Bree said. "Don't worry. I'll put on makeup before the press con."

"Don't." Marge shook her head. "Let them see how much you're sacrificing. Everyone rallies behind a wounded hero."

Bree bristled. "I'm not acting here."

"I know, and that's why people trust you. But like it or not, you're a politician now." Marge set down the papers and pointed to a line marked with a blue sticky tab. "You want money for renovations to the station?"

"Yes." Bree scanned the paper and signed her name.

Marge flipped the page. "The more popular you are with the public, the more leverage you have with the county board of supervisors. They'll be less able to put you off if you have public support."

Bree signed several more papers. "I don't like playing games."

"I'm not suggesting you be anything other than genuine. You don't need to be. But you can use circumstances to your advantage." Marge collected her papers and hugged them to her body. "Remember, the games are there whether you like them or not. The only choice you have is to try to beat them or let them win."

"I don't like to lose," Bree admitted.

"Then you have to stay ahead of those cagey bastards that control our budget. You need to anticipate how they're going to try to screw this department out of money. They will only support you if it's in their own best interests. You have to make that so. Remember, they've been at this a very long time. They know how the game works, and they are always thinking a few moves ahead."

A bright spot of anger bloomed in Bree's chest. She hated politics, but Marge was right. She had to play chess, not Candy Land. "I want that damned locker room."

"That's better." Marge raised a penciled eyebrow. "Now, Angela Beckett is here. Where do you want her?"

"Interview room one." Bree gathered a pen and notepad, though she didn't rush. She didn't mind letting Angela, a woman accustomed to getting her own way, wait. In Bree's experience, wealthy people often felt above the law. Bree wanted Angela's feet firmly on the ground. "When Noah Beckett arrives, please put him in room two immediately. I don't want his mother to see him."

"All right." Marge turned and left the office.

Bree turned to Matt. "Let's go talk to Mrs. Beckett." She tucked her notepad under her sling. "I need coffee and sugar."

They stopped in the break room. Bree bought a pack of M&M's from the vending machine and ate a few pieces of candy while Matt made two cups of coffee. The sugar and chocolate perked up her brain. Then she bought a second pack.

Coffee in hand, they went down the hall and opened the door to the conference room. Angela sat with her back to the wall. She wore gray slacks, a blue silk blouse, and gorgeous gray pumps that cost more than a regular person's mortgage payment. Delicate, understated silver jewelry decorated her earlobes and wrist. A bottle of water sat unopened in front of her. Despite her put-together appearance, her nerves were showing. She was twisting her wedding band around and around on her finger.

Bree turned on the video camera. "This interview is being recorded."

Angela nodded.

"Are we waiting for your attorney?" She eased into the chair at the head of the table, diagonal from Angela. Matt dropped into the seat opposite her.

"No." As if suddenly aware of her fidgeting, Angela stopped playing with her ring and folded her hands on the table. "He was unavailable."

"Are you sure you want to proceed without him?" Bree asked, wanting nothing to invalidate Angela's statements in court later.

"Yes. I just want to get this over with." Angela looked up, her face blank. "I still can't comprehend Paul's death."

"Again, we're sorry for your loss." Bree recited her Miranda rights and slid a paper across the table. In a *this is routine* voice, she said, "I need you to sign that you understand your rights." She offered her pen.

Angela took it, carefully read the paper, then signed it, her tight mouth locked in a brittle half smile.

Bree matched her smile and slid the second pack of candy across the table. "Mrs. Beckett, thank you for coming in to speak with us during what must be a difficult time." She always liked to seem as if she were on the suspect's side, at least in the beginning.

"Call me Angela. I haven't decided if I'm dropping the Beckett yet. I hate the name now, but it's my boys' name so . . ." Angela touched the bag of candy with one finger, as if it would burn her. "I haven't had a piece of candy in . . . I don't even know how long. I was always worried about gaining weight. Paul liked me thin and fit. I play tennis five days a week."

Bree ate a chocolate from her own bag. "Did Paul play tennis?"

"No." She pursed her lips. "He liked golf and fishing, but he didn't have much time for hobbies. The only thing he truly loved was his company."

"But your sons play tennis?" Bree asked.

"Yes." Angela's face lit up in a smile. "They were both on the high school tennis team. They're natural athletes." Her voice rang with pride.

"You must miss them. When were they last home?" Matt asked.

"Christmas." She frowned at the M&M's. "Paul sent them to Florida for spring break. He didn't want to drag the boys into our problems."

Bree made a note. "How did you feel about that?"

"I don't know." Angela looked away. "As much as I wanted to see them, I also didn't want to upset them. But I felt terrible when I had to tell them about the separation over the phone. Some things should be done in person." She sniffed. "I had to tell them about their father's death over the phone too. That was awful for them. But they weren't supposed to come home for two weeks. I couldn't have them hear it from someone else or on the news."

"Then why not wait to tell them about the separation until they came home for the summer?" Matt asked.

"Because if they talked to Paul, he would slip, and I wanted them to hear it from me. I was afraid Paul would be . . ." She waved a hand, as if searching for the right word. "Abrupt. Paul wouldn't have understood the boys being upset. He would have told them to *suck it up*." She bit off the last three words with venom.

Or had she wanted the boys to hear *her* story before they heard Paul's?

Matt's shoulders tipped forward, his posture attentive. "It sounds like Paul was insensitive with his sons."

"He believed men should be tough," Angela backtracked.

"You disagreed on parenting styles," Bree said in an understanding voice.

Angela paused to think before answering. "Paul thought I was too soft on the boys. Maybe he was right."

She was cagier than Bree had expected and was trying to downplay her disagreements with her husband.

Bree shifted topics, hoping to throw Angela off guard. "So, Paul asked you to leave? That doesn't seem right. It was your home too."

"He didn't ask. Not exactly." Angela visibly gathered herself. "A friend told me she'd seen him with another—younger—woman." She took a deep breath. "The really strange thing is that *I* was ashamed. My husband had been seen running around with another woman, yet *I* was the one who was embarrassed." She went quiet, as if contemplating this oddity. But inside, Bree could see turmoil, rage that Angela was working hard to conceal.

"Had you ever considered leaving him?" Bree asked.

"Yes. When the boys were home, I had a purpose. I didn't want to break up their home." Her gaze dropped to her hands. "But unlike Paul, I decided to give our relationship one last try. I admit I'd been so focused on the boys that Paul—and our marriage—often took second place. But I'd invested more than two decades into our relationship. After the boys left for school this year, I suggested Paul and I take a long trip. There are so many places I want to see, but we've always been too busy. Paul with his work. Me with the kids. Suddenly, we had this empty nest."

"What did Paul say?" Bree prompted.

"He couldn't take off from work. He had too many jobs, and we had tuition bills to pay. When I pressed the issue, he called me selfish and lazy. He said I had no idea what kind of pressure he was under to keep the money coming in while I played tennis and organized charity events." Anger flashed in her eyes. She dumped a few candies into her palm and closed her fingers tightly around them. "I knew this was just an excuse. I knew it. But I let him guilt me into backing off because I didn't bring in an income. Ironically, it was Paul who didn't want me to work when the kids were young." She slammed the handful of candy into her mouth in an angry gesture. She chewed, her jaws working harder than necessary. Then she forcibly pulled herself together and smoothed out her expression.

Matt leaned closer. "What did you do before you married Paul?"

Angela swallowed. Her expression turned wistful. "I was a teacher. Third grade."

"So, you gave up your career for him?" Bree poked at the wound.

"I did." Angela reached for the water bottle. "However, I also loved being home with my kids. But now that they're grown, I need to do something meaningful. Playing tennis isn't enough." She sat back. Her shoulders dropped as she relaxed. "And now I won't have to entertain clients or anyone else." She didn't look upset about that. "For the first time in decades, my time is my own."

"When did you tell your sons about the separation?" Bree asked after a minute of silence.

Angela shook her head. "I called them about a week after I moved out."

"You told them the truth," Bree prodded.

"I didn't get specific." Angela's chest heaved. "That's not the kind of information children need."

"They aren't children," Bree pointed out. "They're grown men."

"Why Paul and I separated isn't any of their business," Angela snapped. "It isn't *anyone's* business."

Matt jumped in. "Are the boys close to Paul?"

Angela jerked a shoulder. "He didn't have much time for them when they were young. He was always working, and when neither showed any interest in the family business, Paul was annoyed." There was a slight pause before the word *annoyed*.

"We met Paul." Matt's shoulders shifted forward. "He had a temper. I'll bet he was more than annoyed."

Angela didn't answer. Caution—maybe even calculation—narrowed her eyes. She wasn't stupid. She wouldn't confirm anything that shined a suspicious light on her or her boys.

"Paul was an alpha male." Angela lifted her chin, feigning confidence she clearly didn't feel.

"He was an asshole," Matt added.

Angela's eyes heated, but she didn't comment.

Bree steered the questioning away from the boys, hoping Angela would talk more freely. "Where were you between seven forty-five and eight o'clock yesterday evening?"

Angela picked at the candy wrapper. "As I told you last night, I'm staying with a friend, but she left for work by six thirty."

"I'll need the contact information of your friend." Bree lifted her pen.

"Of course." Angela gave Bree her friend's name and address.

Bree made a note, then dropped her big question. "Where were you last Friday evening?"

"When? Why?" Angela's brows puckered with confusion.

"One of Paul's employees was killed then." Bree watched her eyes.

Angela's mouth dropped open. "Holly," she whispered, almost to herself. She stared down at the bag of candy in her hand, but her attention was inward. "I thought it was suicide. I saw it on the news."

"The reporter was speculating," Bree said. "Holly was murdered."

Angela gaped. "I didn't know. I haven't watched the news since I saw that report. Does this mean Holly's death is related to Paul's?" She cocked her head.

"We don't know." Bree mirrored her movement. "How well did you know Holly?"

"Not very." Angela tilted her chin down, letting her bangs fall across her face. "My only contribution to the business was helping Paul entertain clients. I don't know anything about construction."

"But you *knew* Holly?" Bree pressed.

Angela nodded without lifting her gaze. "I'd met her a couple of times when I'd stopped at the office to speak with Paul, but I didn't know her well."

"I find that hard to believe," Bree said. "She worked for your husband for seven years."

Angela stiffened at the challenge but said nothing. She sat still and averted her gaze. She knew more than she was saying. Holly's name—and murder—had definitely triggered an emotional response Angela was trying to cover. Bree could feel it. She glanced at Matt. He too was patiently waiting, his shoulders deceptively relaxed. As if by mutual agreement, they let the quiet spin out.

"I guess you're going to find out anyway. There's no point in hiding it." Angela tore off a small piece of the candy bag. "One night he said he was working late. I called him, and the line went to voice mail. I texted and he didn't answer. Stupid me. I started to worry about him." Her voice turned bitter. "I called his office, and his secretary said he'd left at five." She stripped off another piece of label. "That's when I started to get suspicious."

Neither Bree nor Matt moved a muscle. When a suspect was on a roll, you let her go.

"A few nights later—" She paused, her face flushing. "I went to bed. Paul was in his home office. I woke up hours later, and he hadn't come to bed. I went downstairs to look for him. He'd fallen asleep at his desk in the past and always woke up with a stiff neck." She bit her lip, holding back tears. "I heard his voice from the hallway." She took a deep, shaky breath. "He was trying to calm her, telling her he'd do whatever she wanted. I listened at the door. He said, 'Don't worry. We won't have to do this much longer. My marriage will be over soon.' Hearing him saying those words to another woman was devastating. Then, the next night he told me he had a meeting." The tears she'd been holding back began to flow. Sobbing, she dropped her head into her hands. A minute later, she lifted her face.

Bree suspected her sadness was real, but it was grief over her lost lifestyle, not over her husband's death. She got up, fetched a box of tissues from a table in the corner, and set them in front of Angela.

Angela sniffed and plucked a tissue from the box. "Thank you."

Bree sat down and angled her body toward Angela, trying to create a connection. "Did he call her by name?"

Matt stayed still and quiet, clearly sensing Angela was not likely to connect with a man in her present state.

"Yes." Angela blotted her eyes. "He said her name twice. Holly."

Bree nudged the water bottle closer.

"Thank you." Angela picked up the bottle and took a swallow. "I confronted him. He didn't even try to deny it. He was glad I found out. Then he laughed and told me I was stupid." Humiliation brightened her eyes. "I was so mad—" She stopped suddenly, as if realizing she shouldn't have admitted that. "Am I a suspect? You didn't answer the last time I asked you."

"Did you shoot your husband?" Bree asked.

"No." Angela didn't break eye contact.

Truth or lie?

"Then you shouldn't have anything to worry about." Bree flattened her hands on the table.

Angela didn't look like she was buying it. She plucked another tissue from the box and pressed it to her face.

Drying her tears, or covering her expression? Bree couldn't tell, but something about her demeanor didn't ring true. Angela's reactions seemed calculated.

"If my spouse was cheating, I'd be furious. Maybe angry enough to kill them both." Bree leaned in and asked the question Angela had avoided earlier: "Where were you on Friday evening?"

"I was home, alone. My friend's home, I mean." Angela's lips flattened and her eyes narrowed in an assessing expression. She was making a decision. She lowered the hand with the tissue. "Look, I can see why I'd be a suspect, since Paul and I were in the middle of a divorce. But I wouldn't have hurt Holly. It wasn't her fault. In fact, it's highly possible Paul harassed or pressured her into their . . . liaison." She looked at Matt. "As you said, he was an asshole. Also, Holly wasn't the only woman he was sleeping with."

"How do you know that?" Bree asked.

"Because after I moved out, I went right to a lawyer. He wanted to document Paul's cheating and hired a private investigator."

CHAPTER
TWENTY-FIVE

Matt watched Angela Beckett's eyes. She was playing them, or at least she thought she was. He had been trying to keep an open mind until she'd confessed about the lawyer and PI. If her story was true, then Paul had deserved to be taken to the cleaners. But Angela seemed more calculated about the divorce than she was pretending to be. She hadn't been shocked to find out Paul was cheating, he reminded himself. She'd been angrier that he'd stopped being discreet about his affairs. She was more concerned about her reputation than her marriage.

"Who did your attorney hire?" he asked.

"Sharp Investigations." Angela opened her purse and pulled out a business card. "I worked with Lance Kruger and Lincoln Sharp."

Matt waved it away. "No need. I know them."

Angela's eyes narrowed with displeasure. She didn't like that he knew Lance and Sharp.

Bree continued to pressure her. "Did the investigators find out who Paul had been sleeping with?"

Angela studied her tissue. "It wasn't just one woman. There were many just in the few weeks he followed Paul. I have to assume there were many more before that."

"Did you know any of the women personally, other than Holly?" Bree asked.

Angela dabbed at her eye, covering her face. "I didn't even look at the list."

Right.

Matt didn't believe that for a second. "The investigators didn't give you a report?"

Instead of answering, Angela said, "I didn't want to know the details. Paul was clearly not in a relationship. He was whoring around." She shuddered. "I went to the doctor that week and got tested for everything. God only knows what kind of diseases he exposed me to."

Bree tapped her pen on the paper. "If I were you, I would have wanted to know everything. I would be plenty angry, and I'd want to get even."

"I'm not a violent person." Angela's gaze dropped to Bree's gun. She shook her hair off her face. "I'd like to go now. Last night was a terrible shock."

"We'd like a copy of the investigators' reports," Bree said. "To verify your statement."

Angela hesitated.

Bree continued. "Unless you've been less than truthful."

"Or you have something to hide," Matt added.

"I don't," Angela snapped. She breathed, clearly weighing the risks and benefits. "I'll forward you the reports."

After she potentially altered them?

Bree shook her head. "We'd need them directly from Sharp Investigations."

Sharp Investigations would have photos and detailed data about Paul's movements and liaisons. No matter how much the sheriff's department preferred gathering all information themselves, they couldn't recreate surveillance on a man who was now dead.

Generally, facts that pass from a PI to an attorney are covered under the attorney's client privilege. If Angela had hired the PIs directly, that wouldn't necessarily have been the case. Either Angela was smart or she had an excellent divorce attorney. Maybe both. The sheriff's department would have a hard time getting the document without her consent.

Angela's words became measured. "Then I'll call my lawyer and have him give the investigator permission to forward you that information."

But not everything.

"Thank you. I have only a few more questions," Bree said. "Who benefits financially from Paul's death?"

"I don't know." Angela looked up, her gaze sharpening. "He doesn't have a will. I tried to drag him to an estate planner years ago, but he refused to consider the fact that he could die. Thankfully, I have my own money, family money in a trust that Paul couldn't touch. I'm not wealthy, but I'll survive." She let go of the water bottle and sat back, her hands falling into her lap. "I guess I'll have to contact an estate attorney."

Matt knew the answer, but he kept quiet. In the state of New York, assets would be divided by a set formula between the spouse and children. It wouldn't all automatically go to the wife, although the distribution would be far easier than in a divorce, unless the business ended up in bankruptcy.

She straightened her shoulders and reached for a small purse on the chair next to her. "Are we finished?"

"Almost," Bree said. "Was there anyone else who might want Paul dead?"

Angela gripped her purse in her lap. Her knuckles were white. She looked ready to bolt. "Holly's husband, the husbands of other women Paul might have slept with."

Bree made a show of writing down that idea. "What about business associates or clients?"

Angela just shrugged. "I wouldn't know."

Matt asked, "Was Paul involved in any shady deals?"

"It's possible," Angela admitted. "Paul wasn't a good husband, but he was a very good contractor. He grew up in the business. He knew every aspect of it from drawing to completion, and he had an incredible eye for space and design. That's why he made a lot of money. He had a waiting list for quotes. People got in line to have Paul remodel their houses." She sighed. "That said, he clearly wasn't the most honest man in the world. I suspect he was cheating on taxes. He was also very vague about other aspects of the business, so not much would surprise me."

"You think he cheated on taxes?" Bree asked.

Angela bared her perfect teeth in a predatory smile. "I might have alerted the IRS."

"But you'll owe money too, and maybe suffer penalties," Matt said.

Angela nodded. "Now that Paul is dead, that is regrettable, but at the time I really just wanted him to pay for humiliating me. I was hoping he'd go to prison." She waved a hand. "It doesn't matter. Paul made sure I wasn't on any of the business paperwork. He refused to share it with me, so I doubt I'll be criminally liable for tax fraud. They can take back taxes and penalties out of Paul's estate. Like I said, I have my own trust fund. I'll be fine. Suing him for divorce wasn't about money. It was about payback."

"So, you had motive to kill him," suggested Matt.

"No." Angela shook her head. "I didn't want him dead. I wanted him to *pay*. There's a difference. Dead, he gets away with everything."

Bree asked, "But you don't know anyone specifically who would have a reason to shoot Paul?"

"Not in our personal life." Angela stood. "I don't know anything about day-to-day running of the business."

Matt didn't believe that for a second. While Angela might play dumb, she'd proven she was anything but.

She clutched the purse in front of her belly in both hands. "You should talk to his secretary. She knows everything about clients and such. She's been with the company for decades. She worked with Paul's father too."

Bree asked, "When did Paul buy his gun?"

"Years ago, after walking in on two burglars at a jobsite."

"Where does he keep it?" Bree asked.

"The glove compartment of his truck," Angela said. "He was always worried about vandalism and theft. Sometimes he'd stop at jobs late at night on his way home."

"How many other people know about the gun?" Bree asked.

Angela lifted a thin shoulder. "I have no idea."

"What kind of gun does he own?" Bree asked.

Angela shrugged again. "I don't know. I don't like guns. He never brought it into the house."

Bree flattened her right hand on the table. Matt recognized the *going in for the kill* gleam in her eyes. She tilted her head. "Did the boys know about it?"

Angela's face went pale, and her lips compressed into a bloodless line.

She was not happy about that question. Not happy at all.

"This interview is over." Angela lifted her chin in defiance. "I won't speak to you again without my lawyer."

Bree had found her weak spot.

Matt rose. Since she was acting like a devastated woman, he pretended to believe her. Putting her on notice would only make her more defensive. "Are you all right to drive?"

"Yes." She nodded, pressing her crumpled tissue to the corner of her eye. "Thank you."

"We'll be in contact," Bree said.

Neither Matt nor Bree mentioned that Noah was in the next room. The mere mention of her kids in the context of Paul's gun had brought out the mama bear in her. If Angela knew they were going to question one of her sons next, she definitely would have gone ballistic.

"Of course." Angela tucked her purse under her arm and left the conference room in long strides.

Matt escorted her to the station lobby. Outside, the media still gathered. Matt turned to Angela to offer her the option of leaving through a different, more discreet, door. But Angela Beckett pushed through without hesitating. They swarmed her like ants on a crumb. She raised a teary face toward the cameras. Matt cracked the door so he could hear.

"The sheriff has promised to find my husband's killer." Angela sniffed and blotted her eyes. No ugly crying for her. "I'm doing everything I can to help."

A reporter shoved a microphone in her face. "Weren't you and Mr. Beckett separated?"

"Yes." A few tears rolled down Angela's cheek. "But that doesn't mean I didn't still love him. He was the father of my children." She raised a hand to block the camera. "I'm sorry. I just can't." Sobbing, she turned away. A few reporters followed her, but she hurried to a silver BMW sedan.

When Matt returned to interview room one, Bree had jotted down a quick list of bullet-pointed notes. She set down the pen and drummed her fingers on the table. "I'm not sure what to make of her. How much of her performance was an act?"

"Most of it." Matt closed the door and described the parking-lot scene. "It was Oscar-worthy. She summoned tears and everything."

"In here, despite all her crying, her mascara didn't run. Her lipstick didn't even smudge." Bree added, "What did you think of her saying she didn't read the PIs' report?"

"I can't see anyone *not* reading that report. Who could resist knowing who their spouse was banging? Everybody wants the dirty details."

"Right?" Bree huffed. "I call bullshit on that too."

"On the bright side, I know Lance Kruger of Sharp Investigations. He used to work for the Scarlet Falls PD. He's a good guy. I only know his boss by reputation, but it's solid. Whatever information they have will be valid. We could get a list of possible new suspects."

Bree tapped her pen on her pad. "If Paul was shot with his own weapon, then whoever killed him knew he had one and where he kept it. They didn't break into his garage and truck and conveniently find a gun."

"Chances are, he knew his killer."

"I agree." Bree turned over the page of her notepad. "On that note, shall we talk to Noah?"

"Yes. The one question Angela flat-out didn't answer is whether or not the boys knew about Paul's gun."

"It would be hard to believe Paul owned a weapon for many years without his adult sons knowing it existed." Bree got up and led the way into the next interview room.

Matt had seen photos of the twins, but in person, Noah looked remarkably like his mother, tall and leanly athletic. His jeans, striped button-down shirt, and loafers had a nerdy/preppy vibe. But he was displaying none of his mother's calculation. Noah was pacing the room, chewing on his thumbnail when Bree and Matt entered. She pressed a button, and the light on the video camera mounted in the corner turned green.

She introduced them and sat at the table, where she read Noah his Miranda warning. "I need you to sign that you understand."

Noah faced them. "Why?"

"It's the law, Mr. Beckett." Bree adjusted her sling and winced.

"Please don't call me that." He yanked out the chair and plopped into it. "Mr. Beckett is my dad's name. I don't want to be him."

"OK, Noah." Bree's tone softened. She had an instinctive ability to read people and tailor her interview style. For Noah, she'd morphed into a mother figure because that's what he responded to. She handed him her pen, and he signed the paper without reading any of it.

He checked his phone. "I tried to call my mom, but she's not answering."

Bree gave him a stern look. "I'm going to ask you to turn off your phone during our interview."

Noah responded with a respectful nod. "Sure. I'm sorry." He switched the phone to silent and shoved it into his pocket.

Matt exhaled. He didn't want Angela to return Noah's call in the middle of their questioning session.

"You're staying with a friend?" Bree began.

"Yeah." He raised his thumb to his mouth and chewed on the nail. "At my girlfriend's place."

"I'll need her name and address." Bree poised her pen.

"Chloe Miller." He gave them the address of an apartment in Scarlet Falls.

"When did you get back to town?" Bree asked.

"Last week. Thursday." He dropped his hand into his lap. "I should have told Mom. But I know there's nowhere to stay at her friend's place, and I didn't want to stay with my dad." He sighed. "I just thought this would be easier."

"You were going to have to tell her eventually," Bree pointed out.

"I know." Noah's gaze fell to his hands. "I'll talk to her later today. She's going to be hurt that I've been here a week and didn't see her." He picked at his nail. "And that I lied to her when we talked last night."

Bree's mouth turned up in the corner. "She loves you. She's going to be happy to see you no matter what."

"Yeah. I know." But Noah looked worried.

Matt jumped in. "When did you see your parents last?"

"I was home for Christmas," Noah said.

"Did they both seem normal?" Matt asked.

"Yeah." Noah's answer sounded half-hearted, but he didn't elaborate. He seemed distracted, as if he was having an entirely different conversation in his own head. Was he replaying events from his holiday break? Or was he simply unwilling to talk about his parents' marriage problems?

Matt changed topics. "Did you know your dad had a gun?"

"Uh-huh." Noah's brows furrowed.

"I used to go shooting with my dad," Matt lied. His dad was more comfortable with a wooden spoon. "Did your dad ever take you?"

Noah frowned. "Yeah. He took me and Timothy out a couple of times. Dad liked all that *man's man* stuff. Fishing, shooting, football . . . He didn't like that we played tennis."

"Do you still play tennis?" Matt asked.

"Sure." Noah nodded. "There's courts at my girlfriend's apartment complex. I'm teaching her to play."

Bree shifted her chair an inch closer, making their proximity more intimate. "But you didn't like those activities your dad liked?"

"Not really. We used to go fishing with him once in a while, just to make him happy. But it's not my thing." Noah flushed. Was he embarrassed at not meeting his father's idea of a "man's man"?

Matt sat back and sighed. "It's hard when you can't live up to your dad's expectations. My dad was disappointed when I became a cop." None of this was true. Matt's dad was an *I love you no matter what* parent. He loved to cook. He watched *Chopped* instead of football, but Matt needed to connect with Noah.

Noah bobbed his head. "When me and Timothy picked majors, Dad lost his shit."

Slightly different from Angela's story.

"What's your major?" Bree asked.

"Education. I'm going to be a teacher."

"Like your mom," Matt said.

Noah brightened. "Yeah."

"What's your brother's major?" Bree asked.

"Law." Noah winced. "Tim will make money. At least Dad respected that."

Melinda Leigh

"But your dad didn't respect education," Matt prodded.

"No. He wanted me to major in engineering or business so I could take over the company. He threatened to cut off my tuition. He would have too, but Mom stopped him." Noah's eyes focused inward. "She didn't do that often. Usually, she found a way to work around him, most of the time without him ever knowing it. She doesn't like confrontation, and Dad could be a bully."

Matt took that to mean Angela was sneaky. "How so?"

Noah glanced away, his face locked in conflict.

"Was he mean to all of you, or just your mom?" Bree asked.

Noah's jaw tightened.

Bree said, "My dad had a temper. He did nothing but yell and scream—and worse." She swallowed. "When I was little, I used to think his blowups were my fault. That I'd done something to make him angry. Now that I'm an adult, I know that wasn't the case. He was a bully not only because he was bigger and stronger, but because he wanted to be one. He enjoyed making us feel small. He liked to be mean."

Noah's eyes locked on hers, and there was the connection they'd needed. Matt wished it had been something different—he could hear the truth in Bree's voice. She wasn't bullshitting Noah.

Bree's voice was soft. "Did he hit your mom?"

Noah shook his head. "I don't think so."

"Did he ever hit you?"

Noah sighed. His body caved forward in surrender. "No, but he was so fucking intimidating. He wasn't a huge man, but when he got mad, he seemed bigger somehow. I can't explain it."

"Because it always seemed like he was going to hit you." Bree clearly understood. "Even when he didn't."

Noah froze. "Yeah. That was it." His gaze dropped. "So, why was he still intimidating when I'd grown up to be as tall as him?"

She said, "Sometimes we still see things through the eyes of the children we once were."

204

Noah nodded. "I guess that makes sense." His mouth went pensive, and he remained quiet. After a few seconds of time ticked by, most people couldn't stand silence, but Noah didn't seem to care.

"We talked to your mom earlier today." Bree raised her hand. "Don't worry. We didn't tell her you were in town. That's up to you."

"My mom was here?" The blood drained from Noah's face. "Why?"

"Oh, we're talking to everyone who was close to your dad." Bree's tone was artificially nonchalant, and her body language suggested there was more to it than that.

Noah's body slammed forward, the legs of the chair hitting the floor with a bang. "My mom wouldn't hurt anybody."

Bree didn't move. "We didn't say that she would."

Noah's entire body went tight. His face reddened, and the tendons on the sides of his neck stood out like steel cables. "My dad was the aggressive one, not Mom."

Bree lifted one hand, the palm facing Noah. "If you say so."

Noah leaped to his feet. The rubber chair feet squeaked on the old waxed floor. "It was me."

Matt was on his feet before he could process any thought, the reaction to Noah's sudden movement automatic. Then his brain processed what the kid had said.

Wait. What?

Was that a confession?

Bree hadn't moved. She blinked once in surprise. She hadn't expected the outburst either.

She kept her eyes on Noah and recovered her shock in less than one breath. "Please sit down."

Noah eased into the chair as if in slow motion. His gaze darted from Bree to Matt, then fell to his lap, where his fingers were clenched into fists on his thighs.

Mirroring Noah, Bree sat very still. "What did you mean by 'it was me'? I need you to be very clear here, Noah."

Noah raised his chin, but he couldn't quite meet Bree's gaze. His voice went robotic. "I killed my father."

Bree sat back, quietly studying him. Under her scrutiny, sweat broke out on Noah's forehead. He was entirely still, except for the jiggling of one leg.

One long minute passed. Then Bree shifted her shoulders just an inch forward. "Convince me."

Noah's eyes widened. Dark rings of sweat appeared under his arms. His voice trembled. "What do you mean?"

"How did you kill him?" Bree's head tilted.

"I shot him." Noah's statement rose at the end, almost like a question.

"Are you sure?" Bree asked.

"Yes." He nodded once, then repeated in a more confident voice, "I shot him."

Bree picked up her pen and held it over her notepad. "Where?"

Noah licked his lips. "In the garage."

Bree made a note. "What did you shoot him with?"

A tiny flash of alarm scrambled in Noah's eyes, then he exhaled, as if just remembering something. "His gun."

Bree's pen scratched on her pad. "How did you get the gun?"

"I took it from the truck," Noah said. So, he knew where Paul had kept his gun.

"Was the truck locked?" she asked.

Noah thought about that. "No."

Bree lifted an eyebrow. "Are you sure about that?"

Noah's jaw jutted forward. "The truck wasn't locked. It was in the garage."

"How did you get into the garage?" Bree asked.

"I have a key." Noah's voice was uncertain. He probably did have a key. His dad's house was his permanent address, but he didn't know about the glass panes that had been cut out of the window.

She lifted her pen. "Where was your dad standing when you shot him?"

"I don't remember exactly." Noah's jiggly leg was bouncing like crazy, and the sweat stains under his arms grew larger.

"OK," Bree said. "How about approximately?"

"I don't remember." Panic clouded Noah's eyes.

"What about Holly Thorpe's death?" Bree asked.

Noah's eyes went as wide as hubcaps. His mouth dropped open.

"You know who she was, right?" Bree asked.

"Of course I know," Noah snapped. "She worked for my dad."

"How did you kill her?" Bree held her pen over her notepad, as if patiently waiting.

Noah's mouth slammed shut. Matt could see his brain working. The kid clearly hadn't thought through his confession.

Matt leaned in. "Did you stalk Holly before you killed her?"

Another flash of fear lit Noah's eyes, then he crossed his arms over his chest. "I'm not saying anything else without a lawyer."

Now the kid gets a clue? Matt sighed.

"Do you want to recant your confession?" Bree asked.

Noah stared straight ahead, his posture rigid, his jaw locked.

Bree finished writing a few notes, then picked up her notepad and pen and stood. "I'll have a deputy book you, and then you can make your call."

The blood drained from Noah's face.

Bree took her handcuffs off her duty belt. "Mr. Flynn, would you cuff him?"

"Yes, ma'am." Matt took the cuffs. "Stand up. Turn around and extend your arms out at your sides."

Noah's body shook as he complied. Matt snapped the cuffs on one wrist, then the other. "Let's go."

Matt marched him out into the squad room and handed him off to a deputy. "Book Noah Beckett on the first-degree murder of his father, Paul Beckett." He gave the kid a hard look.

Noah moved like he was in a daze.

Todd walked in from the back hallway and stopped short. His brows rose.

Bree waved Todd and Matt into her office.

"Close the door," she said, sitting behind the desk.

"What happened?" Todd turned both palms toward the ceiling.

"He confessed." Bree set her notepad in front of her.

"To killing his own father?" Todd's eyes widened.

"Yep. People kill their loved ones all the time." Bree knew better than anyone that blood was not thicker. You couldn't count on someone just because you shared DNA.

"Yeah, I guess they do." Todd winced and examined his ugly black shoes as if he felt bad for forgetting about Bree's parents' deaths.

Matt paced, irritation rushing through him. "The kid is lying his ass off."

"Yep." Bree tugged on her sling. Small pain lines formed around her eyes.

Todd eased into a guest chair. "How do you know?"

"He barely knew the basics of Paul's death, and he didn't know shit about Holly. Whoever killed her did their homework to attempt to make her death look like a suicide." Though it was a poor attempt, in Matt's opinion. "Holly's killer knew where her father had died."

Bree nodded. "That's public information, but he or she had to go looking for it."

"Why would Noah confess if he didn't do it?" Todd asked.

Matt stopped behind the empty guest chair and leaned on it with both hands. "To protect his mother."

The corners of Bree's mouth turned up just a hair, like a cat with a chipmunk in its sights. "It was a drastic—even desperate—move."

Matt met her eyes.

The predatory gleam no longer reminded him of a house cat, but a mountain lion. "There's only one reason Noah would be willing to take such an extreme step."

"Why is that?" Todd sounded exasperated.

Matt broke away from Bree's gaze to face Todd. "Because he's certain his mother is guilty."

CHAPTER TWENTY-SIX

Bree rolled her head on her neck. Pain radiated like heat from her wound. She reached into her desk for a bottle of ibuprofen. She swallowed two with some water from a bottle, though it felt like using a flyswatter on a bear. She'd save the stronger meds for overnight.

"Can we hold him if we know he's innocent?" Todd asked.

"Yes. For a while, anyway." She fished a package of half-crumbled crackers from her desk drawer. "There's evidence that could support his guilt. Noah didn't give us an alibi for his father's death or Holly's, and he does play tennis." She opened the crackers and ate one. "Also, he has an estranged relationship with his father. Plus, Noah doesn't want to recant his confession. Why lawyer up after he already confessed unless he didn't want us to know his confession was bullshit? He wants us to think he did it. But we need to verify our theory." Bree inclined her head at Todd. "Noah lives with his girlfriend. Go talk to her. See if she knows where Noah was when Holly and Paul were killed."

"Now?" Todd asked.

"As soon as we're done in here, yes. We need to get to her before word of his arrest gets out. Just tell her Noah is a suspect in his father's murder. See if she voluntarily provides him with an alibi."

"Before he tells her not to," Matt added.

Bree nodded. "Exactly." She dumped cracker crumbs into her palm.

"Angela is still our number one suspect," Matt said.

Bree nodded. "She doesn't have an alibi for either murder, and she was angry at Paul. Green clay was found in Holly's trunk and in Paul's garage. Angela plays tennis. We definitely need to question her again. Now that we've arrested her son, I'm hoping we'll get a stronger response from her." Bree chewed another cracker and set the package aside. She was not hungry. She'd only eaten to keep the ibuprofen from making her nauseated. Her arm wound felt dry and hot. "Have a deputy verify a midnight phone call between Holly and Paul that Angela claimed to have overheard a couple of months ago. I doubt she'd lie about something so easy to confirm, but you never know."

"What about Owen Thorpe?" Todd asked. "He had equal motive to kill Holly and Paul."

"He has an alibi for Holly's death. We haven't questioned him about Paul's murder yet. We'll do that today." Bree frowned at Todd. "I didn't have a chance to ask you earlier. How did it go at the Grey Fox last night?"

Todd shrugged. "Deputy Collins and I spent two hours there. We found several people who remember Owen from Friday night. None of them saw him leave. All said he was very intoxicated and not fully functional. I wrote up a report and filed it in the case book."

"So, we have not been able to crack Owen's alibi for Holly's murder." Bree ate the cracker crumbs and washed them down with water. "Todd, go see Chloe Miller. I'm going to call in Owen Thorpe and Shannon Phelps for follow-up interviews. Owen owes us a signed statement, and we can ask him about Paul's murder while he's here. I also want to know what Shannon thinks about a possible affair between Holly and Paul."

"Whoever killed Paul used the same method to break into Shannon's house. But why did Holly's killer leave that doll floating in the sink? Why frighten Shannon?"

Bree readjusted her sling. The pain in her arm was giving her an ache in the base of her skull. Her brain felt just as dull. "Is it possible that Shannon knows something? Even if she doesn't realize it?"

"Like something that might help us identify the killer?" Todd asked on his way to the door.

"Maybe." Bree honestly didn't know. That was the piece of the puzzle that didn't fit.

Todd reached for the doorknob. "What do you want me to do with the kid after he's booked?"

"For now, just have him put in the holding cell here. I want him handy for questioning." Bree also didn't like the idea of an innocent nineteen-year-old in the county jail with real criminals. Noah was being stupid, but she understood his motive. He thought he was protecting his mom.

After Todd left, Matt asked, "What do you want me to do?"

"Go talk to your friends at Sharp Investigations. I'd come, but I promised Kayla I'd stay in the office today." Bree wouldn't break that promise, but she was regretting making it. "I need to write another press release. I don't want to issue a statement to the media until you have that information from the PI. When Angela finds out we've arrested Noah, she's going to stop cooperating. She could change her mind about sharing the PI's reports with us."

Bree fully expected Angela to go into a full panic at the thought of her son in prison. But would it be enough for her to confess?

CHAPTER
TWENTY-SEVEN

Matt drove to Scarlet Falls and parked in front of Sharp Investigations, a converted house a few blocks off the main street. Two plaques outside the front door read SHARP INVESTIGATIONS and MORGAN DANE, ATTORNEY. The front door was unlocked. Matt went into the foyer and called out, "Hello?"

Lance Kruger appeared in a doorway holding a little girl upside down in his arms. Lance was a big guy with short blond hair. He shifted the child to his left arm and held out a hand toward Matt. "Good to see you, Matt." He turned the child to face Matt. "This is my daughter, Sophie."

Matt shook his hand and grinned down at the little girl. "It's nice to meet you, Sophie."

The child was giggling too hard to answer.

"Let me pass this little monster off to Morgan." Lance headed down the hall. He ducked into another room and returned in a minute without the child. "Come into my office."

In the corner of Lance's office, a chair was covered in picture books. Lance closed the door and took his seat behind his desk.

Matt sat in a plastic chair facing him. "How is life with a family?"

A former officer with the Scarlet Falls PD, Lance had recently married defense attorney Morgan Dane. Randolph County law enforcement agencies often cooperated. When Matt had been a sheriff's deputy, he'd worked with Lance occasionally.

"Things couldn't be better." Lance settled back into his chair. "If you had told me two years ago that I was going to marry a woman with three kids and turn into a happy husband and father, I'd have said you were nuts." He spread his arms out. "But here I am."

"I'm glad to hear things are good with you," Matt said. "Did Angela Beckett contact you?"

"Her lawyer did." Lance turned to his computer. "He asked me to give you the report on her husband's infidelities." A printer hummed on a credenza. Lance turned and snagged a few pages. He handed the report across the desk.

Matt leaned back and skimmed the pages. "Busy man."

Lance sighed. "We followed him for three weeks. In that time period, he had encounters with seven women. Six of those, he picked up at bars."

Matt lowered the page and pointed toward a paragraph. "Number seven was Holly Thorpe. We heard from another employee that Paul was having an affair with her."

Lance frowned and shook his head. "I don't think he was having sex with Holly."

"No?"

"No." Lance's chair squeaked as he shifted forward and rested his elbows on the desk. "Six times, Paul went to a local bar, picked up a woman, and took her to a motel. They stayed inside the room for about two hours. Then they both left. He did not see any of those women again during that time period."

"One-night stands."

"Yes." Lance nodded. "When Paul met with Holly, the situation was different. One, she drove to his house, not a hotel. Two, she only stayed about fifteen minutes. Three, this happened twice."

"If Paul wasn't having sex with Holly, why was she at his house?"

Lance lifted a shoulder. "We don't know. That wasn't part of the scope of our investigation. The six other women gave Mrs. Beckett's attorney more than enough proof of infidelity."

"Does Mrs. Beckett know the details about Holly's meetings with Paul?"

"I don't know. We sent our report directly to the attorney. We've never met with Mrs. Beckett."

Matt stared at the report again. "Do you have pictures of these women?"

"Yes." Lance tapped his keyboard. The printer whirred again. "The pictures are labeled with names and dates." Lance took a manila file from a drawer and slid the pictures into it. He handed it to Matt, who stuffed the original reports inside.

"Thanks, Lance," Matt said. "Good to see you."

"Same." Lance followed him out of the room.

In the foyer, a tall, dark-haired woman in a navy-blue skirt and white blouse juggled a briefcase, a suit jacket, and her child. The little girl had both arms wrapped around her mother's waist.

Lance introduced Matt to his wife, Morgan.

"I'm done for the day," Lance said. "Hey, Sophie, get your stuff. We'll go home and ride bikes."

The child abandoned her mother without a backward glance. "Yay!"

"Thank you. I have a meeting at the courthouse in an hour." Morgan tossed her jacket over one arm. "It was nice to meet you, Matt."

Matt left them gathering the child's toys. For the first time in his life, he wondered what it would be like to have his own family. Where had that come from? He'd always assumed he would have a wife and kids someday—in the unspecific, distant future—but those assumptions had never been concrete.

But then again, why was he surprised? He came from a close, stable family. He liked kids. He'd always preferred relationships to dating. He was a one-woman kind of man. But for the past few years, he'd been too preoccupied with his career, his injury, and the upheaval after his shooting to think about the future.

Until now.

Putting deep thoughts about his future aside, he stopped at a deli on his way back to the station. Bree and Todd were in the conference room. Matt brought in the deli bag. "Turkey subs."

"Thank you." Bree reached for a paper-wrapped sandwich. "A deputy verified that Paul called Holly around midnight in the first week of March. I called Deb Munchin. She says she was working at the diner Wednesday through the dinner shift. I spoke with her manager, and he confirmed it. So, she has an alibi for Paul's murder but not Holly's."

Matt summed up his discussion with the PI. "Lance doesn't think Paul and Holly's relationship was sexual."

"Does he know why she went to his house?" Bree asked.

"No." Matt handed Bree the file and explained Lance's theory.

She opened it and skimmed the written sections. "This is interesting. Deb saw Holly at Paul's house last week, on Tuesday." Bree flipped through the murder book for the notes on their interview with Owen. "That's the same night Owen said Holly was going to meet with Deb."

"Is it?" Matt hadn't made the connection. "Holly didn't want Owen to know she went to Paul's place."

Bree tapped on the report. "Clearly, but why? Sharp Investigations' report says she was only inside the house for fifteen minutes. If the PI doesn't think Holly and Paul were having sex, why would she need to lie to her husband?" She flipped through the photos. "All of these women are young with long dark hair." She frowned. "Wasn't the hair you found in Paul Beckett's bed long and dark?"

Matt nodded. "Seems he has a type."

"Holly was blonde." Bree unwrapped her sub. "So is Angela Beckett."

"Paul was married to Angela for more than two decades," Matt said. "Maybe he wanted something different."

"Tired of one flavor, looking for another?" Bree wiped her fingers on a napkin.

Matt lifted a shoulder.

"Todd, fill Matt in on your interview with Chloe Miller." Bree took a bite of her sandwich.

Todd grabbed a sub. "Chloe was very upset to learn Noah was a suspect. She was desperate to prove he couldn't have done it. She says they were together all week."

"All week?" Matt picked up half his sub.

"What were they doing for a whole week?" Bree swallowed and reached for her water bottle.

"Um. She said they'd been apart for months, so they had some catching up to do." Todd blushed.

"Oh." Matt grinned.

Todd cleared his throat. "Anyway, she swears she was with him 24/7, and they left her apartment only once. She had a bunch of food delivery receipts. I checked with the manager of her apartment complex. They have surveillance cameras in the parking lot. He gave me a copy of the videos for the past week. Noah's car arrives last Thursday. The only time the vehicle moves is on Sunday for about two hours. Chloe said they went for coffee and stopped at the grocery store. She didn't have receipts, but she showed me the payments on her credit card app. The surveillance video confirms what time they left and came back, and their cars stay put until today."

Bree set down her water bottle. "So, Noah didn't do it. His girl-friend's statement and the videos give him alibis for both murders."

"Do we release him?" Todd asked.

"Not yet." Bree took another bite of her sandwich and chewed thoughtfully. After she swallowed, she said, "I know the coincidence would be huge, but is there any possibility that Holly and Paul were killed by two different people? Holly was choked, and Paul was shot."

"A very slim one." Matt's instincts told him the crimes were related. "The victims knew each other. They were engaged in something that required a late-night phone call a couple of months ago and a more recent visit from Holly to Paul's house. And there's the green clay found in Paul's garage and Holly's trunk. So, we have a link between the crime scenes as well."

Bree's lips flattened as she considered his points. "Can those correlations be explained in another way? Is it possible that Paul killed Holly, then Angela or someone else killed Paul?"

"Angela says he didn't play tennis," Todd said. "Noah confirmed it."

"He has a court on his property. Paul could have picked up traces of clay without playing the game," Bree argued. "Maybe something blew onto the court and he went to retrieve it. Or one of the landscapers could have walked on the court and tracked clay to another place, where Paul picked it up on his shoes."

"It's possible." But the explanation didn't sit well in Matt's gut. "Why would he kill Holly?"

"Don't know yet." Bree shrugged, then winced and rubbed her injured arm below the bandage. "It doesn't seem Paul was concerned about hiding his affairs any longer. He was open about them. How do we explain the two different methods of killing?"

"Holly was a small woman, easily overpowered by a stronger woman or man," Matt said. "Paul was not a small man, and he worked construction. He might have been carrying some extra weight, but he was still strong."

"Right. I just wanted to make sure we're not making invalid assumptions." Bree rubbed her forehead. "On that note, I'm going to do the press conference now. I want Owen and Shannon to feel secure enough to talk about Holly and Paul's relationship. We need more evidence on Angela Beckett."

CHAPTER TWENTY-EIGHT

"Last night, Paul Beckett was shot to death at his home." Bree faced the press and gave a quick recap of the crime. "Today, his son Noah Beckett has confessed to the murder. I cannot comment on the validity of the confession, as we are still investigating."

Video cameras whirled, flashes went off, and reporters fired questions. Bree nodded toward a tall man in the front.

"Sheriff, did Noah Beckett also kill Holly Thorpe?" he asked.

"We don't have the answer to that question yet." Bree pointed to another reporter. "This is still an active investigation."

A woman asked, "Are the deaths of Holly Thorpe and Paul Beckett related?"

"We are looking hard at the possibility that they were killed by the same person," Bree said. "But at this time, we cannot confirm that."

The blonde woman followed up. "Didn't Holly Thorpe work for Paul Beckett?"

"Yes," Bree said. "There is a definite link between the victims. But we need hard evidence to connect their deaths as well."

"So, Noah didn't confess to killing Holly Thorpe?"

"No, he did not." Bree summoned patience, then took three more questions and ended the press conference. The ibuprofen she'd taken before the press con had barely made a dent in her pain.

Back inside the station, she grabbed Matt from the conference room. "I want Owen to relax. I'll interview him solo. I want you to watch from the monitoring room."

"OK." Matt headed for a closed door down the hall.

Bree tugged on her sling but could find no position for her arm that was comfortable. Ibuprofen wasn't touching the pain. She took a deep breath and went into the room.

Owen was waiting inside, watching the screen on his phone. He looked up and set his phone on the table as she entered.

Bree sat next to him and turned her chair to face him. He looked rough, with bags under his eyes big enough to hold groceries. But he was sober and showered. His jeans and T-shirt looked clean with just a few normal wrinkles, not the kind that came from sleeping in your clothes for several days.

"How are you?" she asked.

He sighed. "I don't know. It doesn't feel real, you know?"

"I know. It will in time."

"I'm not sure I want it to feel real." He pulled out a paper and slid it across the table. "I answered those questions like you asked."

"Thank you." Bree skimmed his answers. His statement was brief but matched what he'd told her verbally. She pushed the page back to him. "I'll need you to sign your statement."

"OK." He picked up a pen from the table, signed the paper, and gave it back to her.

Bree slid it into her folder. "I have a few additional questions." She handed him a Miranda form, read his rights, and asked him to sign the acknowledgment.

Owen balked at the form. "Didn't somebody confess to killing Paul Beckett? I kind of assumed the same person killed Holly. I was feeling better that you'd caught the guy."

"Yes," Bree lied. "But I still have to cross all my t's and dot all my i's. We can't take the risk that a defense attorney would claim we didn't do a thorough job and get him off."

"I guess." Owen signed the Miranda form, but he seemed reluctant.

"This interview is being recorded." Bree took the form. "You obviously know Paul Beckett was killed last night."

Owen nodded. "I saw it on the news."

"You said you assumed the same person killed Holly and Paul. Is there a reason?"

He lifted a hand. "Considering Holly worked for Paul, it just seems crazy to think they were both killed within days of each other by different people. Maybe it's all about Beckett Construction." Owen's brows furrowed. "Maybe Paul was doing something illegal."

Bree watched him closely. "I don't know. His son is the one who confessed to killing him."

"Did he say he killed Holly too?"

"No. Why would he?"

Owen shook his head and stared at his hands. "But he did it, right? He killed Paul."

"We can't say with one hundred percent accuracy at this time. You understand."

"Of course." He exhaled. "But why would Paul's son kill Holly?"

"We don't know. Did you know Holly went to Paul Beckett's house?"

"No." Owen's shoulders snapped straight.

"She did."

"How do you know?" he asked.

"The Becketts were involved in a divorce. Mrs. Beckett had a private investigator following her husband."

Owen was quiet for a few seconds. "What does that have to do with Holly? She could have been dropping off something for the business. She did work for him."

"If it was that simple, why did she lie to you about it? You said that Holly was going out with Deb for drinks Tuesday night. Deb says Holly blew her off to drive out to Paul's house."

Owen shook his head. "I don't know."

"Did you ever suspect Holly was having an affair with Paul Beckett?"

"No!" Owen jumped to his feet, his face red. His chair scraped backward on the linoleum. "How can you even ask that? She would never have cheated on me."

"I'm sorry, but I have to ask the question. It's my job."

Owen slowly lowered himself back into the chair. "It just doesn't seem fair to attack Holly's reputation when she isn't here to defend herself."

"I know, but a good defense attorney will explore all angles, and you can bet Noah's mother will hire the best attorney she can find for her son."

Owen frowned. "Rich people always get off."

"I don't want Holly's killer to get away with anything. Noah has only confessed to his father's murder. I have to prove he also killed Holly, and I have to be thorough. Please bear with me. I'm doing this for Holly. You want her killer caught, right?"

"Right." He rolled his shoulders and cracked his neck, as if preparing for a fight. "OK."

"Do you know of any special relationship between Holly and Paul?"

"No."

"Did Holly ever mention any illegal activities at Beckett Construction?"

"No." Owen shook his head.

Bree tossed out another zinger. "Do you have any idea why Holly and Paul would have talked on the phone at midnight back in March?"

Owen stiffened, and he looked away as he answered, "No."

Was he lying? Or simply defensive at the idea that his wife had cheated?

Bree continued. "Where were you last night between seven forty and eight p.m.?"

"I was home," Owen said.

"Alone?"

He nodded. "My brother had to go back to work. I showered and shaved and did some laundry."

"I'm glad to hear that." Bree meant it. "Did you order any takeout or talk with anyone on the phone?"

He shook his head. "After I got cleaned up, I was really tired. I slept for twelve hours straight."

"OK, Owen. If you think of anything else, please call me."

He gave a single stiff nod. "OK."

Bree escorted him to the lobby. The news vans had cleared out after the press conference, and Owen walked across a mostly empty parking lot. After he left, Marge caught Bree's attention. "Shannon Phelps is in interview room two."

"Thanks." Bree stopped in the monitoring room, where Matt sat facing two screens. She closed the door behind her. "What do you think?"

"He seems sure Holly didn't cheat." Matt stroked his beard, which was on the long side. Usually, he shaved or trimmed it at this point.

"I agree. So, what were she and Paul up to?" she asked. "Maybe Shannon knows."

"Want me to watch from here?" Matt asked.

Bree considered the question. "Actually, I'd like you to do the interview. She connected with you more than me. I want her talkative." When Matt stood, she took his chair. It was still warm from his body.

"You're feeling OK?"

"No," she said, surprised at her own honesty. "But I'll live. Go interview Shannon. See what you can get out of her."

"Will do."

CHAPTER TWENTY-NINE

Matt walked into the interview room. Shannon's eyes were still red and sore-looking, as if she'd been crying for days. But then, he supposed she had.

"Thanks so much for coming in." Instead of sitting across the table from her, Matt took the chair beside her.

She sniffed and looked down at the crumpled tissue in her hand. "I keep thinking I'll feel less sad tomorrow, but every day I wake up and it's the same."

"It'll take time." Matt read her rights. "Do you understand?"

Shannon nodded.

Matt slid a Miranda form toward her. "I need to ask you some more questions. Did you know someone confessed to killing Paul Beckett?"

Shannon nodded. "Did he kill Holly too?"

"That's what we're trying to determine." He nudged the form closer, then set a pen on top of it. "First I need you to sign this form."

She stared at it as if it were a big fat bug. "Why? Am I a suspect?"

He gave her a nonchalant shrug. "The sheriff insists."

"OK." Frowning, she signed her name.

"Thank you." Matt pushed the paper away. "I also need to tell you that this interview is being recorded. In case you give us any important information, we don't want to get any of the details wrong."

Shannon nodded.

Matt continued. "So, Paul Beckett's son confessed to killing his father. Do you have any idea why he'd want to kill Holly too?"

Shannon shook her head hard. "I don't even know him."

"Holly worked for Paul. Are you aware of any other special relationship between them?"

Shannon's brows came together. "What do you mean?"

Matt leaned closer. "Holly was seen at Paul's house. There was also a late-night call between them."

Shannon shifted her weight back. "Are you asking me if Holly cheated on Owen? Because if you are, the answer is no."

"But Holly had left Owen multiple times."

"She always went back. As much as they fought, when they were together, they were really together."

"So, why might Holly have gone to Paul's house?"

"It must have been something to do with the business." Shannon blotted her eyes. "I only met Paul Beckett twice, but I didn't like him much. He was an arrogant bully."

"How did he treat Holly?"

"She was always complaining about him. He yelled at people, but he paid pretty well. She got good benefits, and he wasn't in the office much. Some days she didn't interact with him at all." Shannon squirmed, and her gaze shifted to the floor. She knew something she wasn't saying. "A few weeks ago, Holly told me something that made me worry."

"Like what?"

Shannon looked at the ceiling. "She said, 'I hope I don't get in trouble.' Like he was asking *her* to do something illegal. I asked her what, but she wouldn't say. She changed the subject."

"I also need to ask you where you were Wednesday evening between seven forty and eight o'clock." Matt could not think of any motivation for Shannon to have killed Paul, but then again, they didn't know why he'd been murdered yet. An alibi would make it easier to cross Shannon off the list.

"I took Chicken to the vet." She lifted her purse off the table. "His appetite has been off. I think I still have the receipt here." She produced a crumpled piece of paper and smoothed out the wrinkles.

"I'd like to make a copy of that." Matt glanced at the paper. The register receipt was time-stamped seven forty-six. He would follow up, but it seemed Shannon hadn't killed Paul Beckett.

"Sure. Go ahead."

Matt left the room and ran off a copy on the machine in the conference room. He came back and gave her the original, which she shoved into her purse.

"What did the vet say?"

"She didn't find anything wrong with him." She lifted a shoulder.

"Rescues, especially nervous ones, can take months to adjust to their new homes." Matt frowned.

"She said he might be picking up on my emotions." She worried her lip.

"Dogs can be very sensitive," Matt said. "I'm sure he'll be OK. Thanks again for coming in."

She smiled back at him. "Thank you for working so hard to find my sister's killer."

Matt walked her out, then returned to the monitoring room. Bree was holding her arm against her body as if the pain was getting worse. "You heard her alibi?"

"I did." Bree sounded doubtful.

"You don't believe her?"

"I don't know." She chewed on her lip. "But there's something nagging me about her interview."

"I know the vet. Let me call them." Matt lifted his phone. After speaking with the receptionist, he texted a photo of Shannon to the vet's office to confirm her ID. He set down his phone. "It was her."

Bree shook her head, rewound the interview, and watched it again. "She didn't give us any new information."

"Except she didn't think Holly was having sex with Paul either," Matt said. "And she has a solid alibi."

"So, we're back to Angela." Bree checked the time on her phone. "Who will be here with her attorney any minute. She left a message while you were interviewing Shannon. Angela sounded angry."

"This should be fun." Matt scratched his chin.

Bree lifted a folder in her lap. "We received the financials for Beckett Construction. Holly was Paul's bookkeeper. She also had more cash than she should have. Could Paul have been paying her to do something illegal for him?" She shook the file. "Maybe the answer is in here."

"Do you want me to go through them?" Matt offered.

Bree shook her head. "No. I need to go home tonight. I promised Kayla." Her small smile was wry. "But I'm going to review these later. Do you want to come for dinner?"

"Yes. What's Dana making?" Matt had finished his dad's pot roast, and he wasn't in the mood to cook. Besides, Dana was a master in the kitchen.

"I'll ask." Still smiling, Bree picked up her phone and sent a text. Her phone vibrated a few seconds later. "Tortellini with prosciutto and peas."

"I'm in."

Someone knocked on the door, and Marge stuck her head in. "Angela Beckett and her attorney are here."

Matt rubbed his hands together. "How do you want to do this?"

"We'll both go in. Two on two. Besides, I wanted Owen and Shannon to feel comfortable to get them talking. Angela needs a different approach."

"Let's do this."

Bree shook her head. "I need coffee, and Angela needs to marinate for a few minutes."

They stopped in the break room for two coffees.

"Do you want another pack of candy?" Matt asked.

"No, thanks. I've had more than enough."

He handed her the coffee. They sipped for ten minutes before heading to the interview room. The attorney sat at the table. Disappointment slid through Matt. The lawyer's eyes were steely gray and sharp. He wore a custom-fitted suit of deep navy blue and a pricey pale-blue silk tie, but the briefcase on the table in front of him was battered and worn. He was expensive, confident, and experienced. There would be no bullshitting him or goading his client into her own confession.

Angela paced the narrow aisle behind his chair. She spun on one heel as they entered the room. If her eyes could have shot laser beams, then Matt and Bree would have been sliced into bloody ribbons.

"How. Dare. You." Angela started toward them. Her face was red and blotchy, and she bit the words off with gritted teeth. "You arrested Noah."

Matt stepped in front of Bree's wounded arm. But Angela's attorney caught his client by the elbow and stopped her movement. He shook his head and gave her a look of warning. She lifted her chin and glared down her nose at Bree and Matt with a nastiness that Matt hadn't expected. Angela was an attractive woman, usually composed and elegant, but now, her mouth was curled in an ugly snarl. She looked like she wanted to rip off their heads with her teeth.

She looked like a woman capable of committing murder.

Her attorney tugged her into the chair next to him, leaned over, and whispered in her ear.

She sat completely stiff and unmoving. When the attorney straightened, she exhaled hard. If she were a dragon, she would be breathing fire. She said nothing, but Matt could see that she wanted to let loose.

Bree and Matt took the chairs opposite.

The attorney slid two business cards across the table. "I'm Richard Sterling. I'll be representing Mrs. Beckett."

They skipped the handshakes. Bree introduced herself and Matt. Then she went through the Miranda rights spiel and handed the acknowledgment to Angela. She ignored it.

"This interview is being recorded," Bree said. "Let the record show that Angela Beckett was informed of her rights, and that her attorney is present for questioning."

The attorney opened his briefcase and removed a single piece of paper. "This is a signed statement from Miss Chloe Miller. Noah Beckett was at her apartment. They were together when Paul Beckett was shot. Noah couldn't have killed his father."

They'd moved fast.

"Noah confessed." Bree might have been responding to the lawyer, but her gaze never left Angela's eyes.

"I spoke with him a few minutes ago," the attorney said. "He will be withdrawing that confession."

"Have you shot Paul's gun in the past?" Bree asked Angela.

She opened her mouth, but the attorney held up a hand.

"Mrs. Beckett will be exercising her constitutional right to remain silent," he said. "If you want to bring her back to the station, you'll have to arrest her. If you had any evidence, you would already have done so." With one hand under Angela's elbow, he stood, pulling her up with him. "I expect Noah to be released immediately."

"We'll see," Bree said.

"We all know he didn't do it, Sheriff." The attorney sounded bored. "You'll have no evidence except his confession, which is invalid."

"Then why did he give it?" Bree asked. She had a good poker face, but Matt could see frustration in the lines fanning from her eyes.

"I didn't ask." The attorney didn't blink. "Because it doesn't matter. He's innocent. He has an alibi, which I'm sure can be confirmed by electronic means. We're all wasting time here."

Bree and Angela stared at each other for three awkward breaths. Then Bree said, "He'll be released within the hour."

"Thank you for being reasonable. Good day." The attorney steered his client out the door.

Bree turned off the camera. Her body was rigid. When she started for the door, it was with jerky strides instead of her usual graceful motions. Matt wouldn't have been surprised if she kicked the trash can. But she didn't, of course.

She swept one hand over the top of her head. "I didn't expect him to get to Chloe that fast."

"He's no novice."

"No," Bree agreed. "He didn't let Angela say one word."

"What now?"

"We let Noah go. Then we go home for dinner." She stopped in the conference room for the murder book. She tucked the Beckett Construction financials inside. "Maybe we'll find another motivation for killing Paul."

Bree checked in with Marge and Todd before leaving through the back door.

"Do you want me to drive?" Matt asked.

Bree sighed. "Please."

He drove the SUV to her house. She was quiet on the short ride. When Matt turned into her driveway, he glanced over. Her head lolled back on the headrest. Early-evening sunshine hit her face, highlighting the shadows under her closed eyes.

He shifted the vehicle into park. She lifted her head and blinked hard a few times, as if she'd dozed off. She winced as she climbed out of the vehicle.

Matt fell into step beside her. "Before we get started, have you taken anything for that? I've been shot. I know what it feels like."

"Ibuprofen. I'm saving the strong stuff for bedtime." She held her arm stiffly at her side.

"Have you changed the bandage?"

"No."

"Isn't it time?"

"I guess." Bree folded her good arm across her injured one. "Are you offering to do it?"

"Yes."

They stopped and stared at each other for a couple of breaths.

"Fine." Bree started toward the door again. "But you'll have to come upstairs. I don't want the kids to see it."

They went into the kitchen. Ladybug trotted over to greet them, the stump of her docked tail spinning in a crazy circle. Dana was bent over a cutting board, slicing prosciutto. The dog circled back to sit at her feet and drool. Matt sniffed the air like a hungry dog—the kitchen smelled like Dana had been baking. A square pan sat on a cooling rack in the center of the island. Bree's black cat, Vader, judged her work from the counter across the room.

"You're early." Dana's sharp gaze swept over Bree.

Bree rubbed the cat's head. "I'm going to take a shower and change."

"Do you need help with the bandage?" Dana glanced at Matt with worried eyes.

"No." Bree adjusted her sling. "Matt will do it."

"I've done it before," he said.

Dana nodded. Vader leaped from the counter to the island. Raising his nose, he sniffed in the direction of the meat. Dana narrowed her eyes at him. "Back off, mister."

Vader was not impressed. Matt scooped him off the counter and set him on the floor. The cat gave him an annoyed look. He jumped back to his original perch and began washing all the places on his body that Matt had touched.

"Where are the kids?" Bree asked.

Dana pointed her knife toward the window that overlooked the barn and pasture beyond. "Feeding the horses."

"We'll be down soon," Bree said.

Matt followed her to the second floor. He stopped in the doorway to her bedroom, surprised. "This is different from the rest of the house."

"I've kept my sister's things everywhere else. I didn't want to change the kids' environment. They've had enough upheaval. This house should still feel like their home. This furniture came from my apartment in Philly. I needed one room that felt like my space."

The design wasn't exactly modern, just clean-lined and sleek compared to the farmhouse look in the rest of the house.

"Close the door. I don't want the kids walking in." She slipped off the sling and flicked open the top button of her uniform shirt.

Matt knew since the hospital that she wore a tank top under her uniform shirt, but seeing the buttons open one by one was still damned sexy, even under the current circumstances. He couldn't help it. He was just a man.

"I'll wash the wound in the shower." She tossed her shirt into a nearby hamper. "But I'll need help rebandaging it."

"Need help removing the bandage?"

"Sure." She flexed her nicely muscled arm as if it was stiff. Then she ducked into a closet, grabbed fresh clothes, and walked into the bathroom.

Matt followed. A totally different kind of hunger stirred. *Focus.* He washed his hands, carefully removed the old bandage, and examined the stitched wound. "It doesn't look red. I don't see any sign of infection, but I'm sure it hurts like hell."

Bree craned her neck over her shoulder to see the back of the wound in the mirror. "That's going to leave a mark."

"This tattoo is amazing," Matt touched the dragonfly on the back of her shoulder. Under the artwork, he could feel the raised flesh of the old scar. He turned her to face him. Her gaze was on his face, but he was studying her tattoo and scars. He traced a vine—and scar—that snaked over her shoulder. It passed dangerously close to her neck and continued for several inches. As the son of a doctor, his knowledge of anatomy was above average. His fingertip brushed her collarbone. Just below it, a flower was centered over a round, puckered dot, likely where a canine tooth had sunk into her flesh. So close to the artery that ran through the armpit and into the arm.

So close to killing her.

"You were lucky." His voice was hoarse. "I know it probably didn't seem like that at the time."

"Oh, I know." She frowned. "The ER doctor said if the bite had been a half inch to the side, I would have bled out in under a minute."

"I'm sorry, and I'm sorry the doctor told you that. It must have been terrifying."

Bree smiled. "He didn't mean to. He was angry at my mother. Her story about the attack was inconsistent. He could tell she was lying. She wasn't very good at it."

"Then why didn't she tell the truth? Why not try and get away from your father?"

The tattoo shifted as she shrugged. "Because she knew he'd kill us all if she left him." A small shudder passed through her. "I'm going to have a new scar, and it's going to be ugly. Maybe I'll have the vines extended farther down my arm."

"You don't need to cover anything." He tugged her closer, until her body pressed against his. "Your scars are part of you. You're a survivor."

"I'd still prefer not to have them."

Matt pressed his lips to hers. He closed his eyes and let the kiss spin out. When he lifted his head and looked down at her, her eyes were still closed. They fluttered open, and she smiled. They'd kissed before, but somehow this felt more intimate. It wrapped around his heart and squeezed.

She could have died last night. The realization hit him like a blast of Freon, and he went cold straight to his soul. Falling in love with her—he couldn't even pretend that wasn't what was happening—meant gambling his heart on a woman who would always take risks. Could he accept that? He kissed her again, letting it spin out as he held her closer. Her body fit against his in a way that he could only describe as right.

He answered his own question with a resounding yes. He was all in. She was worth risking everything.

Dana's voice sounded from downstairs, disrupting the moment. "Dinner in fifteen minutes."

Bree broke the embrace and reached into the shower to turn on the spray.

Matt didn't trust his voice. He cleared his throat and swallowed. "I'll wait in the bedroom." The words sounded husky, almost harsh.

He backed out and closed the door behind him. As he listened to the water run, he pictured her . . .

Nope. Don't go there.

Their relationship was progressing toward a physical one, but he would not rush a single step, and this was not the time. Still, it was a nice thought. Very nice.

His phone vibrated in his pocket. He pulled it out and glanced at the screen. Todd.

"What's up?" Matt answered.

"We have the license plate number for the vehicle of the man who accepted the envelope from Paul Beckett last night." Todd's voice sounded tight.

"Who is it?"

"The building inspector."

"Does the inspector have any previous allegations for accepting bribes?"

"Not that I know of," Todd said. "What now?"

"I'll talk to the sheriff." But Matt was sure she'd want to launch a quiet investigation.

CHAPTER THIRTY

Cady wiped sweat from her forehead. "Awesome workout! Thanks for coming, ladies!"

Her kickboxing class filed out the front door. Her brother, Nolan, stepped onto the mat in his full white Brazilian jujitsu Gi. "Great class, Cady."

He ducked, weaved, and snagged her by the waist, lifting her off her feet as if she were tiny, which she was definitely not.

"Nolan, put me down," Cady said. With two older brothers, she'd learned to sound bored when they teased her.

He set her on her feet. "You're no fun anymore."

Cady rolled her eyes. "You need to grow up." She poked him in the chest.

"Never." He grinned. Despite his bald head and full sleeves of tats, when he smiled, she could still see him as a twelve-year-old. Equally badass-looking men filed in, and Nolan started them on warm-up drills. He stretched his arms over his head and winced, quickly covering the pained look on his face. A career as a professional MMA fighter had left him physically broken. The human body could take only so much abuse before it rebelled. He was only forty, but his body had high mileage.

Cady moved closer. "You take it easy tonight. Make them do all the work."

He waved and moved off to teach class.

But she knew he wouldn't. At least he'd given up fighting.

She collected her gear and pulled on a zip-up hoodie over her tank top and leggings. Then she headed for her car. She'd stop home, shower, and feed her own dogs, then head to the kennel to feed the rescues. At Matt's request, she'd hired Justin to clean the kennels and hang out with the dogs, but she wasn't ready to trust him with more responsibility yet. He hadn't been out of rehab long enough for her to know if sobriety had stuck. He had a bad record with drug dependency and relapse. Plus, his wife's death had left him fragile. She'd known him since childhood, and it saddened her to know what opioids had done to him.

But as bad as she felt for him, she would take no chances with the dogs in her care. The rescues were Cady's responsibility. She would check every single night to make sure they were settled with full bellies, clean water, and warm beds. Those dogs had suffered too much for her to allow them to be anything but comfortable.

As she crossed the parking lot, she zipped her hoodie against a chilly evening breeze. Her workout clothes were soaked. As usual, her kickboxing class had kicked her own ass. She drove home and parked in the driveway. She could hear her dogs barking. One great big woof sounded, then some barking from the pit bulls. Above it all was the high-pitched yapping of little Taz going ballistic. He was always reactive, but today he sounded particularly angry.

Juggling her purse, duffel bag, and phone, Cady hurried from her minivan. She didn't need more complaints from the neighbors. As she went up the walkway, she shifted her bag straps over her shoulder and dug into her purse for her house key. "I'm coming," she called through the living room window, but the dogs continued to bark. The pitties cranked up the volume. Even Harley got involved. She found her keys and separated her house key from the rest.

A shadow fell over her. Before she could turn around, pain exploded through her head. Her vision dimmed, and she felt her legs fold like an ironing board. She dropped her phone, and it bounced under a bush.

When her knees hit the concrete, she barely felt the impact. On her hands and knees, she gagged a few times. Each time she retched, the pain in her head ratcheted up a notch. The agony was all encompassing. She curled into a ball on the pavement. Something warm and wet trickled into her eyes. Then everything went dark.

CHAPTER THIRTY-ONE

Bree stood under the spray, rinsing her hair and trying to clear her head. The encounter with Matt had short-circuited her brain. If she hadn't been recently shot . . .

But she had.

She turned to let the warm water rush over the wound. It burned. Gritting her teeth, she washed it tentatively, surprisingly squeamish about the stitches. She turned off the water and stepped onto the bathmat. One-handed drying proved challenging. When she was mostly dry, she stepped into jeans and a fresh bra and tank top. She opened the door, her bra still open in the back. Matt was leaning against the wall in the bedroom.

He moved back into the bathroom to inspect the wound again. "This actually looks pretty good."

"If you say so." She rubbed a towel over her hair.

When she'd finished, Matt took it from her and hung it over the shower door.

"Would you mind hooking this?" She spun and pointed at the hook of her bra.

"This feels wrong." But he did it. Then he opened the bag containing the bandages and discharge instructions from the hospital.

"The hospital supplied me with everything I need. Being sheriff has its perks." She gritted her teeth as he read the instructions and dressed the wound.

He rolled gauze around her arm and taped it in place. "How's that feel?"

"Better." She flexed her arm and winced.

"Liar," he said.

"I'll take ibuprofen with dinner." She rolled her wrist and moved her fingers. Her muscles were stiff, and everything hurt from her shoulder to her elbow.

"You have antibiotics?"

"Yes." She sighed. "I'll take those with dinner too."

"You're supposed to keep your arm still for a few more days." He handed her the sling, and she put it on.

She reached for her hair dryer.

"Let me help." Matt took it and aimed it at her head. He ran his fingers over her scalp, fluffing her hair at the roots.

Bree let him. She was tired and aching, and it felt nice to have someone take care of her, even if it was only for a few minutes.

When it was mostly dry, she said, "That's good enough."

Matt shut off the dryer and ran a brush through her hair. "The man who met Paul was the building inspector."

"Paul was probably bribing him." She wasn't surprised. Paul had no respect for the law.

"We can't prove it."

"Yet," Bree said. "Let's go eat, then we'll brainstorm."

They went downstairs. Dana was just putting out dinner when they entered the kitchen. Bree's arm throbbed. Despite what she'd told Matt, the washing and rebandaging had hurt, and the pain was beginning to wear her down. She started on her pasta, knowing the food would help. Kayla, excited to have company, chattered. Luke and Matt talked about baseball.

"Any more dates on the horizon?" Bree asked Dana.

Dana took a small sip of her red wine. "Maybe. I've messaged back and forth with another man. We'll see how it goes. I'm in no rush."

Bree shook her head. "I can't wrap my head around dating apps."

"It's actually kind of fun." Dana grinned. "You should see some of the profile pics. I want to message half the men over fifty and tell them to ask their daughter to take their picture."

"Bad?" Bree forked a piece of prosciutto into her mouth. The bacon-y taste melted in her mouth. Bacon really did make everything better. The more she ate, the better she felt.

"You have no idea." Dana passed a basket of garlic bread.

Twenty minutes later, Bree carried her almost empty plate to the sink.

Dana followed her.

Bree turned to her best—only—friend. "Are you OK here?"

"I'm fine, why?" Dana set her own plate in the sink. "Because I'm using a dating app?"

"Frankly, yes."

Dana turned to face her. "I love being here with the kids. I never had a family of my own. But I admit I'm a little lonely, and maybe a little bored."

"I appreciate all you do for me and my family, but I don't want you to be unhappy here."

"The way I feel has nothing to do with my geographical location." Dana paused. "I just retired five months ago. It's a major life change. I'd need to make decisions about the rest of my life regardless of where I live. Two divorces have left me a little jaded, and I didn't expect to want to date. But I see you and Matt . . ." She sighed. "And I see something worth putting up with some bullshit for. So, I'll try this app and see what happens."

"Let me know if there's anything I can do."

Dana laughed. "Does Matt have a brother?"

"Actually, yes."

Dana laughed harder.

On the other side of the kitchen, Matt's chair scraped as he stood. "My ears are burning."

Dana grinned at him. "I made lemon bars. Do you want coffee, tea, espresso, cappuccino . . ."

"Just coffee, thanks." Matt pointed at Bree, then at her chair. "You sit. I'll clear."

He began collecting dishes from the table. Luke jumped up to help. Kayla fetched the platter of lemon bars on the kitchen island, walking with slow and careful steps toward the table. Ladybug stood, her eye on the dessert. Bree blocked the dog with her foot before she could intercept the child. Dessert was consumed in about sixty seconds. Then Luke went to his room to study, and Kayla settled at the table with spelling homework. Matt and Bree carried their mugs into her home office.

Bree sat behind her desk and opened the file containing Paul Beckett's financial statements.

Matt took a chair. "I'll take the personal accounts."

She passed them over. "I get the corporate statements?" She eyed the stack of pages. "This is going to take forever."

"I could text my sister and ask her to help," Matt offered.

"Cady?"

He nodded. "She used to be an accountant, and she does the book-keeping for my brother's business."

Bree brightened. "That would be great."

Matt sent a text. "She's probably feeding and exercising the dogs right now, but she'll get back to me."

"In the meantime . . ." Bree opened the first report.

Two hours later, Dana knocked on the door. "Kayla is ready for bed."

"I'll be back in a few." Bree ran upstairs, read to Kayla for fifteen minutes, then tucked the little girl into bed. When she returned to the home office, Dana handed her a mug of fresh coffee. She and Matt were already sipping theirs.

"I offered to help." Dana perched on the corner of the desk and waved a financial statement. "Matt brought me up to speed."

Matt stretched. "So far, I've found two things. Paul decreased his salary over the past two years. His personal expenditures stayed about the same. There were a few months he used personal assets to cover business expenses."

"What about his fancy cars?" Bree sipped coffee and returned to her seat behind the desk.

"Leases," Matt said. "The truck payment goes through the business. The others are personal leases. He doesn't own any of the vehicles. He rents the business office space."

"He drew down on a working capital line of credit a few times too," Dana added. "He's only paying the interest. There's a letter from the bank saying he needed to pay the credit line off for thirty consecutive days once a year. He hasn't done that."

"Why has the company been less profitable?" Matt asked.

"I'm not sure." Bree stepped back from the bank statements to look at Beckett Construction's financial statements. A number caught her eye. She skimmed backward through the pages. She'd been looking at individual monthly bank statements instead of the big financial picture. "The expense for plumbing doubled in the last two years, but gross income remained about the same."

"Why would plumbing costs increase that significantly without a corresponding increase in revenue?" Matt set down the page he was reading and leaned over the desk. "Did he have one particular job with a plumbing disaster?"

"No. It's spread out over time and jobs." Bree pointed to the line item, and he pulled the corresponding bank statements for the first quarter. "Let's take a look at the plumbers Paul used."

Matt made a list and began researching. "This plumber doesn't seem to exist. Or this one."

Dana leaned over the papers on the desk. "How much of the plumbing expense went to those two companies in the first quarter?"

Matt grabbed his phone and opened his calculator app. "Almost half."

"What about the fourth quarter of last year?" Dana asked.

"Same," said Matt.

Bree drummed her fingertips on the desk. "So, Paul was paying two plumbers who don't seem to exist."

"Is it possible the companies operated under different names?" Dana asked.

Matt shrugged. "Holly did the books, and it was Paul's company. Who else could we ask?"

"Deb Munchin?" Bree suggested. "She helped Holly with the accounts sometimes."

Matt frowned. "Didn't she say she went to Paul with questions and he wouldn't answer?"

"She did." Bree grabbed her phone and dialed Deb's number. She explained her question.

"Funny you ask about that," Deb said. "There were multiple plumbers assigned to several jobs. For most residential work, we usually use one plumbing subcontractor per job, unless something unusual happens. I thought someone messed up the invoices."

"What did Paul say?" Bree asked.

Deb snorted. "He said to pay the fucking bills. If he wanted me to think, he'd let me know."

Nice.

Bree highlighted the line item on the statement. "What do you think happened?"

"I think he was funneling money out of the business," Deb said. "To cheat on his taxes and/or take the money out of play in his divorce. Knowing Paul, he would love the two-for-one aspect."

"But the Becketts just split up a couple of months ago," Bree said. "And Angela left Paul, not the other way around."

"Paul planned everything." Deb paused. "He knew exactly how to make her leave him. It wouldn't surprise me if he started hiding money from Angela years ago."

"Why would he do that?" Bree asked.

"So there would have been less in total assets to split. He reduced his salary over the past two years. If she sued him for alimony, his monthly income would also be lower, so he'd have to pay her less. The business was still profitable, but just enough to maintain his standard of living. Paul wouldn't want to sacrifice his lifestyle."

Bree ended the call and related Deb's responses to Matt and Dana.

"According to Angela, Paul told her the company was having financial trouble," Matt said. "But that could have been a lie. We need to follow the money. Pass me that laptop."

"One minute." Bree emailed Todd to request yet another subpoena to track the financial transactions. "It's almost always about money. People are so predictable." She hit "Send," then handed the laptop over the desk to Matt.

He typed on the keyboard. "What do you want to do about the building inspector?"

Bree leaned back in her chair and closed her eyes. The ibuprofen had eased her headache, but the pain radiating up her arm was growing tiresome. She wanted to put on her pajamas, take a pill, and go to bed. "I can't think of any reason the building inspector would kill Paul. Why eliminate the source of your extra cash flow?"

"But it's more evidence that Paul was engaged in illegal business practices." Matt scrolled on the laptop touchpad.

Bree tapped the statements in front of her. "We have plenty of proof of that right here."

He smiled. "And here." He clicked the mouse. "Is your printer on?"

Bree reached behind her and switched on the machine. It whirred and spit out two pages. She plucked them off the tray. "What is this?"

"Guess who owns those two plumbing companies?" Matt asked.

Bree skimmed the printout from the NYS Department of State Division of Corporations Business Entity Database. She skipped down to the section that named the chief executive officer. "Noah Beckett." She turned the page. "And the second company is registered to Timothy Beckett."

Dana lowered the page she was scanning. "So, to summarize, Paul was probably guilty of bribing a building inspector, tax evasion, and hiding assets from his wife."

"But did Angela know?" Bree asked.

Matt lifted a shoulder. "If she did, it would give her more motivation to kill him."

"She was already angry with Paul," Bree pointed out.

"How much money went to those two fake plumbers over the last two years?" Matt asked.

"Close to a hundred thousand dollars." Bree went back to the statement. "I know that's a lot of money, but given Paul's lifestyle, there must be more fake accounts. His net worth has dropped by over a million dollars."

Matt set her laptop on the desk and closed the lid. He lifted his phone. "My sister should have answered my text by now." Worry creased his forehead. He tapped his screen and put the phone to his ear. "She still hasn't responded." He picked another number. "Maybe her phone is dead. I'll call Justin and see if she's at the kennel."

Bree could hear the faint sound of the line ringing.

Matt said, "Hey, Justin. Have you seen Cady?"

Bree couldn't hear Justin's answer.

Matt's face grew grim. "Thanks." He ended the call and swept a hand over his head. "Cady didn't show up to feed the dogs, and she's not answering her phone."

He was already headed for the door. "Cady is always at the kennel at feeding time, and if she is going to be late, she calls for me or Justin to feed the dogs."

"Give me one minute to grab my weapons." Bree stood.

Matt opened his mouth.

She gave him a pointed look. "Do not tell me I should rest."

"Don't worry. I won't. In fact, I was going to apologize for asking, but I need your help."

"I wouldn't have it any other way." Bree started gathering papers to return to the murder book.

Dana held out her hand in a *stop* gesture. "Leave the financials with me. I'll keep digging for more fake vendors."

"Thanks." Bree turned to Matt. "Let's go."

CHAPTER THIRTY-TWO

Matt stopped at home. He slammed the sheriff's vehicle into park and jumped out. Bree was right behind him. Brody greeted Matt at the door.

Justin was in the kitchen, snapping a leash onto Greta's collar. "I fed your dogs and took them outside. I was just going to take Greta for a walk. I know she gets antsy."

"Thanks. I appreciate that." Matt grabbed Brody's harness. As soon as he lifted it from its peg, the big shepherd's body snapped to attention. "I'm taking Brody with me."

Matt had debated driving straight to Cady's house, but he was almost passing his own place on the way. Brody was an important tool, and Matt needed every bit of help he could get.

He had a terrible sensation in the pit of his stomach. Something was very wrong. He'd called his sister's cell and left a message. He'd also texted her, just in case she was in an area with poor cell reception. He'd also called her landline. Nothing. It was not like her to be out of reach. Ever.

Matt transferred the dog's ramp from his Suburban to the sheriff's SUV. With his harness in place, the dog was all business. He knew. Bree sat quietly in the passenger seat. She hadn't argued when he'd asked to drive. She could drive with one arm, but he could drive faster with two.

Matt pulled up at his sister's one-story house. He could hear the muffled barking of Cady's dogs. Her minivan sat in the driveway. He unfolded Brody's ramp, and the dog jogged down to stand obediently at his side. The three of them walked to the front door. Inside the house, Cady's dogs went ballistic. He tried the front door. It was unlocked.

The hairs on the back of his neck stood straight up. Cady lived in a nice neighborhood, but all the years he'd been a deputy, he'd hounded her about personal security. She never left her doors unlocked.

Scenarios ran through his head, each one more dire than the last. Had she fallen and hurt herself? Had she been burglarized?

Standing aside, Matt pushed the front door open. Bree drew her weapon. Cady's dogs were gated in the back of the house. The Great Dane mix cowered at the rear of the pack, while the Chihuahua snapped and growled at the gate. The pit bulls simultaneously barked and wagged their tails.

With one wary eye on the dogs, Bree hung back at the front door. Matt told Brody to stay. The Great Dane gave one loud, deep bark. Bree stepped closer to Brody.

Matt stepped over the gate into the kitchen. "The big dogs are harmless. Watch the little one, though. He has a temper, and those little teeth are damned sharp."

"I'll wait here," Bree said.

Matt scanned the kitchen. No Cady in there or the adjoining family room. The dogs' water bowls were low. Someone, probably the Chihuahua, had peed on the floor. The pitties ran to the pantry and barked at the closed door.

"I don't think they've been fed." Worried, Matt collected stainless-steel bowls and dished out their food. The dogs practically inhaled their kibble. Matt cleaned the floor and wrote his sister a quick note so she would know her dogs had eaten if she returned. Then the dogs lined up at the back door. "I'm going to take the dogs out back and check the yard."

"OK. I'll check the rest of the house." Bree turned and walked toward the short hall that led to the bedrooms.

"Brody." Matt swept one hand toward Bree, and the big shepherd followed her. A six-foot fence surrounded Cady's yard. She was not outside. The dogs did their business and ran back into the house. Matt tried the garage, but his sister wasn't among the dog crates, pallets of food, and other supplies for her rescue organization.

Matt went back into the house. Bree and Brody came down the hallway. "She's not in any of the bedrooms."

Panic knotted in Matt's gut. "I don't like this. Cady would never be this late with her dogs' dinner." He pulled out his phone and called his brother. "I can't find Cady. What time did she leave there?"

"Right after her class ended at six," Nolan said. "I'll call her kick-boxing students in case she decided to go out for drinks with them."

"Good idea." But Matt didn't believe Cady would have dropped her car at her home and not fed her dogs. Maybe he'd been wrong? Had he fed the dogs a second time?

"Maybe she's out rescuing a dog," Bree suggested.

"Her van is here."

"Does she ever go in one of her volunteers' vehicles?" Bree asked.

"I don't know." Matt pulled out his phone and called Maxine and Ralph, the two volunteers who worked with Cady at the rescue. "Neither of them has seen her."

"What about your parents?" Bree prompted.

"I should have called them first. I'm not thinking straight." Matt dialed his mom's number.

"Matt." His mother's voice rang with pleasure.

"Hey, Mom. Is Cady there?"

"No." His mom's tone shifted to worried. "Why?"

"I'm looking for her. That's all."

"Don't lie to me. That is not all," she said in her schoolteacher voice.

Dad was a pushover, but Matt had never been able to hide anything from his mom. "She's not home, but her minivan is," he said.

"Did you try Maxine and Ralph?"

"Yeah. They haven't seen her."

Mom's tone shifted to her most efficient. "What can I do?"

"Call her friends," Matt said. "Call me back if you hear anything."

"You do the same," Mom said.

"I will." Matt ended the call. Then he dialed his sister's number again. The tinny sound of "Who Let the Dogs Out" drifted through the open front door. Matt ran toward it. Outside, he followed the music to the front flowerbed. Pushing aside an overgrown shrub, he saw Cady's phone under the bushes.

He reached for it.

"Matt!" Bree said. "Use a glove."

The thought that his sister's phone might need to be fingerprinted tightened the knot in his belly. But he put on gloves and picked up the phone by the edges. The screen was cracked. It must have bounced on the concrete walkway. He touched the screen, and the phone brightened.

Behind him, Bree and Brody walked the front yard with a flashlight, searching the grass. Matt was surprised to see Bree holding the dog's leash. The dog lifted his nose, then lunged forward. Bree quickened her steps to keep up with him, and he led her toward Cady's minivan.

Matt punched in his sister's passcode and called up recent texts. They all seemed related to dog-rescue business.

Brody whined, a high-pitched and plaintive sound.

"Matt, over here!" Bree called from the driveway. He hurried over. She pointed her light at the driveway. Dark red spots colored the concrete. Blood. One was as large as Matt's splayed hand—too big to have been caused by a trivial injury. Brody whined again.

Matt opened Cady's recent calls and everything inside him went cold. "Guess who Cady called last?"

"Who?" Bree asked.

Brody pulled at the leash, and she held him back.

"Shannon Phelps."

"What?"

Matt scrolled. "Cady actually called Shannon three times today. The first two calls were short. Maybe she hung up or left a brief message. The third call was a little before four o'clock and lasted nearly two minutes. She must have talked with Shannon. If she'd left a message, the call would have been shorter." He paced a few feet away and back. "Cady saw Shannon's name on a file I brought home the other night. Cady's rescue placed that little dog with Shannon. Cady recognized her name."

"And?"

"And she probably called her to ask how the dog was doing." Matt's brain whirled. "Cady is very empathetic. She felt awful about all the loss Shannon has suffered. Knowing Cady, she wanted to see if she could help."

Bree stared back at him. "Shannon has an alibi for Paul's death, but not for Holly's."

Matt's gaze fell to the broken phone screen and dropped to the spots of blood. His heart contracted. "We have to find Cady."

CHAPTER
THIRTY-THREE

Worried, Bree called for backup. The broken phone and blood made Cady's house a likely crime scene. Bree looked at Matt. "Two things. One, Cady could have fallen and hurt herself. Maybe she called a friend to take her to the ER."

"She would probably have called me or my brother, but my mom is calling her friends just in case."

Bree continued. "Two, I know this link to our current murder case is disturbing as hell, but we shouldn't make assumptions. Is there anyone else in your sister's life who might cause her harm?"

Matt stopped pacing. "Maybe her ex. Cady ran into him this week. She said it was weird. I can't think of anyone else. Cady spends ninety percent of her time with her rescues or working in my brother's studio."

Matt's phone rang. "It's my brother." He answered the call. "Yes, Nolan? Damn. OK. Good idea. Keep me in the loop." He ended the call and turned back to Bree. "None of Cady's students have seen her. Nolan is going to drive around to her favorite spots."

Brody sat at Bree's feet, looking up at her with dark, soulful eyes. He gave her another thin, sad whine. She stroked his head. If she didn't have a crisis in front of her, she would have been in awe at her lack of fear, and very impressed with herself for picking up the leash. While she'd been searching Cady's bedrooms, Brody had made her feel more secure, not less.

The barking from Cady's dogs, however, was making the hair on her arms stand straight up.

Brody pulled on the leash and looked back at Bree.

"Go ahead," Bree said and dropped the leash.

Brody went to Matt and pawed at his leg. Matt patted his dog. "We'll find her."

A few minutes later, a patrol car pulled up to the curb. Bree put Deputy Collins in charge of using a field test to confirm the substance on the driveway was actually human blood. She also put out a BOLO on Cady.

She turned to Matt. "Do you want to go see Cady's ex or Shannon Phelps first?"

Matt closed his eyes for a few seconds. When he opened them, his face was drawn and tight. "Greg's place is the closest. We'll stop there first. If she's not there, we'll go on to Shannon's."

Leaving Collins in charge of the scene, Bree, Matt, and Brody climbed into the SUV. Agitated, Brody paced the back seat.

"What can you tell me about Cady's relationship with her ex?" Bree asked.

Matt drove away from his sister's house. "I didn't like Greg the first time Cady introduced him." Barely slowing the vehicle, he steered around a bend in the road. "He seemed emotionally stunted to me, a boy in a man's body. He did some modeling and followed a strict diet. If Cady ate anything that wasn't grilled chicken breast or broccoli, he'd comment. Cady's never been overweight, but she isn't a waify-model type either." He lifted a broad hand and frowned at it. "The Flynns are not small people."

No kidding.

He continued. "I didn't want to get between her and Greg, but more importantly, I didn't want to put her in a position where she ever felt like she had to choose between a boyfriend and her family." Regret tightened Matt's face. "She's a grown woman. It wasn't my place to tell her who to date. And I knew she wouldn't take his shit for long. They only dated for a couple of months when she found out she was pregnant."

"So, that complicated everything."

"Yeah. Cady was thrilled. To be fair, the pregnancy seemed to make Greg act like an adult. He started cooking for her instead of encouraging her to eat practically nothing." He swallowed, darkness coming over his eyes. "She was four months along when they skipped off to Vegas and came back married." His lips pressed in a tight line. "At just over five months, Cady lost the baby, and Greg went back to being a jerk."

"I'm sorry."

Matt shook his head. "Greg blamed Cady, even though it was no one's fault."

Bree couldn't hold back her anger. "What an ass."

"Yeah. As upset as Cady was, she knew he was off base. She left him."

Bree sensed the story wasn't over.

"Greg took the breakup like a nasty four-year-old who was angry because someone had taken away one of his toys. He followed her. He harassed her. He alternated between sending her flowers and leaving nasty notes on her car." Matt shook his head. "Even grieving, Cady did everything right. She used her head and got a restraining order. I tried not to get involved. I tried very hard."

"Until?"

"Greg crossed the line. He started following her, always staying just beyond the required hundred feet. Cady looked out her window one night, and he was parked just up the road. He was watching her. She called the sheriff's department, but Greg was more than a hundred feet away. Technically, he was obeying the order."

With a man like that, a restraining order was about as useful as cardboard body armor.

Bree fumed. "He wanted to punish her."

"Cady was grieving, and the man who should have been supporting her was acting like a dick." Matt swallowed. "I'm not particularly proud of what I did next."

"You encouraged him to leave her alone?"

"Yeah. Let's go with that. I strongly *encouraged* him to leave Cady alone." He curled a hand into a fist. "He never bothered Cady again."

I'll bet he didn't.

Some people only respected physical superiority.

Bree glanced at Matt's profile. It wasn't just his height and coloring that always brought Vikings to mind. He was big-boned and powerful-looking, from his square jaw to his hands. She could easily picture him swinging a broadsword or battle-ax.

Matt's fingers curled tightly around the steering wheel.

"I assume you know where he lives?" she asked.

"I might keep track of him."

Bree turned on the dashboard computer. "What's his last name?"

"Speck."

Bree confirmed his address with Matt. "Gregory Speck, age thirty-eight. No priors. Except for that restraining order you mentioned, his criminal record is clean."

"What does he do for a living?"

"He works at a gym."

Matt parked and they stepped out into the street. Bree smelled rain in the damp night air. She squinted at the sky, where clouds drifted like heavy fog in front of the moon. More storms were forecasted. Rain washed away evidence.

"Hold on." She opened the back of the vehicle and removed their vests.

Matt waited, impatience vibrating through his body. She tossed her sling into the back of the vehicle and shrugged into the vest. Her bullet wound throbbed. Matt put on his own armor and helped her with the straps of hers. Then he turned toward the house.

"Hold on." Bree stepped in front of him and held out both hands. "You wait here."

Matt folded his arms across his chest and glared at Greg's front door.

"Please," she said. "Your presence will not make him more cooperative, and you're wasting time."

Matt returned to the SUV. He used the ramp to let Brody out of the back seat and stood in the street with the dog at his side. She sighed. Matt and Brody were damned threatening even from a distance.

Bree wasn't in uniform, but she was wearing her badge on her belt, and her marked SUV was parked at the curb. She knocked on the door. The man who answered it was about six feet tall with the chiseled face and body of a male model. He coughed into his fist, the sound wet and nasty. Bree took a quick step backward.

"Mr. Speck, I'm Sheriff Taggert." She showed her badge. "When was the last time you had contact with your ex-wife, Cady Flynn?"

He didn't answer. His gaze lifted over her shoulder. He bristled and stepped forward.

Bree assumed he'd seen Matt.

Brody barked, and Greg's forward motion stopped as if he'd hit a force field. "Get him off my property," he said to Bree without taking his eyes off Matt.

Bree glanced over her shoulder. Matt was still in the street.

"He isn't on your property," she said.

Greg walked out of his house, letting the screen door slap shut behind him. His chest puffed as he pointed and yelled at Matt, "Get the hell out of here, or I'll sue you!"

"For what?" Bree asked. "He's on public property."

A vein in Greg's forehead pulsed.

"Mr. Speck." Bree commanded his attention. "I'm looking for Cady Flynn. Have you seen her?"

"No." He jabbed his finger at Matt again, then did a quarter turn to face Bree again. "Did he say I did something?"

"No. But Cady is missing. We're checking with all of her acquaintances. You're just one person on the list. We know you saw her at the pet supply store."

His eyes went small and mean as he glared down at her. "That was an accident. Before I ran into her there, it'd been, like, six years since I've seen her. I wrote her off a long time ago." He jerked his chin at Matt. "Cady and me might have gotten back together if *he* didn't interfere."

"Where were you tonight?" Bree asked.

"Home." He backtracked to his door and yelled, "Jenn, get out here!"

A brunette appeared behind the screen door. She held a baby on her hip. She was a tiny thing, and young. Really young. In ripped jeans and a T-shirt with a spit-up stain on the shoulder, she didn't even look old enough to be served at a bar.

"Come out here," Greg commanded. "Tell them I was here all evening."

Jenn pushed the screen door open and stepped outside. She nodded, her eyes huge, dark, and just a little fearful. Her voice quivered as she said, "He's been here all week. He's just getting over the flu."

Greg propped his hands on his hips and squared off with Bree. "Get off my property or I'll call my lawyer. I'll sue the sheriff's department for harassment."

If not for the flu germs, Bree would have gotten in his face. She would not be intimidated by this jerk. "Do you want to take this discussion down to the station?"

He glared at her. Bree maintained eye contact.

Ten seconds later, he backed down. "Like Jenn said, I've been here all week."

Typical bully. He didn't have the courage to face someone who would stand up to him.

"Thank you for your time," Bree said.

Greg waved an angry hand at his front door. "Go inside."

Jenn dropped her gaze to the ground and scurried back into the house. Greg followed her. He shut the door with a firm bang.

Bree hurried back to her vehicle. Matt's eyes were flat and cold. He loaded the dog into the SUV and jumped into the driver's seat. The SUV shot away from the curb with a small squeal of tires.

"He's an ass," she said. "But I don't think he took Cady. He looked genuinely confused when I asked about her." Bree grabbed the door handle as Matt barely slowed for a bend in the road.

"I agree." Matt was trying to maintain his cool, but Bree could sense emotions gathering inside him like the storm clouds thickening in the sky. Tension corded the muscles in his forearms and neck, and his jaw was clenched tight.

She couldn't blame him for losing control. She remembered her sister's call asking Bree for help, the burning anxiety in her gut on the long drive from Philly to Grey's Hollow, and the punch of grief when she'd learned Erin was dead.

Please, don't let anything terrible happen to Cady.

CHAPTER
THIRTY-FOUR

Shannon Phelps's house was dark when Matt parked down the street. Worry burned in his belly as if he'd swallowed fire. They stepped out of the vehicle. Wind gusted, and dead leaves tumbled along the gutter. Overhead, the sky darkened with thickening clouds.

Matt let Brody out of the back. He slid the ramp back inside and closed the door. "I don't know whether I should hope she's inside or not. If she isn't, we have no idea where to look."

Or who might have taken her.

His scarred hand ached. He looked down to discover he'd been clenching his hands into tight fists. He uncurled his fingers and flexed.

Stop freaking out. Keep a clear head and find Cady.

They walked up to Shannon's front door and flanked the doorway. Bree raised a hand and knocked. Inside, they could hear Shannon's little dog barking. It must have been confined, because the sound stayed in the back of the house.

Bree rang the doorbell. It chimed inside. The dog barked louder. Matt cupped his hands over his eyes and peered through a window next to the door. He saw no one in the dark foyer.

He jogged around the side of the house and looked through the garage window. Empty. He returned to the front step. "Her car isn't here."

Bree stepped back and scanned the front of the house. "Now what?"

Matt paced while Brody watched him. "If Cady was here, Brody would know."

Bree's phone rang, and she pulled it from her pocket. "It's Dana." She answered. "Hey. I'm putting you on speaker. Matt is here." She pressed a button and held her phone between her and Matt.

"I found several more fake payable accounts," Dana said. "In addition to the two owned by Paul's sons, two more are owned indirectly by Paul himself. You'll never guess who owns the last one."

"Who?" Bree asked.

"Shannon Phelps," Dana said. "About thirty thousand dollars went into that account over the past year."

Matt looked up at Shannon's house. "Holly did the payables. She must have known what Paul was doing. What if she was blackmailing him?"

"That would explain her late-night phone call and the brief visit to his house," Bree said.

"We already suspected Paul liked to buy people with envelopes full of cash," Matt added.

Bree frowned. "Maybe Holly decided that wasn't enough. She really liked to spend money. Maybe she started funneling some money to her sister."

"But why use her sister?" Matt asked. "Why not just put the company in her own name?"

"Too easy to trace." Bree shook her head.

"So, was Shannon in on it?" Dana asked.

Matt turned back to the house. "She must have been. But why would she have taken Cady?"

A few seconds of silence ticked by.

"Do you have anything else for us, Dana?" Bree asked.

"No," Dana said. "I'll call you if I do."

"Thanks." Bree lowered her phone. "How does all of this translate to Shannon killing Holly?"

"I don't know." Matt resumed his pacing. "Shannon had an alibi for Paul's murder."

"Maybe Angela killed Paul."

"But why would Shannon kill Holly?"

Bree grimaced. "Shannon was angry that Holly wanted their mom to go into hospice. We learned that the very first time we talked to her."

Matt glanced back at the house. "We know Cady called Shannon. Maybe she remembered something about her. Something incriminating."

"What could Cady know?"

Matt shook his head. "I don't know, but I don't have time to analyze all the data. Cady is missing. I'm going into that house to see if Shannon left any clues of where she was going. You don't have to come with me."

It was a gamble. They had no probable cause, other than the fake account in Shannon's name collecting money from Beckett Construction. But they had no way to connect that activity to Cady's disappearance. But Matt didn't care. He'd do whatever was necessary to find his sister.

Bree stared at him. "We're doing this together."

"Are you sure? You could get sued."

"Cady is more important," Bree said. "I'll take my chances."

"The alarm will go off."

"And the alarm company will call my department." Without hesitating, Bree pulled her flashlight from her pocket and used the handle to break a small window near the front door. She reached in, unlocked the door, and opened it.

They both halted, waiting for the alarm to sound. Most security systems allowed only thirty seconds to a minute to turn them off.

But they heard nothing. Matt looked for the alarm panel. The lights were green. "She didn't turn on the alarm."

"If she's the one who killed Holly, then she doesn't have a reason to be afraid."

"The break-in here and doll in the sink were fake," Matt said.

"It's possible she wanted to throw off the investigation. If that was her goal, I'm sorry to say it worked."

He led Brody inside, making sure the dog didn't step on broken glass.

Bree drew her weapon, and they swept through the house. Brody's presence made the search quick and easy. He'd been trained to clear rooms, and he could sense people who were hiding.

Back downstairs, Bree stood in Shannon's kitchen, her gaze scanning the room.

"I'll look in the home office." Matt walked toward the small study.

"Wait." Bree picked up a framed photo of the two girls with their softball bats and balls on the shelf. She looked up at Matt, her gaze stunned. "I've figured out what was bugging me about Shannon's last interview. Now everything makes sense."

CHAPTER THIRTY-FIVE

Bree shoved the picture at Matt and pulled out her phone. Nerves roiled inside her. She wavered between horror at what she was thinking and exasperation that she could have missed something so basic.

Matt took the photo. "What is it?"

"Give me a second. I want to verify this. It feels crazy." Bree called Dana. "Could you open the murder book? Find a picture of Holly with her sister as kids. Would you take a picture of it and send it to me?"

"Sure," Dana said. "Anything else?"

"No." Bree ended the call and waited. A few seconds later, her phone beeped. She stared at the image on her screen. Next, she called the sheriff's station. A deputy answered. "I want you to access the video recording of the interview with Shannon Phelps. Stop at the spot when she signs the Miranda acknowledgment, take a photo of the screen, and text it to me."

She lowered the phone.

"What are you thinking?" Matt asked.

Bree turned her phone screen to him. "Here's the photo Mrs. Phelps gave me." In the picture, two little girls sat across from each other, drawing. "Shannon is the younger, smaller child." She pointed. "She's holding her crayon in her left hand."

Her phone beeped, and she downloaded the picture of Shannon's interview that her deputy had sent.

"She signed with her right hand," Matt said.

Bree nodded. "It's not Holly lying in the morgue. It's Shannon."

Matt drew back, shock widening his eyes. Then he tugged on his beard. "That explains so much."

"Holly was going bankrupt. Angela had called the IRS on Paul. She was hoping he'd go to prison. What if Holly was guilty too? She's the one who transferred the money to the dummy corporations. What if she was also blackmailing Paul and stealing from Beckett Construction?"

"By killing her sister and switching places with her, she avoids all penalties, financial and criminal. She takes over her sister's life and starts fresh with a nice bank account and business." Puzzle pieces fell neatly into place in Bree's mind. Not all of them, but enough.

"But her mother would recognize her."

"She hasn't seen her mother since before she killed her sister," Bree said. "Remember, she said she had a cold. Plus, her mother's vision is terrible."

Matt shook his head. "A mother would still know her own daughter."

"But would she turn her in?"

"What about Owen? He'd recognize his own wife, and wouldn't he be mad if he knew his wife was abandoning him to their bankruptcy?"

Bree remembered their original interview with Owen. "He and Shannon hated each other. Maybe she was hoping to avoid him. Or maybe he knew about the plan."

Matt frowned. "Did Holly kill Paul, or did Angela do that?"

"I don't know. Could have also been Owen." Bree could see any of those options working. "Angela didn't have an alibi for Paul's death.

Holly, masquerading as Shannon, was at the vet with the dog. Owen didn't have an alibi."

Matt froze. "I know why Holly took my sister. Shannon adopted her dog through Cady's rescue. Cady met her just a few months ago."

Horror curled inside Bree's chest, wrapping its fingers around her heart and squeezing. "Your sister would know she wasn't Shannon. Until now, we haven't met many people who personally knew Shannon. They look enough alike to fool someone who didn't know either of them well. Shannon worked for herself from home, so she has no coworkers and no boss. She wasn't close to her neighbors. She didn't seem to have many friends either."

"Cady said she was very shy." Matt looked devastated. "We have to find them. Where would she take her?"

Bree met his eyes. "I can only think of one place. The same place their father died. The same place Holly tried to fake her suicide."

"The bridge." He headed for the front door, Brody at his heels.

Bree hurried to keep pace with his longer legs. "I hope we're right."

"We don't have anywhere else to look," Matt said.

Outside, they ran for the SUV. Brody didn't wait for his ramp. He leaped into the back seat.

Bree fastened her seat belt. "Do I call for backup now, or wait until we confirm they're at the bridge?"

"What if we're wrong? What if Holly took Cady somewhere else?"

"I'll call in a BOLO." Bree used her radio to put out the alert. "Since we're operating on our guts, it's better to have the deputies looking for Shannon's vehicle than sending everyone to the bridge."

She set down the radio mic. Her deputies were searching the county for Shannon's Ford Escape. If she called them all to the bridge, they wouldn't be actively searching.

She'd wait. If they found Holly and Cady at the bridge, then she'd call for backup.

Her belly cramped. Holly had killed her own sister and left her in the trunk of her vehicle until she was ready to dispose of the body. Bree said nothing to Matt. There was no point in driving his anxiety higher with speculation.

But if Holly was consistent, Cady was already dead.

CHAPTER THIRTY-SIX

Pain rocketed through Cady's head. She blinked, but all she could see was darkness. She moved her legs, and a wave of nausea swept over her. She lay still for a few minutes, breathing.

Where was she? What time was it?

One side of her face pressed into a flat napped carpet, and it suddenly lurched under her. The sound of an engine accelerating followed. She was in the back of a vehicle. Something lay across the other half of her face. No. It was draped over her whole body. Underneath, the air was stifling. She lifted a hand to move the canvas from her face and discovered her hands were bound together in front of her body.

The attack came rushing back. The blow to her head. Her falling to the ground. Being dragged. Darkness.

Whoever knocked her out had kidnapped her.

Her breaths quickened, and her stomach spun. She probably had a concussion. On the second attempt, she managed to move the heavy canvas off her head. Fresh air hit her face, and she gulped it down. A minute later, her stomach settled. She turned her head to examine the vehicle. She was in the back of a small SUV. The night sky showed through the back window.

The vehicle slowed. The tires grated, and the vehicle bumped as it left the smooth surface of a road. The SUV stopped. She heard the driver shift gears. The engine went quiet. Then the door opened.

Shit.

No time to plan an escape. She'd have to play dead. She pulled the tarp back over her head and held still.

The back of the vehicle opened, and the canvas was pulled off her. Raindrops fell on her face. Cady kept her eyes closed and tried to control her breathing, but it felt ragged in her chest.

She heard her kidnapper's breaths come closer. Cady opened her eyes to slits. A shadow leaned over her. She rolled to her back, pulled her knees to her chest, and kicked out with both feet. But her movements were slow and clumsy. Her kidnapper ducked and grabbed her legs. A fist struck out and slammed into Cady's temple.

Dizziness rolled over her. The cloudy sky spun. She closed her eyes against another bout of nausea. Breathing through her mouth, she opened her eyes. A woman stared down at her. Her face was blurry. Her hair was a fuzzy blonde halo.

Shannon Phelps?

Cady squeezed her eyes closed and opened them again. The blurriness cleared, and the face came into focus. It wasn't Shannon, but someone who looked remarkably like her.

The woman reached out and grabbed Cady by the ponytail. "Get out."

Pain tore across Cady's scalp. She reached her bound hands toward the base of her ponytail and held it against her head to minimize the force.

"I said get out." The woman yanked harder.

Cady's head jerked, and her scalp screamed in agony. Tiny lights sparked in front of her eyes. Fighting the dizziness, she sat up. Everything swirled around her. Before her brain could settle, the woman dragged her from the back of the vehicle. Cady untangled her legs and swung them over the raised lip of the cargo area. Her sneakers hit the pavement and she stood. The woman released her. With wobbly knees, she leaned her butt against the back of the vehicle. She pressed her bound hands to the top of her head and the pain that throbbed beneath her skull.

Rain bathed her face and soaked her hair and clothes. The cool water and fresh air cleared her head. After the world stopped spinning, Cady heard something beyond the beat of her own heart: the rush of water. She glanced around, taking in the road, the surrounding woods, and the iron beams overhead. The car was parked in the middle of the bridge on Dead Horse Road.

One thought dominated Cady's mind: this woman was going to kill her. She didn't have time to figure out who this woman was or why she had kidnapped her. She needed to stall as long as possible. She needed to get away.

But how?

"Who are you?" she asked.

"None of your fucking business."

Cady followed the yellow line painted down the center of the road. The blacktop was a ribbon of darkness, winding up the hill and disappearing into the forest. It wasn't a busy route, but a car *could* come along at any moment. Even if no one came to help her, Cady's balance was improving as she stood upright. Every second she delayed a physical confrontation, her chances of survival increased.

"You're not Shannon."

"No, and that's why you have to die." The woman reached into her pocket and pulled out a gun. She aimed it at Cady. "Move away from the truck."

Cady took a tentative side step. Her legs were shaky, but they held.

"All the way to the railing." The blonde woman jerked the gun's barrel toward the river.

Cady stared at her. Her eyes had adjusted to the dimness, and her brain was finally waking up enough to add two plus two. If this blonde woman wasn't Shannon, there was only one person she could be. "You're Shannon's sister, aren't you? The one everyone thinks is dead."

"Shut up!"

Cady took that as a yes. "You killed your sister."

"She was a pain." Holly sounded bored. "Now climb up on the railing."

"Why?" Cady peered over the side. Thirty feet below, the water churned black in the night.

"Because you're going to jump."

Cady assessed her chances. The bridge wasn't high enough that dying in the fall was a sure thing. Once she climbed up on that railing, she was willing to bet Holly was going to shoot her. After all, she needed to make sure Cady was dead.

Fuck that.

Cady would not make it so easy.

"Go on. Climb," Holly said.

Cady raised one foot toward the railing, then pivoted on the ball of her other foot and dived at Holly's feet. The impact with the pavement rang like a giant bell in her head, and Cady's vision dimmed.

CHAPTER THIRTY-SEVEN

Matt took the turns on two wheels. Panic scrambled for a foothold in his chest. He breathed his way through it. He had to find his sister. Rain pattered on the windshield, and he switched on the wipers.

In the passenger seat, Bree pulled out her phone when it rang. "It's Collins." She answered. The call lasted for twenty seconds. "Thanks." She lowered her phone. "Collins had no luck with the ERs. No one meeting Cady's description was brought in today."

Matt hadn't believed that scenario anyway. If Cady had gotten hurt, she would have called a family member.

"What if they aren't at the bridge?" Matt would have no idea where else to look for Cady.

"Then we keep looking until we find them. My deputies are actively looking for Shannon's vehicle."

He didn't respond. How long would Holly keep Cady alive? The only way to guarantee her silence was to kill her.

Matt slowed as he navigated the downhill switchbacks of Dead Horse Road that led to the bridge. A half mile from the bridge, he killed the headlights. The combination of dangerous terrain, darkness, and rain forced him to slow the vehicle. Sweat broke out on his palms as he navigated the last few turns in the dark. When they emerged from the woods, he stopped the car at the crest of the hill. The bridge loomed in the dark.

Bree exhaled hard. She took her binoculars from her glove box and looked through them. "I see a compact SUV." She adjusted the binoculars. "Looks like Shannon's Ford Escape is parked in the middle of the bridge." She used her radio to call for backup, instructing two of the responding deputies to approach from the opposite side of the bridge. "We'll box her in. She won't get away."

"ETA on backup?" Matt took the binoculars and aimed them on the vehicle.

"Six minutes. We won't wait."

He squinted through the binoculars, but rain and darkness obscured his view. "I can't tell if anyone is in the vehicle."

"What about on the bridge?"

"It's too dark." He lowered the binoculars. "But where else would they be?" Matt wouldn't consider the possibility that Cady was already dead and in the river. "I'm going in."

Bree extended an upturned palm for the binoculars. "Let's go."

He handed them to her, she turned off the dome light, and they slipped out of the vehicle. Matt lifted Brody from the vehicle and kept him on a short leash. Bree met them at the back of the SUV. She opened the hatch slowly and quietly.

Rain came down in a steady drizzle. The sound would help cover their movement and approach, but it also reduced visibility. He patted the flashlight in his pocket. The hackles on the back of Brody's neck stood up, and the dog growled softly in the direction of the bridge.

Matt handed Bree a black nylon windbreaker with the word SHERIFF printed on the back. Her light-gray T-shirt would stand out in the dark. She slipped into it, setting her jaw as she worked her wounded arm into the sleeve. Then she stuffed the binoculars into a pocket.

He hated that she was out here, injured, in the rain, but with Cady's life on the line, he didn't have a choice, and he trusted Bree to have his back.

She removed the AR-15 from its gun vault and handed it to him.

He slung the strap over his shoulder. "Let's go."

They jogged down the hill toward the bridge. Bree jogged next to him, her rubber-soled shoes quiet on the blacktop. Brody was quiet, no whining or barking. Matt scanned the darkness ahead.

Where are they?

At the base of the bridge, he went down on one knee behind a support beam. He set a hand on his dog. Brody vibrated with focus like a tuning fork.

Bree pulled out her binoculars. "I see shadows moving. Two people are on the ground on the other side of the SUV. Damn. They're near the edge."

Matt sprinted onto the bridge. He ran past the small SUV. The two bodies rolled on the pavement.

"Stop!" Holly yelled at him. She knelt near the railing, holding Cady by the ponytail. His sister was on her knees, her head drawn back, the muzzle of a revolver pressed against her temple.

She's alive.

Matt put on the brakes. His feet slid in dirt on the pavement. "Hello, Holly."

Brody lunged against the end of the leash. Matt held him back, and the dog planted all four feet and leaned into his harness, waiting, his attention riveted on Holly and Cady.

"So, you figured it out." Holly got to her feet, dragging Cady with her and keeping her body behind Cady's. Her eyes darted nervously to Brody.

Matt had no shot. Pain and fear radiated in his sister's eyes. Blood matted her hair and dribbled down her forehead. Anger and fresh fear rose into Matt's throat.

Bree came around the other side of the Escape, her Glock aimed at Holly. "Freeze!"

"You can't get away," Matt said.

Desperation widened Holly's eyes. She backed toward the railing, pulling Cady with her. "Stay back. All of you. And call off that dog. Or I'll shoot her. I'll do it. I've killed before."

The only thing keeping Cady alive was her ability to shield Holly.

"Don't do it, Holly." Bree leveled the gun.

Holly's lip curled, and she pulled on Cady's hair. Anger stoked high in Matt's chest. But he couldn't shoot Holly without risking hitting his sister. If he turned the dog loose, Brody could knock them off the bridge. Or Holly could shoot Cady or Brody on reflex. Holly dragged Cady up onto the railing. They stood on the bottom rung, the top of the railing level with their thighs. Cady was taller and stronger, but she was also wounded.

Cady grabbed the base of her ponytail and resisted, sinking her butt low and using her body weight to try to pull Holly back onto the bridge. She knew how to use leverage instead of strength.

"Stop it!" Holly dug the revolver deeper into Cady's skin. "I'll blow your fucking head right off."

Cady met Matt's gaze. Her chin moved in a tiny nod. She was going to do something. Matt held his breath and raised the AR-15. He didn't want to shoot a woman, but he would if that's what it took to save his sister.

Holly had killed her own sister. Matt had no doubt she would pull the trigger. She was evil.

At her side, Cady extended three fingers, then two, then one. She spun, brushing her hand along her hair and knocking Holly's gun away from her head. The gun went off into the air. Cady continued her turn, both hands striking out to shove Holly. The gun flew from Holly's hand, over the railing, and disappeared.

Brody bolted, tearing the leash from Matt's hand.

Holly teetered. She looked over the side where her gun had disappeared. With a terrified glance at the huge dog racing at her, she grabbed Cady, pushed her over the edge, and ran toward the opposite end of the bridge. A splash followed. Brody didn't hesitate. He ran straight at the railing and leaped over it, following Cady off the bridge and into the darkness. A second later, Matt heard a second splash as the dog hit the water.

He sprinted to the railing. His gut hit the top rail just in time to see his dog disappear under the rippling black surface of the river. There was no sign of Cady.

Chapter
Thirty-Eight

No!

Horrified, Bree rushed forward.

"Call an ambulance." Matt kicked off his shoes and climbed over the railing. "And get Holly."

He jumped.

Cursing, Bree leaned over the railing. He splashed into the water, then she saw nothing but blackness. Her eyes searched the river downstream, but all she saw were occasional light-colored rocks and spots of white water. The rest of the river was too dark. No Cady. No Matt. No Brody. She turned back toward the road. She couldn't swim with a bullet hole in her arm. Matt would end up needing to rescue her as well.

Damn it.

Holly was racing toward the other end of the bridge. Bree went after her. As she ran, she pulled out her cell phone and called for an ambulance, a water rescue team, and additional backup. "The kidnapping victim and Investigator Flynn went over the edge. I'm in pursuit of the suspect."

Bree's arm ached, but there was nothing wrong with her legs. She tucked her arm close to her side and turned on the speed. Adrenaline pumped into her bloodstream. Ahead, Holly was stumbling. She'd sprinted the first fifty feet on pure instinct, but her lack of fitness was showing. Bree gained on her.

She caught up with her before the end of the bridge. Headlights approached.

Backup!

Charged with anger and determination, Bree dived forward. She threw an arm around Holly's waist and took her to the ground. They hit the pavement in a tangle of arms and legs. Bree felt her stitches pop. Warmth rushed out of her wound, but she didn't care. After a quick burst of white-hot agony, adrenaline blunted the pain. She flipped Holly to her stomach.

"You're under arrest." Bree pulled the handcuffs from her belt. In her peripheral vision, she saw the headlights of the approaching vehicle come to a stop. She glanced over her shoulder at the approaching vehicle, but the LED lights blinded her.

Holly tried to crawl away. On her hands and knees, she kicked out at Bree's face.

Bree caught the kicking foot and yanked hard. Holly went down on her face, and blood spurted from her nose. Panting, Bree planted a knee into her back.

Holly lifted her face from the road and spat blood. "Fuck you."

Bree snapped one cuff around a wrist, then reached for the second.

"Hold it!" a male voice shouted.

Bree froze.

Not backup. Owen.

She looked over her shoulder. He stood about fifteen feet away, a gun in his hand. Rain plastered his hair to his head.

"Is that Paul's gun?" she asked, trying to stall. Backup should be there any moment.

"Yep," he said. "Slide your gun toward me."

Bree slid her Glock from its holster, set it on the road, and gave it a half-hearted push.

Owen frowned as the weapon stopped just three feet from Bree, a dozen feet short of him. "Get off my wife."

Slowly, Bree slid off Holly. Bent forward, she rested her hands on her thighs and worked to catch her breath. Holly turned, sat up, and slapped Bree across the face. Bree overexaggerated her response, falling to the side and onto her hands and knees on the wet road. Holly jumped forward and kicked her in the ribs. Pain exploded in Bree's abdomen. Her lungs expelled all their air and locked up. She dry heaved in the road.

Holly spat on her. "Get up, bitch." She turned toward Owen. "Love you, baby."

"Love you too." He smiled. A siren sounded in the distance. Bree braced one foot under her body, as if ready to lever herself to her feet.

"We'd better kill her quick and get out of here." Owen held out his free hand for his wife. "Come here, baby."

"One second." Holly kicked Bree in the thigh. "You broke my nose."

Bree drew her backup piece from her ankle holster and dived for the street. Owen fired at her. A bullet ricocheted off the blacktop a few feet away. Her good shoulder hit the pavement. She rolled over once, leveled her weapon at Owen, and pulled the trigger three times. His body jerked. Three dark spots bloomed on his chest. He dropped his gun, collapsed onto his knees, and face-planted in the road.

"No!" Holly's voice echoed with despair. Water and blood sluiced down her face.

Bree walked to her and grabbed the handcuff dangling from one wrist. She spun her around and levered the other behind her back. The second handcuff closed with a resounding snap.

Bree tightened the cuffs, then forced Holly onto her knees. "Don't move."

She leaned down and pressed two fingers to the side of Owen's neck, but his blank stare told her he was dead.

Bree didn't allow herself to process what had just happened. This nightmare wasn't over yet. Matt, Cady, and Brody were still in danger. Bree clamped down on her emotions.

Later.

The blue and red lights of a cruiser approached. Todd got out of his vehicle, and Bree called him over. "Lock her in the back of your vehicle and bring a rope down to the riverbank."

Bree ran around the side of the bridge and scrambled down the bank toward the river. She headed toward the place where Shannon's body had washed up and hoped that was where the current would deposit Matt, Cady, and Brody.

CHAPTER THIRTY-NINE

Matt broke the surface of the water and gasped for air. "Cady!"

Treading water in the shifting current, he scanned the surface but didn't see his sister. He looked up at the bridge overhead and estimated where she had hit the water. A few bubbles broke the surface. Matt dived, his hands sweeping out in the darkness. Nothing.

He shot for the surface again, tossing water off his eyes and yelling over the river. "Cady!"

As a rower, Cady was very strong. She had to be here. Unless she hadn't survived the fall. But he would not give up until he found her.

"Matt!" a weak cry sounded.

For the second time that night, he thought, *She's alive!*

He followed the sound and saw her—and Brody—next to a cluster of rocks. The dog had the back of Cady's hoodie in his mouth, and his front paws were on a boulder. Cady was neck deep in water. The upper half of her face was barely above the surface. She had to tip her face backward to breathe. Without Brody holding her afloat, she would have been swept under the surface. The current lapped and a small wave broke over her face. She sputtered as Matt swam over.

"I'm—stuck," she said between mouthfuls of water.

Matt went under and followed her leg to the end. Her foot was jammed between two rocks.

He came back up. "I need room. You have to go under so I can free you."

Cady nodded.

He gave Brody the release command, and the dog opened his mouth.

"One, two, deep breath in, three." Matt inhaled and dived under, pulling Cady with him.

He tugged her foot down and pulled it from between the rocks. They surfaced together in the middle of the current. It swept them into the center of the river, right toward a cluster of boulders. A splash sounded behind Matt. A few seconds later, Brody's head appeared next to him. Weak, Cady floundered and almost went under again. She was barely conscious as Matt pulled her closer.

White foam churned around them. Matt turned her in his arms and put her back to his chest. Then he wrapped one arm around her and turned his back to the rocks. Brody grabbed Matt's sleeve in his mouth and stroked toward the bank, pulling Matt off a direct collision course with the rocks. Matt's shoulder glanced off the boulder instead of hitting it head-on. He took the impact across his back, shielding his sister in his arms. The blow knocked the air from his lungs. He wheezed as the current swept them through an eddy. It tugged them under. Water closed over their heads and sucked them toward the bottom. His chest burned with the need for oxygen. Matt pushed off the bottom with both feet, holding tight to Cady and propelling them back up. His head broke the surface. He coughed and gasped.

Brody was right there at his side, pulling them both toward the shore.

"Cady?" Matt yelled.

She didn't answer. Her body was limp in his arms. He turned on his back, hauled her against his chest, and stroked with his free arm.

They'd popped out of the eddy at the foot of the rapids. Just ahead, the river forked. To one side, the rapids continued. The other branch led to a quiet, flat inlet. With Brody's help, Matt headed for the calm water. He spotted Bree and Todd on the shore near the place where they'd found Shannon's body.

"Almost there, Cady," he shouted.

His sister didn't answer. He turned her face to him. Panic pushed him to swim faster. Her lips were blue, and she wasn't breathing.

CHAPTER FORTY

As Bree and Todd waded out toward the trio, Todd made a lasso and flung the coil into the water. Matt grabbed it, and they pulled him and Cady in. As soon as she was within reach, Todd pulled Cady closer. He bent over her face and started rescue breathing while he towed her on her back in the water. When he was only thigh deep, he scooped her up and carried her to dry ground. Laying her on the rocky shore, he went back to mouth-to-mouth. Bree rushed from the water, dropped to her knees beside Cady, and checked her pulse. Nothing. She began administering chest compressions.

Matt stumbled out of the water and fell to his hands and knees beside them. His shirt was torn and bloody across the backs of his shoulders. Brody emerged and shook himself, sending water spraying in all directions.

Bree counted compressions and stopped for Todd to breathe into Cady's mouth. They had completed two cycles when Cady choked, gasped, and coughed. Todd rolled her to her side and held her as she retched and coughed up water. Bree sat back on her heels. Her pulse hammered in her veins, and nausea swirled in her stomach. Matt collapsed at her side, with what seemed to be tears of relief in his eyes. Brody barked and wagged his soaking-wet tail.

On the road above, more lights and sirens signaled the arrival of the ambulance and rescue crew. Todd lurched to his feet. "I'll get them." He turned and jogged up the slope and into the trees.

Cady coughed. A hard shiver shook her whole body. Bree took off her windbreaker and draped it over her. The rain stopped, but the night air remained cold and damp.

Matt crawled closer to his sister. "You're going to be OK." He turned to Bree. "What happened with Holly?"

"Long story short, Holly is handcuffed in the back of Todd's vehicle, and Owen is dead." Bree gave him a quick summary.

Matt lifted his brows. Then he took her hand and held it against his chest. "But we survived."

What would she have done if he hadn't? Her heart stuttered. *Don't think about it. Not even for a second. He's fine.* Bree locked away her fears. At this rate, she was going to need an internal vault to compartmentalize all her emotions.

"We're a pretty good team." She squeezed his fingers.

The EMTs followed Todd to the riverbank. Todd glanced at Matt's and Bree's joined hands. He smiled, then coughed into his fist to hide the grin. Embarrassed, Bree released Matt's hand, stood, and backed up to give the EMTs room to work on Cady.

Lights and sirens signaled the arrival of additional emergency vehicles on the road above. Deputies scrambled down the embankment. Someone brought blankets. Matt took one and rubbed down Brody before accepting a blanket for himself.

A short time later, Cady was carried to the road on a gurney. Bree and Matt climbed up the slope behind the EMTs. The bridge was full of deputy vehicles. An ambulance was parked on the shoulder, and the medical examiner had arrived. Cady was loaded into an ambulance.

Matt hesitated at the back doors. He clearly wanted to go with his sister. "I need someone to take Brody."

"I'll do it," Bree said.

Matt shook his head. "Your arm is bleeding. You need to go to the ER."

She glanced at the wet, bloody bandage. "I know."

"I've got Brody, Matt." Todd stooped and picked up the end of the leash, which was dragging in the mud.

"We'll also need someone to pick up Shannon's dog," Bree said.

"I can call one of Cady's volunteers to take him," Matt offered. "If you send a deputy to pick him up."

"I'll take care of that too," Todd said.

"Thanks. We'll find him a new home." Matt climbed into the back with his sister. He pointed at Bree. "I expect to see you at the ER ASAP."

"I'll be there." She gave him a short wave as the ambulance doors closed. As much as she wasn't looking forward to having her arm cleaned and restitched, she wanted to face Owen's dead body less. But she walked toward the bridge and the medical examiner's van. She had a job to do. As usual, she would put aside the emotional fallout over killing a man until the work was done.

The medical examiner stepped away from the body and walked to the rear of her van. She removed her gloves and set her kit inside.

Bree approached. "Do you need anything?"

"No. You'll get my report, but I didn't see any surprises." Dr. Jones assessed Bree. Her gaze stopped on Bree's arm. She raised a brow.

"I know," Bree said. "I'm headed to the ER next."

"Good." Dr. Jones closed the back of her van. "Take care, Sheriff. We need you."

Bree turned and scanned the swarm of law enforcement personnel for her chief deputy. She spotted him standing next to his vehicle, talking on the radio. Brody sat at his side.

Bree crossed the pavement.

Todd leaned into his vehicle and replaced his radio mic. "Deputy Oscar took Holly Thorpe to the station and put her in holding."

"Good. I need to interview her tonight."

"Sheriff," Todd said. "No offense, but I think you should get that arm seen to."

Bree scanned the scene again, then looked back at Todd. He was perfectly capable of doing the job, and it was time she let him. "You're right. You're in charge, Chief Deputy."

"Oh. OK." He blinked, as if surprised she'd agreed. "Any instructions?"

"You know what to do." Bree gave Brody a pat on the head, then turned toward the direction of her vehicle. She glanced over her shoulder. "I'll see you at the station later."

Todd stood straighter. "Yes, ma'am."

CHAPTER FORTY-ONE

Matt stood outside Cady's ER cubicle. A nurse had found him a set of dry scrubs. A plastic bag held his wet clothes. The abrasions across the backs of his shoulders had been cleaned and dressed. Except for his wet socks and shoes, he felt almost human.

The doctor emerged from behind the curtain. She raised her glasses and looked Matt over. "Your sister has a concussion, two broken fingers, and a whole bunch of bruises. Between that and possible complications of near drowning, we're going to admit her tonight for observation. As long as the CAT scan comes back clear, she can probably go home tomorrow. Someone should keep an eye on her for the next few days."

"She'll be going to our parents' house." Something Matt had not told Cady yet. "My father is a retired physician. She'll be in good hands." Their parents had been insistent—their dad was a softy, but not when it came to their health.

"Excellent."

"Thanks." Matt knocked on the wall next to the curtain's edge. "Cady? It's Matt."

"Come in." She reclined on the gurney. Blankets were piled on top of her, and an IV dripped into the back of her hand. A small patch of hair on the side of her head had been shaved, and an inch-long gash stitched.

"Nice hairdo." He perched on the edge of the gurney and took her hand.

She smiled. "Maybe I should shave my whole head."

Matt grinned. "You'd still be cute."

"Thanks for saving me."

"You're welcome." He squeezed her fingers. "Mom and Dad and Nolan are on the way."

"I need clothes."

"The 'rents just left your house. They packed you a bag."

"I'm going home with them tomorrow, aren't I?" Cady grinned.

"Yep."

She rested her head back. "Maybe Dad'll make his homemade mac and cheese."

"I'm sure he'll make whatever you want."

She closed her eyes. "Sweet."

"Cady?" Mom's voice sounded from the hallway.

"In here," Cady called out.

The curtain opened and Matt's parents and Nolan walked in. At seventy, George Flynn hadn't lost an inch of his broad six-foot-two frame. His thick white hair and trimmed beard made the blue of his eyes look even more brilliant. Their mom was only a few inches shorter and robustly built. No one would call her frail.

"You should have called me sooner." Nolan ran a hand over his bald head.

"There wasn't time," Matt said.

Dad immediately checked Cady's vital signs on the monitor. Another knock sounded outside the cubicle, and Bree stuck her head in. "I just wanted to make sure you were OK."

Cady smiled. "I am. Do you need to question me?"

"No." Bree shook her head. She still wore her wet clothes but held a small duffel bag in one hand. The bandage on her arm hadn't been changed. "Tomorrow will be soon enough. You rest tonight."

Matt introduced his parents and brother. They all shook her hand.

Their dad held on an extra few seconds. "We'd like to thank you with Sunday brunch."

"This weekend is Mother's Day," Bree said, her eyes turning sad. "But I'll take a rain check."

Matt's dad held up a hand. "Don't answer now. Think about it." He nodded. "Bring your whole family. I'll make extra cinnamon buns."

"Thank you." Bree stepped back.

A nurse came in. "Sheriff. We're ready for you in bay six."

Bree excused herself. "I need to get this restitched. It was nice to meet you." She ducked out into the hallway.

"Go with the sheriff." Matt's dad motioned toward the exit. "We know you want to. Your mom and I have things in hand here."

"Thanks." Matt kissed his sister on the head and went looking for Bree.

The curtain was closed in bay six. When it opened, Bree had changed into a dry uniform. She smiled at him as she hopped onto the gurney to sit sideways. "I wish I had dry shoes."

"Same." His shoes squished as he walked in. He closed the curtain behind him. He leaned down and kissed her softly, then he wrapped both arms around her, careful of her injured arm. She leaned into his chest for a minute. When the squeak of rubber soles signaled a nurse's approach, they broke apart.

Matt stepped back.

"Knock knock." The curtain opened and a nurse entered. She cut away the bandages.

"I'll be questioning Holly Thorpe after this." Bree held out her arm as the nurse inspected the wound. "You want in?"

Matt straightened. "Damned straight I do."

Chapter Forty-Two

Bree watched the screen in the monitoring room. On the display, Holly Thorpe sat in the interview room, handcuffed to a ring mounted in the center of the table. Her eyes were red-rimmed and swollen.

"It'll be interesting to see how she reacts to you." Matt stood next to Bree, still wearing the scrubs he'd been given at the hospital.

"It will be."

"You want me to watch from here?" he asked.

"Yes. I want her to talk, and I think she might be more comfortable one-on-one."

"I'm surprised she hasn't asked for a lawyer."

"Me too." Bree left the monitoring room and went into the interview room.

Holly looked up, her sad eyes flaring with rage. "You killed Owen."

Bree didn't answer. She sat across from Holly and went through the Miranda routine. Holly signed without commenting. She seemed flat, emotionless.

Bree folded her hands on the table. "When did you decide to kill Shannon?"

Holly sniffed.

Bree shrugged. "Doesn't matter. We don't need a confession. We have you cold on kidnapping, assault, and attempted murder, among other things. You're not going anywhere. You're going to spend the rest of your life in prison. We have plenty of time to investigate Shannon's murder."

Holly glared.

"I have to admit," Bree said. "I'm impressed. You almost had us. If it hadn't been for Cady . . ."

"Stupid do-gooder." Holly rolled her eyes. "I tried to ignore her, but she kept calling. Finally, I answered and told her I was busy. But she wouldn't let up. She wanted to be friends." She said this as if it were the most ridiculous idea in the world.

"And she'd seen Shannon recently, so she would have known immediately that you weren't her." Bree sighed. "If Cady hadn't gotten in the way, your plan would have worked. No one would have known. It was brilliant, really."

"Stupid bitch." Holly preened at the compliment. She didn't look stable. But then, normal, stable people didn't usually kill their own sisters.

"Was Paul cheating on his taxes?" Bree asked.

"Paul cheated on everything. He bribed inspectors. He funneled money out of his joint accounts and buried it. He hid money from Angela and the government. When he was ready, he pushed Angela's buttons to make her leave him. He believed possession was nine-tenths of the law like it was the eleventh commandment."

"And you helped him."

"I did it all." Her voice rang with pride. "Paul didn't know anything about bookkeeping."

"And he paid you in extra cash?"

Holly snorted. "He gave me cash, and I took more. He never even suspected. It was his own fault. He got greedy. He had so many fake transactions flowing through those books, I could barely keep track. It seemed simple to skim off some extra money for my rainy-day fund."

"Paul wasn't that smart. How did he figure out who you really were?" Bree bluffed. It was the only explanation that made sense.

"*He* didn't figure out anything. You're right. Paul wasn't that smart. His tax attorney found the business I set up in my sister's name."

"I'll bet he was impressed. It was an elaborate plan." Bree continued to stroke Holly's ego.

"Paul showed up at Shannon's house and saw me through the window."

"What did he want?" Bree asked.

"He said I had to fuck him, or he'd call you." More anger snapped in Holly's eyes, then a tear rolled down her cheek. "I would never have cheated on Owen. He was the only man for me. I loved him." She leveled a bone-chilling gaze at Bree.

"So, instead of fucking Paul . . ."

"Owen killed him. He was mad that Paul would try to blackmail me into having sex with him. Paul needed to go. He threatened our plan. It would have worked out fine, except Owen panicked when you showed up." Holly let out a deep sigh. "I loved him, but he couldn't react in a crisis. It was stupid to shoot you. He should have run."

Bree agreed. "How long did it take you to look like Shannon? That was the genius part."

"The hardest part was gaining weight. That took a couple of months. I didn't like letting myself go like that, but Shannon was dumpy, so . . ." Holly shrugged. "The rest was easy. I cut my hair and curled it. Unless someone looked really close, I passed. I even switched our makeup, toothbrushes, and hairbrushes. I knew the medical examiner would do a DNA test." Holly was bragging outright now.

"What about your mother? Didn't you think she'd notice?"

"She's mostly blind." Holly bit her lip. "I did worry about her recognizing my voice. That's why I'd been avoiding her. I never had a cold.

I was hoping she'd die before I had to deal with it. But even if she did figure it out, what would she do? Call the police on her only living daughter?"

Bree kept her interested poker face intact, but inside, she was thinking, *wow*.

"Owen helped you," Bree said, trying to sound impressed. Holly seemed narcissistic, and narcissists love praise.

"Of course he helped me. This was our big chance. Shannon had a nice cash cow going. She hardly worked. She made good money. I went through her files. It didn't seem very hard."

"But Owen would still have to deal with the debts."

She shrugged. "He was going to declare bankruptcy. The only bad part of the plan was we had to live apart for a while. But we figured in a year or so, Shannon would move. She didn't have any friends or coworkers. She hardly knew her neighbors. She was wasting her life. She didn't travel or have fun. She was such a freak."

Shannon was the freak?

"Your plan really was perfect." Bree tossed out more flattery. "It's almost a shame you got caught."

She suspected Holly was a sociopath as well as a narcissist. She couldn't resist boasting about her superior intelligence.

Holly sighed. "I put so much work into it. Paul had forged his kids' names on corporate documents. He gave me the idea to steal more money from Beckett Construction. I started a new corporation in my sister's name, and Owen opened an account at the bank. We planned this for years."

Another piece of the puzzle clicked into place: Owen's job had enabled him to illegally open accounts.

"Why not just take the money and run?" Bree asked.

"And do what? Live on the run?" Holly's tone was filled with contempt, as if Bree were an idiot. "This isn't a TV show. How could we travel without passports? Do you know how hard it is to get fake documents these days? Everything is digital."

"You're right." Bree nodded. "To have a good quality of life, you need documentation."

Holly's single nod was arrogant. "I wanted Shannon's business, her nice house, the whole cushy life she'd built." Jealousy laced her words.

"You deserved it," Bree said.

"I did." Holly shook her head. "I should have killed Angela. She tipped off the IRS. They started sending Paul audit notices. He was freaking out. I was afraid I'd go to jail with him. *I* did most of the work. It's easier to get away with murder than cheat on your taxes."

Bree did not point out that Holly had failed on both counts. "Did you make Shannon's dog sick so you'd have an alibi with the vet?"

"I would never hurt a dog." Holly's posture and tone turned indignant. "I'm not a monster."

"I'm glad to hear that."

"Someone needs to get Chicken," Holly added. "I'll miss that dog. He's ugly, but he's really sweet." She blew a frizzy curl out of her eye. "He didn't like me that much, though. He missed Shannon, but he would have adjusted over time."

"So, Owen had an alibi for Friday night. Did you kill Holly alone and dispose of her body?"

"Do I look like I could have tossed that much deadweight over the side of a bridge?" Holly rolled her eyes. "We killed her early Friday morning—before I went to work—and dumped her Friday night before Owen went to the bar."

And because the real Holly showed up for work on Friday, Bree had gotten the time of death wrong.

Bree said, "I don't think I've ever solved a better-planned murder."

Holly huffed. "And it would have worked perfectly if that rescue-dog woman hadn't been so determined to be so fucking nice."

Bree finished the interview and left the room. She found a deputy and instructed him to take Holly to the jail and book her for kidnapping, assault, attempted murder, and first-degree murder. There was no question her crimes had been premeditated.

Matt met her in her office. "Wow."

"Right?" Bree asked. "I'm betting psychopath, sociopath, *and* narcissist."

"The psych profile should be interesting." Matt's head tilted. "Do you need to go home?"

Bree shook her head. "The kids are asleep. I talked to Dana to let her know we were OK." She looked at her desk. "I should get started on the paperwork."

Matt grimaced. "The paperwork can wait. You need sleep."

"Sleep would be nice." Her arm was still numb from the local anesthetic. "I would really like a shower too." She sighed. "I'm not sure I'm ready to go home. I need to decompress." She looked up at him. "Can I come home with you?"

Matt's eyebrows shot up.

"To sleep," she specified.

"Of course you can." He looked a little disappointed.

They didn't talk on the short ride back to his house. Inside, Matt greeted the dogs and took them out into the yard. He sniffed Brody. "I think Todd gave him a bath. He doesn't smell like river water."

He brought the dogs back inside. Greta headed for her bed. Brody came to Bree for a head scratch.

"Come on." Matt led her back to a guest room. He brought her a pair of sweatpants and a ridiculously large sweatshirt. He taped a plastic bag around her arm to keep her bandage dry. "Keep that out of the spray. Towels are in the bathroom."

"Thanks." Bree took a long, hot shower. Then she wandered into the kitchen. Matt's short hair was damp. He handed her a mug of hot chocolate and a ham sandwich. She finished both in three minutes. "I didn't even know I was hungry."

He took her empty dishes. "Go to bed." He kissed her on the forehead.

Bree slid between the sheets of his guest bed and stared up at the ceiling for an hour. Every second of the night replayed in her mind. Finally, she gave up. Padding barefoot through Matt's house, holding the waistband of the sweatpants up with one hand, she found his bedroom and knocked softly.

"Yeah," he answered.

Without a word, she opened the door, crossed the wood floor, and slid into bed with him. "I can't sleep."

Matt rolled over and tucked her against him. The solidness of him dispelled her loneliness. She'd never been one to seek the comfort of another. When stressed in the past, she'd always chosen to be alone. But peace settled over her as she curled into his body. Times change, sometimes for the better. With the heavy weight of his arm across her body, Bree finally slept.

CHAPTER FORTY-THREE

Mother's Day

Sunday morning, Bree and Kayla rode Pumpkin double. Their combined weight wasn't a problem for the sturdy little horse. He plowed steadily through the meadow. Adam followed on Cowboy, while Luke and Riot took the lead. The more spirited bay gelding tossed his head and pranced. On his back, Luke wore a backpack, its contents bulky.

They crested the hill at the rear of the farm. They stopped near a tall oak tree. Luke stepped off his horse and collected the reins. Adam lifted Kayla down. Bree's arm was still in a sling, and her dismount wasn't pretty.

"Are you sure?" Bree asked Kayla and Luke.

They both nodded.

"This was Mom's favorite place." Luke wiped a tear from under his eye and set the backpack at his feet. He opened it, took out the wooden box, and handed it to Bree. Did he need her to start?

"Mommy used to bring us here for picnics." Kayla's lip trembled. "Can we have a picnic here with her someday?"

"Whenever you want." Bree swallowed the grapefruit-size lump in her throat and wiped sweat from her forehead. Today felt more like summer than spring.

When Luke had suggested the meadow, Kayla had immediately agreed. Overhead, the tree's branches were green with fresh spring leaves. The wind swept across the open field. A few early wildflowers swayed. The coolness of the air was a welcome counter against the warmth of the sun.

Bree touched Luke's arm. "You were right. This is perfect."

She glanced at each one of them, her family. Her heart swelled. A year ago, she would not have imagined the close bonds they had formed. It was both sad and ironic that Erin's death had brought them closer. Bree would choose to be grateful that goodness had grown from something so horrible. Happiness was still possible. The sun would continue to shine.

"Ready?" she asked.

Luke, Kayla, and Adam nodded. Awkwardly, Bree opened the urn and let some of the ashes fly. She passed the box to Luke, who tipped some into the wind. Kayla and Adam finished. Tears closed Bree's throat as the breeze took the ashes and carried them across the hill and toward the meadow, as if Erin knew where she wanted to be.

Go free.

Luke's head bowed, but Adam turned his face upward to the sun and closed his eyes. Her brother always saw things from a different perspective. Usually, his was a darker outlook, but today, he seemed to crave the light. Maybe that was a sign. Bree wondered if his artwork would reflect change.

Her gaze roamed the pretty landscape. The tall grass and wildflowers bent to the wind. She could see the farmhouse and barn in the distance. Erin had loved this farm. It had given her peace in life. *Please bring her peace forever.* Something in Bree's chest unfurled, the tension unwinding like a coiled spring slowly being released. Her sister was gone, but from here, she would always be watching over them. Bree took comfort in the thought that she could come and talk to Erin whenever she wanted.

Kayla looked up at Bree. "Can we go now?"

Bree looked to Adam and Luke. They nodded. They both looked tired, but also more relaxed. Bree pressed a hand to the base of her throat, where the release of tension had left her feeling a little hollow. They were done here for now.

"We can." Bree boosted her up behind the saddle, then mounted. They all rode back to the house.

After they'd put the horses away, cleaned up, and changed clothes, Bree asked the kids, "Are you sure you want to go to the Flynns' house?"

"Yay!" Kayla jumped up and down.

"Yeah," Luke said. "It'll be good to get out of the house."

And give them all some time to process the morning.

Distraction is good, Bree thought.

They went into the kitchen, where Dana was wrapping fresh focaccia in foil. She'd insisted on contributing to the Flynns' Mother's Day brunch. "I'm ready."

"Thank you."

Adam put the flowers he'd picked in the meadow in a vase. "Let's go."

They climbed into Dana's SUV and drove over to Dr. and Mrs. Flynn's house. Matt's parents lived in a big house on several acres.

Matt's mom steered them into a huge great room. Bree introduced the kids, Dana, and Adam. Brody lay in the grass out back. Matt's brother, Nolan, threw a ball for Greta. The black dog streaked after it. The kids made a beeline for the dogs.

An apron-clad Dr. Flynn—George—had set out a huge buffet on the patio. "This focaccia looks amazing. You'll have to share the recipe."

Dana smiled. "I'll trade you for your cinnamon bun recipe."

"Deal." George's blue eyes twinkled.

Dana grabbed an apron from a hook. "What still needs doing?"

"Can I help with anything?" Bree asked, though her kitchen skills were decidedly lacking.

"Absolutely not." Matt's mom, Anna, put an arm around Bree and steered her out onto the deck, where Cady lounged on a chaise. "Leave the work to George. He is never happier than when he's cooking and entertaining. And you deserve some downtime." She deposited Bree in a cushioned chair overlooking the yard. "Coffee, tea, orange juice, mimosa?"

"Coffee would be great. Thank you." Bree leaned back. Sunshine warmed her skin and melted tension from her muscles.

"Let them fuss." Cady raised a mug. "One, you can't stop them." She grinned. "Two, they thrive on it."

"OK." Bree laughed. "You're feeling better."

"Much. Thanks. You?" Cady asked.

"Better." Bree adjusted her sling. Her arm was still sore but feeling better every day.

"I'll be right back." Cady got up and lifted her mug. "Need anything from the kitchen?"

"No, thanks." Bree turned toward the yard. The kids took turns throwing a ball for Greta. Adam and Nolan drank iced tea and watched the kids. Brody climbed onto the deck and stretched out next to Bree's chair. She reached down and ran her fingers through his fur. He sighed and closed his eyes. Bree did the same.

The chair next to her creaked. She opened her eyes. Matt handed her a cup of coffee. "From my mother."

She took a sip, then set the cup on a table next to her. "I can't thank your parents enough for inviting us today. I was hesitant to commit to anything on Mother's Day, but this was just what the kids needed."

"I'm glad." Matt reached over and put his hand on hers. "And my parents have been wanting to meet you and your family for months. I didn't want to rush you."

"I appreciate that." Bree watched the two families mingle. She felt like the Grinch when his heart expanded three sizes. Then her thoughts turned to Holly Thorpe, murdering her own sister. Had she been born a sociopath? Had she ever had sisterly feelings for Shannon? What Bree wouldn't give to have her own sister back . . . "How did Holly—"

"Nope," Matt interrupted. "No work talk today. None."

Bree smiled. "You're right. I need to learn to step away."

Live in the moment.

"You do." He interlocked their fingers. His grip was strong, warm, and steady, just like him. She wasn't ready to analyze her feelings for him yet, but for now, she was grateful he was part of her life.

Bree leaned back, holding his hand, watching the kids laugh.

Life had its ups and downs. Her job ensured a steady stream of unpredictable events. Today, life was good, and she needed to hold on to that for as long as possible.

Who knew what tomorrow would bring?

ACKNOWLEDGMENTS

It truly takes a team to publish a book, let alone build a career as an author. *Drown Her Sorrows* is my thirtieth published work since my first book released in 2011. As always, credit goes to my agent, Jill Marsal, for plucking my first manuscript out of her slush pile and supporting my career for more than ten years. I'm thankful for the entire team at Montlake, especially my managing editor, Anh Schluep, and my developmental editor, Charlotte Herscher. Special thanks to writer friends Rayna Vause and Kendra Elliot for help with various technical details, moral support, and plot advice. Most of all, I thank my family for their unwavering support back when I hadn't sold a single book. They believed in me long before I did. Ten years ago, I never thought I'd be a full-time writer, but here I am, truly grateful.

ABOUT THE AUTHOR

Number one Amazon Charts and number one *Wall Street Journal* bestselling author Melinda Leigh is a fully recovered banker. Melinda's debut novel, *She Can Run*, was nominated for Best First Novel by the International Thriller Writers. She's garnered numerous writing awards, including two RITA nominations. Her other novels include *She Can Tell*, *She Can Scream*, *She Can Hide*, and *She Can Kill* in the She Can Series; *Midnight Exposure*, *Midnight Sacrifice*, *Midnight Betrayal*, and *Midnight Obsession* in the Midnight Novels; *Hour of Need*, *Minutes to Kill*, and *Seconds to Live* in the Scarlet Falls series; *Say You're Sorry*, *Her Last Goodbye*, *Bones Don't Lie*, *What I've Done*, *Secrets Never Die*, and *Save Your Breath* in the Morgan Dane series; and the Bree Taggert novels, *Cross Her Heart* and *See Her Die*. She holds a second-degree black belt in Kenpo karate, has taught women's self-defense, and lives in a messy house with her family and a small herd of rescue pets. For more information, visit www.melindaleigh.com.